Forever *by* Your Side

Books by Tracie Peterson

WILLAMETTE BRIDES

Secrets of My Heart
The Way of Love
Forever by Your Side

THE TREASURES OF NOME★

Forever Hidden

BROOKSTONE BRIDES

When You Are Near
Wherever You Go
What Comes My Way

GOLDEN GATE SECRETS

In Places Hidden
In Dreams Forgotten
In Times Gone By

HEART OF THE FRONTIER

Treasured Grace
Beloved Hope
Cherished Mercy

THE HEART OF ALASKA★

In the Shadow of Denali
Out of the Ashes
Under the Midnight Sun

SAPPHIRE BRIDES

A Treasure Concealed
A Beauty Refined
A Love Transformed

BRIDES OF SEATTLE

Steadfast Heart
Refining Fire
Love Everlasting

LONE STAR BRIDES

A Sensible Arrangement
A Moment in Time
A Matter of Heart

LAND OF SHINING WATER

The Icecutter's Daughter
The Quarryman's Bride
The Miner's Lady

LAND OF THE LONE STAR

Chasing the Sun
Touching the Sky
Taming the Wind

All Things Hidden★
Beyond the Silence★
House of Secrets
Serving Up Love★★

★with Kimberley Woodhouse

★★with Karen Witemeyer, Regina Jennings, and Jen Turano

For a complete list of Tracie's books, visit her website:
www.traciepeterson.com

Forever *by* Your Side

WILLAMETTE BRIDES · 3

TRACIE PETERSON

BETHANYHOUSE
a division of Baker Publishing Group
Minneapolis, Minnesota

© 2020 by Peterson Ink, Inc.

Published by Bethany House Publishers
11400 Hampshire Avenue South
Bloomington, Minnesota 55438
www.bethanyhouse.com

Bethany House Publishers is a division of
Baker Publishing Group, Grand Rapids, Michigan

Printed in the United States of America

ISBN 978-0-7642-3231-2 (trade paper)
ISBN 978-0-7642-3232-9 (cloth)
ISBN 978-0-7642-3233-6 (large print)

Scripture quotations are from the King James Version of the Bible.

This is a work of historical reconstruction; the appearances of certain historical figures are therefore inevitable. All other characters, however, are products of the author's imagination, and any resemblance to actual persons, living or dead, is coincidental.

Cover design by LOOK Design Studio
Cover photography by Aimee Christenson

20 21 22 23 24 25 26   7 6 5 4 3 2 1

To Care and Bill Tuk.
You have fought the good fight and
inspired so many.
Thank you for your friendship
and continued encouragement.

CHAPTER 1

JUNE 1880

I want this job." Constance Browning looked her interviewer straight in the eye. "I want to do this. And furthermore, I'm the best person for the job."

"But you are a woman," Ulysses Berryton said, as if her gender was somehow unknown to her.

Connie was already frustrated by his condescending nature. "I know I'm a woman. I have been of the female persuasion for twenty-two years now."

He reddened. "And you truly feel qualified for this position?"

"I do. Although my skin is white, I was born on an Indian reservation and have many friends there. The project to catalog and record all Oregon tribes and their cultures is something I'm not only qualified for but would very much enjoy. In addition, many of the people there already know me. It will help speed things up."

He looked again at her application. "The Bureau of Ethnology takes its work very seriously. We must consider what's best for this organization. After all, the government has put a lot of trust in the Smithsonian Institution by transferring the duties of ethnology from the Department of the Interior to us."

Connie had had enough. "Mr. Berryton, I'm a very practical woman. I have never been one to attempt something without being convinced of my capability. I can assure you I am the best person for this job. If you need further reference, you only have to speak to my uncle, Dean Murdoch. He works right here at the Smithsonian."

"I'm very familiar with your uncle, Miss Browning. In fact, I did seek his opinion, and he gave his highest approval."

She nodded. "Of course he did. He's taught me a variety of specialized studies every summer since I was fifteen."

Berryton smiled. "I have my concerns, Miss Browning, but frankly I cannot imagine anyone more qualified for this task than you. Welcome to our department. You will be working with Thomas Lowell. I understand you know each other quite well."

The joy she felt at finally being approved for the job threatened to spill out. Instead, Connie forced herself to remain stoic and professional. "Yes, Thomas and I have been good friends for over seven years. He knows my family, and when he was attending Georgetown, he took numerous classes with Uncle Dean."

"Well, I expect you both to work in cooperation with one another. You will leave in a week for Oregon. I hope that won't be a problem."

Connie rose. "Not at all. I know you won't regret this decision, Mr. Berryton."

He stood and shook her hand. Connie smiled, gathered her things, and exited before he could change his mind.

She knew Tom would be waiting for her in the hall. He had a meeting with Berryton at two o'clock. That meant they only had a few minutes to talk. She caught sight of the tall, lean young man and smiled. He was her dearest friend in all the world, and she had him to thank for this job.

"I got it." She couldn't hold back a giggle. "I'm going with you to Oregon."

Tom grinned. "Of course you are. Berryton is a smart man. He no doubt understood the benefit of having you as a part of the team."

"I doubt he would have if you hadn't put in a good word for me." She juggled her books as they threatened to slip from her grip.

"Here, let me have those," Tom said, taking the books. "You're the most qualified, Connie. A lifetime of experience living among the Indians is something few people can boast."

Connie thought of those years. They were a mixture of pleasant memories and sorrow. The Indians might as well have been in captivity on the reservation. They were forced to remain on reservation grounds unless they had permission to leave, but it was usually for no more than a few hours, unless they were lucky enough to have procured work with the local white settlers. Even then, Connie wasn't sure how lucky it was to work for the white families. They generally paid very little and treated the Indians like the lowest of slaves.

"I was glad to help you," Tom continued. "No one gets ahead in this town without knowing someone and getting their help." He rearranged the books into a better order.

"Well, maybe someday I can return the favor."

"I'll hold you to that. Now, I've got to go, or I'll be late." He leaned down and kissed her cheek, then pushed the books back into her arms. "I'll meet you at four—the usual place. Oh, but if I'm late, it's because I have a meeting with Mr. Van Buren."

Connie's mind was already churning with thoughts and plans. She would have to secure a better wardrobe right away. The clothes she had at her aunt and uncle's house were perfect for Washington's social circles but would be confining and overly formal on the reservation.

"I'll see you then." She started to turn, then glanced back over her shoulder. "Tom, you truly are my best friend."

He grinned. "I know. And you're mine."

She waited until Tom disappeared into Berryton's office before all but skipping down the hall, despite her load. She paused at the flight of stairs that would take her to the second floor, where her uncle's office was located. Smiling, she juggled the books and hiked up her skirt. She had to tell him her news. He'd be delighted.

Moments later, Connie burst into the office without knocking. "Uncle Dean!"

He looked up from behind the stacks of books and papers that occupied his desk. "What in the world? You rush in like there's a fire following you."

She added the heavy tomes she carried to those on the desk. "I got the books you asked for." She gave him a kiss on top of his head. "And I got the job. I'm going home."

Uncle Dean stood to embrace her. "I'm so proud of you, honey. No one is more deserving."

"I'm just so relieved. This will allow me to help Mama and Papa." She pulled away, looking over her shoulder. Seeing she'd left the door open, she went to close it so no one could overhear her words. "There. Now we can talk."

Uncle Dean reclaimed his seat. "I doubt anyone would understand even if they heard you. It's only natural that a child would wish to help her parents." He leaned back in his chair and gave his graying beard a stroke.

Connie lowered her voice. "The very idea that the government thinks Mama and Papa could be a part of the conspiracy to incite the Indians to war just makes me mad. My parents have served faithfully ever since the reservation system came into being. They were there teaching and preaching before the government offered any compensation. They didn't even raise a fuss when the government replaced them with the Catholic Church representatives. They just quietly kept on working to help the Indians, being paid with private funds alone."

"I know, sweetheart. I know as well as you do that they aren't capable of the things they're accused of."

"Well, in time I will find the proof that will clear them altogether. And then"—she shook her index finger at some unseen foe—"I will take them all to task for maligning the good Browning name."

"When do you leave?"

"In a week." Connie opened the draw-string of her reticule and withdrew a small brown paper sack. "I stopped at your favorite candy store." She plopped the bag in front of her uncle. "Toffee."

"What will I do without you? Every day your aunt asks me if I visited the candy store, and thanks to you, I never have to answer in the affirmative. When you go to Oregon, I shall have to do without or find someone else to do my bidding."

"I'm sure there are plenty of interns who would vie for a chance."

Her uncle met her gaze and shook his head. "I shall miss you so much. Your aunt will be heartbroken."

"Aunt Delphinea will write me copious numbers of letters. Maybe you can buy her some beautiful jewelry to soften the blow. I've learned in this town that if you have something beautiful to show off, all your troubles seem far less important."

"Ha. That's hardly the case for your Aunt Phinny, and you know it. You were the only beautiful thing she truly enjoyed showing off. You gave her days purpose."

Connie shrugged. "She could come West with me. In fact, you both could. I know my folks would love to see you."

"We would be hard-pressed to get away. I have my work, as you can see." He waved a hand over the desk. "And Delphinea has her social responsibilities. Goodness, the Independence Day celebration is just a few weeks away, and you know how many committees she's on for that."

Connie had often wondered if anything at all would get done in Washington if her aunt didn't oversee or control the details. She wouldn't have been surprised in the least to have found her aunt in the middle of the president's office, barking out orders to those doing his bidding or seeking his favor.

"Well, it was just a thought," she said. "I know Papa misses his family."

"Perhaps one day. It won't take long for her to miss you. I fully expect by fall she'll be making arrangements for some sort of trip West. That's another reason I must get all of this done first." He gave another wave at the top of his desk.

"Well, then, I should be on my way. I'm meeting with Tom later, and I have a great many things to accomplish before I can leave for Oregon." She kissed him again on the head. "I'll see you at dinner."

"Here, take this." Her uncle pulled a wallet from his coat pocket. He took out several bills and handed them to her. "I want to make sure you have money, just in case you shop where your aunt doesn't have an account."

"I doubt that's even possible," Connie said, taking the money. "But thank you. I must find some more serviceable clothes and shoes, not to mention . . ." She smiled. "Well, we won't mention them."

He laughed. "I am going to miss you, Connie. You have brought such laughter to our home. What a blessing it has been to have you here all these years."

She knew that, after losing their youngest two children to sickness and seeing their oldest off to West Point, her aunt and uncle had been eager to have her live with them. Coming East to attend school, in fact, had been their idea, and Connie had thought it a grand adventure. Of course, her parents had been less enthusiastic. How she longed to see them again, and her brother Isaac as well. Seven years was a long time to be away from home and family.

"I'm going to miss you and Aunt Phinny. You've been my rock all these years. But for now, I'd best let you get back to work."

"Are you sure she doesn't suspect anything?" Mr. Berryton asked.

Thomas Lowell sat back in the leather upholstered chair and casually crossed his legs. He knew it might be considered rude to strike such a pose, but he didn't care. These people were ruthless in their lack of concern for the people in his life.

"She doesn't suspect anything other than that I endorsed her for the position."

"This is critical, Mr. Lowell. This ongoing problem in Oregon must be brought to a halt. Far too many incidents have been instigated, and war is certain to break out if we don't get to the bottom of this. It's important you ferret out all of those who are responsible. Even if it includes Miss Browning's parents, as we suspect."

"I understand the situation, Mr. Berryton. I believe I understand it so well that I was the one to suggest Miss Browning could be of use to us."

"You were." Mr. Berryton took out a handkerchief and mopped his perspiring brow. The heat was still climbing, and Tom knew they'd be lucky if temperatures didn't hit one hundred degrees. Added to that, the rising humidity suggested a storm might be brewing, and it made the day completely unbearable.

Tom was no more comfortable than Berryton, but he wasn't about to show it. He simply stared back at the older man and waited for him to speak.

"You will both receive a stipend, and accounts will be set up for you in Salem, where you can expect regular deposits for your work. I have written detailed instructions to go along with the other instructions I gave you last week. The ethnology work is equally important, but obviously not as time sensitive. I will expect regular reports."

"And you will have them." Tom smiled and waited to see if there was anything else to discuss. He wanted nothing more than to be out of Berryton's office and away from these pompous souls who so easily judged Connie's parents.

"Then I will dismiss you. We should meet again before you leave next week."

"Perhaps you could host a farewell dinner." The heat was making Tom feel testy, and he knew his tone was tinged with sarcasm.

"That's probably a good idea," Berryton replied. "I'll check with Mr. Murdoch and see when he might be available."

Tom got to his feet and extended his hand. "Until then."

"And you're sure he wasn't suspicious?"

Tom gave Connie an incredulous look. "Do you think me so poor an actor that I couldn't convince that old ninny? He believes I'm using you to get to your folks. He thinks we have the perfect situation in place."

Connie leaned back, wishing the shade tree offered more help with the heat. She searched her purse for her fan and rejoiced when she found it. "Oh, I'm so glad for this."

"A hot breeze is better than no breeze, I suppose." Tom pointed to the west. "Once those rain clouds finish building into a thunderstorm, we should have a little relief in the temperature."

"It's never like this in Oregon. Oh, we get thunderstorms now and then and plenty of rain, but we don't have to worry about this much heat. At least not usually. I do remember a summer when it was dreadfully hot. Rosy told me that one of the women in the tribe said she'd used her spirit powers to cause the heat wave in order to punish someone else. I asked Rosy why she would do that when she had to suffer the heat as well. If she was going to punish someone, shouldn't she do something that would hurt that person alone? Rosy said the woman was well known for cutting off her nose to spite her face."

Tom chuckled. "I like your stories about Rosy. Is she still there?"

"She is. Mama wrote recently to say Rosy just celebrated her sixty-sixth birthday in May. She said Rosy has the strength and endurance of a much younger woman and the spirit of a saint. She's always doing things for others and constantly works to keep peace among the women. I can hardly wait to see her again."

"You've missed life there, I know."

"I have." Connie had no reason to be less than completely honest. Especially with Tom. "When I came here, I thought it would be a great adventure. And it was, but I'm tired of adventures. I want to go home." She smiled. "I think you'll love it there, Tom. I'm so excited to show you everything and everyone. There's just so much to do before we leave."

Tom nodded. "You can say that again."

CHAPTER 2

Aunt Phinny, have you ever been ashamed of being Cherokee?" Connie asked as she finished dressing for the fund-raiser ball she would attend that evening. She had battled with that question on many occasions, but she knew she'd had it much easier than her father and his family.

Her aunt looked thoughtful. "I suppose some would say I should be, but that truly isn't why I remain silent about it. There was a time when everyone around me knew that I was a quarter Cherokee, and they did their best to make me miserable. Your father and our other siblings and I were made fun of and challenged at every turn. When I found a man who didn't mind my heritage, I was so grateful. In all honesty, I probably wouldn't have looked twice at your uncle otherwise. He wasn't the type of man I found at all intriguing, with all of his books and focus on ancient rituals and cultures." She smiled. "But he was so unconcerned with my being part Indian that it endeared him to me. And, of course, as I got to know him, I fell in love."

"I don't feel ashamed, but the world makes it clear that I should, and I'm only one-eighth Cherokee." Connie looked into the cheval mirror and adjusted a curl. "But that's the trouble with the world. Certain folks have decided what we should or shouldn't find shameful, and the rest of us have it imposed upon us."

"That's true enough. I've heard the same argument said of religious views," Aunt Phinny declared. "That's why I've always tried to focus more on being kind and loving as a means of getting people interested in better knowing God."

Connie nodded. "In some cases, I've felt compelled to hide my faith along with my heritage. Isn't it sad that people can't just be themselves without fear of retribution?" She stepped back and met her aunt's sad expression. "Few know that Papa is a quarter Cherokee, or that I'm an eighth, and they probably never will. And I can't help but feel that that's not right."

Then, as she always had done, Connie

pushed those thoughts aside and buried them deep.

She twirled like a little girl to show off her dress. "Well, what do you think, Aunt Phinny?"

Her aunt studied her a moment. "It's hard to believe you're all grown up. When you came here, you were just fifteen and so petite—just like your mother." She motioned for Connie to turn again. "This time go slower."

Connie did as instructed. "I love the fit of this gown. Pity I'll have no use for it after tonight."

"We can keep it here for you, and then when you visit, you'll have something beautiful to wear."

Connie studied her reflection in the mirror. The buttery yellow garment was cut from the finest silk, with beautiful inlays in the overskirt that allowed for glimpses of delicate lace. The original bodice had been cut low and square, but Aunt Phinny had arranged for her dressmaker to fashion a more modest décolletage. Connie turned to see the back of the gown as best she could. The bustled train fell in a waterfall effect of gathered silk and lace, spreading out behind her in a most appealing fashion. "Maybe I'll take it with me. There's bound to be some formal occasion."

"You might get married. It would make a lovely wedding gown."

Connie chuckled. "I have no plans for that, Auntie. I see no reason to wed. I have plenty of friends who keep me from growing lonely, and with no one to share my bed, I don't have to worry about sharing my covers either."

"Goodness, child." Aunt Phinny laughed. "I've never heard of a young woman who had such an aversion to marriage."

"It's not an aversion. More simply put, I like being in control of my own life. You and Uncle have taught me that a woman can fare well enough for herself if she gains the knowledge she needs to navigate life. Thanks to you both, I feel I have that."

"Well, I can't help but believe that one day a young man will come along and sweep you off your feet. Now, turn again." Connie did as instructed. "You're absolute perfection, and I like the way the maid arranged your hair with those tiny white roses. Quite stylish yet subdued."

"I wish you and Uncle were coming tonight."

"I do too, but we'd already committed to dinner with the Hamiltons. Besides, I have a feeling this ball will attract more young people than elderly folks like us."

Connie laughed and went to kiss her aunt's cheek. "There is nothing elderly about you and Uncle. You do far more work than many people half your age. I caught Uncle in the garden just yesterday, down on his knees, pruning the roses."

"Keeping busy keeps us youthful," her aunt admitted. "But ballrooms hold little interest for me these days. Your uncle cannot dance as he once could, and I've no desire to dance with anyone else." She smiled. "Now, you run along and have fun. I'm sure Thomas and your friends will be much better company than Uncle or I could be."

"Speaking of friends, Sallyanne asked for a ride to the ball, so I suppose I should hurry."

"There you are. You'll have Sallyanne as your ally."

But Connie knew that once they arrived at the fund-raiser, she'd be left to the mercy of dozens of would-be suitors. Tom couldn't devote his entire evening to her. He was, after all, a very eligible bachelor. Sallyanne loved being seen, so she would be dancing as much as possible.

Connie sighed and gathered her wrap. "I doubt we'll be all that late getting home. Tom and I have so much to do before we leave next week, and we need what sleep we can get."

"Knowing Sallyanne as I do, I doubt she'll want to come home early," Aunt Phinny said in a sympathetic tone.

"Her folks are coming late, so they'll take her home. She only asked for our help in getting there so she could spend as much time dancing and flirting as possible."

"Then you'd best hurry. It's nearly eight."

Connie glanced at the clock. It seemed only moments ago it had read seven. "Goodness, the minutes are just flying by."

"So are the years." Her aunt sighed. "I shall miss you so much, my dear. You came to us when we had suffered such great loss. Having laid Regina and Millicent to rest only months before, we were so grateful to have you stay with us. Then, when Monty went off to West Point just weeks after your arrival, I was even more grateful to have you. I think I would have died of loneliness and sorrow without you."

"Perhaps you should invite another family member to come and keep you company. My cousin Meg, Grace Armistead's daughter, is nearly fifteen. Perhaps she would like to attend Mount Vernon Seminary for Girls." Connie shrugged. "She might not be immediate family, but she is family, in a rather extended way."

"Well, your uncle has promised me a trip West, although it will have to be delayed because of all the responsibilities we have in the immediate future. But I do intend to visit my brother and the rest of the family before too much time passes. I miss them all. Perhaps you could invite your cousin to come spend time with you while we're there."

"I'll do exactly that. I had always hoped Mama and Papa might be able to come here for a visit, but they never seemed able to get away from their work."

"Your uncle is like that as well. But it has paid off. His position with the Smithsonian is quite to his liking. It is, in fact, everything he could have ever hoped for, and spending his days with his books and artifacts pleases him more than anything else in the world. That, in turn, makes me happy."

"Well, perhaps you can entice him with the work the Bureau of Ethnology is doing." Connie gave her aunt another kiss. "No matter what, you're both loved, and I know you will be very welcome in Oregon. Now, I'd better go. I'm sure Tom will be here soon, if he isn't already."

She found Tom and Uncle Dean deep in conversation when she reached the first floor. The men looked up and broke into smiles of appreciation.

"How pretty you are, my dear," Uncle Dean said, coming to embrace her. "Oh, I remember the days of my youth and how exciting it was to see the young ladies all dressed up. The gentlemen tonight will no doubt lose their hearts at first sight."

"Well, I don't need them doing that," Connie said, glancing admiringly at Tom in his black suit. "Speaking of cleaning up nice, just look at you."

He laughed. "I was about to compliment you, but if you insist on poking fun at me, I'll take back all the nice things I intended to say."

"Suit yourself. I wasn't poking fun. You look quite dashing. Someone will be blessed to get you as a husband one day."

She saw the way Tom sobered before he turned away. "I was just telling your uncle how grateful I am for the lower temperature today. I fretted all week about how awful it was going to be to wear this suit, but since the temperature eased, it doesn't seem so bad."

"I thought the same thing." Connie rose up on tiptoe and kissed her uncle. "We'd best be off. I wouldn't want Sallyanne to think something happened to us."

Her uncle followed them outside. "I am glad you're all going together."

"We make quite the consortium," Tom said. "Discussing everything from war battles to fashion."

She laughed. "Not to mention ancient

artifacts and cultural studies. Thanks again for letting us borrow the carriage."

Her uncle merely waved, as if it meant nothing at all.

The carriage and driver were ready and waiting at the curb as Tom and Connie emerged. Tom helped Connie up, then climbed in after her. As she settled into the soft leather seat, she thought of the things she'd miss about the capital city. The hubbub was sometimes quite exciting. There was something about the middle of the day downtown, with all the hustle and bustle, that energized her. She'd miss that for certain.

Tom took the seat opposite her and instructed the driver to head down the street to the Van Buren house. "You look reflective. You aren't having second thoughts, are you?" he asked her.

"Just trying to keep in mind all that I will miss when we go away."

"Like being the belle of the ball to a captive audience of men?"

"Why would you say such a thing?"

"What? It's all true. You are the belle of most balls. Men are quickly drawn to your side. They especially like the fact that you aren't seeking a husband, like the others."

Connie frowned. "Why do you say that? I've never said such a thing."

"Perhaps not with words," Tom replied. "But your actions most assuredly do. Why do you think you're so popular among all the men, young and old?"

"I thought it was my great beauty," she replied, her voice thick with sarcasm.

Tom chuckled. "Well, of course that has a lot to do with it, but it's also your attitude. Most women your age and older are desperately searching for a husband. That makes men uncomfortable. When they walk into a room of women, they immediately feel as though they are prey amongst predators—led to the slaughter by beautiful executioners in Worth gowns."

"Oh, for pity's sake. That's the most ridiculous thing I've ever heard." Connie shook her head. "Men are the ones who seek a mate. Women always have the feeling of being stalked like a prized turkey."

"You might be surprised to know that most women enjoy that sensation. They want very much to be pursued. That's why they dress in elaborate outfits. They fancy up their hair and lower their necklines."

Connie looked away, feeling her cheeks redden. It was embarrassing to think that Tom noticed such things.

The driver pulled to a stop along the curb, and Tom gave a heavy sigh. "I'll fetch

Sallyanne. I'm sure her hair will be a great deal fussier and her neckline much lower than yours."

After a few minutes, Tom and Sallyanne finally emerged. Another young woman followed them. Connie tried to place the young lady but wasn't successful.

"Oh, Connie dear. I'm so happy to see you. It's been ages and ages since we had a nice long talk," Sallyanne declared as Tom assisted her into the carriage. "This is my cousin April. I invited her to come with us. My folks will join us later at the ball."

Sallyanne was resplendent in lavender tulle and taffeta. And just as Tom had suspected, her gown was cut quite low, as was the fashion. Connie thought back to what Tom had said about women being beautiful executioners in Worth gowns.

April was next to climb aboard, taking her place beside Sallyanne. She was a delicate-looking young lady gowned in a bustled fashion that looked much too mature for her age. She couldn't have been older than sixteen, which was soon confirmed by Sallyanne.

"This is April's first big outing since her debut last month in New York. Isn't she pretty?"

"Quite. You're both beautiful. April, I'm pleased to make your acquaintance. I'm

Constance Browning, but everyone calls me Connie."

The younger woman gave a meek smile. "I'm pleased to meet you."

"Sallyanne, that gown is quite, um, fashionable."

"It's my new Worth gown," she said, beaming. "I believe it will capture the attention of every man there. Mama says I should be far more aggressive at seeking a husband. I am almost twenty, after all."

Connie saw Tom's eyebrow raise in his *I told you so* expression. She nearly burst out laughing.

"It definitely suits you, Sallyanne."

Tom jumped up and took the remaining space beside Connie. He smelled of heady spiced cologne. Connie smiled. It reminded her of her uncle Dean's choice of scents. Perhaps Tom had even asked for her uncle's suggestion.

By the time they reached the party, Sallyanne had divulged all the household secrets, shared gossip about the neighborhood, and mentioned several new hats that she'd ordered. April answered a few of Connie's questions about New York, and then Connie shared their plans for Oregon, which shocked both Sallyanne and April's delicate sensibilities.

When they reached their destination, Tom

helped April and Sallyanne from the carriage. Sallyanne waved to friends and dragged April off to meet them. Tom swung back around and helped Connie just before her slippered foot touched the carriage step.

"Are you ready to concede I was right about the husband hunting?" he asked, grinning.

"Well, I knew about the husband hunting. I just didn't know that it made men nervous. That's an entirely different side of things that I never considered."

"Men aren't always looking to marry, you know."

"Oh, I do." She took hold of Tom's offered arm. "That's why we get along so well. You aren't looking for a wife, and I'm not looking for a husband. It makes us the perfect team."

She parted company with Tom shortly after they were announced to the partygoers. Connie found herself gravitating toward the older ladies, while Tom found a gathering of older men. From time to time they each danced with a variety of partners.

The dancing went on until nine o'clock, when a cold supper was furnished along with copious amounts of champagne. Connie, having never been a drinker, declined every offered flute of sparkling drink and sought instead to enjoy the iced lemonade. At supper, she joined a conversation with several senators' wives when she'd have preferred to talk politics with their husbands. The ladies, in contrast, discussed ill children, new draperies, and the complications of finding and keeping good staff.

Connie was bored nearly to the point of falling asleep when the orchestra began to play again, and the dancing started back up. Since Sallyanne's father and mother had arrived, Connie felt free to call it an evening, but Tom seemed particularly engrossed in conversation with one of the congressmen in attendance.

Mr. Berryton approached and gave her an abbreviated bow. "Would you do me the honor, Miss Browning, of the next dance?"

Desperate to be away from the women without causing offense, Connie nodded. Mr. Berryton led her to the dance floor, and they were soon waltzing with the others.

"I hope you aren't sorry for your new position. Now that you can see what you'll be missing, I feared you might want to change your mind," he said, watching her as though he might be called upon to dry her tears.

"Not at all, Mr. Berryton. I'm quite delighted with my decision and your hiring me. I can hardly wait to head home."

"I suppose the fact that it is home makes

all the difference." He moved her gracefully around the room, much to her surprise. If there was one thing men were required to do in Washington, it was dance, and Mr. Berryton had not disappointed.

When the waltz concluded, he led her back to where he had found her. "I'm glad you don't regret your decision. I would be hard-pressed to fight against a woman's tears should you have come to me begging off."

"I honor my commitments, Mr. Berryton, so you needn't fear. I have been gathering my city clothes and am prepared to pack them away or sell them for more appropriate fashions. I have secured my books and other niceties to leave with my aunt and uncle until I might send for them. All in all, I am nearly ready to step onto the train that will take me to Oregon."

"Very good." He seemed relieved and used the handkerchief he'd held against her back as they danced to dab at his lips. "I hope you continue to enjoy the evening. I'd best go in search of Mrs. Berryton."

"Good night, then, and thank you once again for giving me a chance."

He gave another abbreviated bow and departed while Connie searched the room for Tom.

"Miss Browning," a voice said behind her. Connie turned to find Mr. Lynden, a particularly hopeful would-be suitor. "I wondered if I might have this dance."

She saw they were forming up for the Virginia reel. "Of course, Mr. Lynden." Hopefully, with the moves of the dance, she wouldn't have to spend much time in conversation.

"I heard a horrible rumor," he said, leading her to the dance floor.

"Oh, really? Pray, what did you hear?"

"That you're leaving Washington and going to live with the Indians." He looked completely aghast.

"That's no rumor, Mr. Lynden. I am leaving Washington to take on my duties for the Bureau of Ethnology. American politicians and intellectuals have decided that it is important to catalog and maintain an accurate history of the various Native tribes of this great country. You do realize, don't you, that many tribes are already extinct?"

"I didn't." He paused as if considering this fact. "However, that's no place for a delicate young woman such as yourself. I can hardly approve."

She might have laughed out loud had there not been so many other people in the room. The music began, and she curtseyed while Lynden bowed. They didn't continue the conversation until the dance concluded, and by then Connie was more than ready to go home. She gave a quick glance around the room, but there was no sign of Tom.

"Miss Browning, surely you understand the dangers involved in dealing with Indians. It's said that they not only scalp white settlers when given the chance, but that they do other . . . distasteful things. You really shouldn't go. It's not at all appropriate."

Connie gave him a fixed look and fought to hold her temper. "Mr. Lynden, I would be going there whether I had a job or not. My parents live there. I grew up on a reservation, and I assure you that no one was scalped or given to eating human flesh or dissecting bodies to keep the dead from entering the spirit world." She saw him blanch and smiled. "Yes, I've heard all the horrible rumors. My suggestion is that you should come experience the reservation rather than cast judgment on it and the people there."

She left him looking as if he might lose his supper. It was more than a little annoying that people were so prejudiced in their thinking. She knew her circle of girlfriends was no different. No one understood her desire to return to the reservation and renew friendships with the Native people. It was one thing, they had said, to be a child befriending another child, but for an adult woman to carry on with the Indians . . . well, it defied understanding.

Then let me defy it.

CHAPTER 3

It's hard to believe Samuel is gone. Murdered," a stately gentleman declared.

"I think it may be the result of his views on people of color," another added. "They might well be to blame for killing him and Berkshire."

The man they knew only as Mr. Smith walked amongst the gathered elite and smiled. If they only knew.

"Mr. Smith, it's so good to have you join us for our meeting."

Smith tried to remember the man's name. Johnson? Jamison? No, it was Jenson. "Mr. Jenson, it is my pleasure to be here." He tapped his walking stick on the floor.

Smith knew the men gathered here felt as he did. There was no acceptance for people of color polluting the population of Oregon.

There were laws on the books that went widely ignored, and today they were speaking on how to resolve that. The key, most agreed, was to get judges and officials who supported the laws and would pledge to see them upheld in office.

"Some of us plan to share supper after the meeting, if you'd care to join us," Jenson added.

"I'm afraid previous obligations make that impossible, but thank you for the kind invitation."

Generally, at these events, Samuel Lakewood would have been in charge, but Smith had grown weary of the man's failings and inability to motivate his underlings. He had concluded that the only thing to be done was to kill Lakewood and his top man, Gerome Berkshire. He only wished he could stand up and announce that he'd done it and would do the same to any man here who chose to defy him. Unfortunately, he couldn't. He'd never allowed his leadership position to be known, except to a choice few. With Lakewood and Berkshire gone, that left only one man, and he was about to speak to him.

"Mr., uh, Smith," the man greeted nervously. "I had no idea you were attending this evening's meeting."

"I'm sure you didn't," Smith replied.

"Given the current situation, I felt it was necessary. Wouldn't you agree, Mr. Carter?"

Elias Carter was no more than five feet, five inches and weighed nearly two hundred and fifty pounds. He didn't strike an imposing figure, but was rather a rotund, sweating fool. At least in Smith's eyes.

"I—I supposed that you would come eventually." He tried to smile. "I just didn't think it would be here . . . like this."

"Well, wouldn't you suppose that the murder of two of our most prominent members would necessitate my presence?"

"Ah . . . yes. Of course." Carter was perspiring all the more. "But of course, no one knows of your leadership . . . save me."

"Yes, I'm well aware of that. I make myself scarce so as to be less noticeable. A sage such as myself needs to guard his appearance. While it's perfectly acceptable to disagree with our current situation, one needn't make one's self out to be a madman."

"No. No, of course not," Carter agreed. He leaned a bit closer. "Is there anything I can do to aid you at this time?"

"Not here. I would, however, like you to come to my hotel after this meeting adjourns." He handed Carter his card. "I've written the hotel and room number on the back. I'll slip out of the meeting before anyone can corner me for discussion. See that you are there without delay after the meeting concludes."

"Yes. Yes, of course. I'll be there," Carter said.

Smith tried not to notice that the man's hand was shaking. It was good that Carter was afraid. He should be. If he counted his life precious, he would do what he was told and not interfere or improvise with the plans. After all, not following orders to the letter hadn't served Lakewood or Berkshire well at all.

"I'm so excited to see Connie again. She's been gone for far too long." Faith Gratton crossed the kitchen of the boardinghouse to the icebox and took out a pitcher of lemonade.

"I'm excited to see her too," her cousin Nancy Carpenter agreed. Nancy had just finished feeding her baby son, Jack, and was attempting to burp him. A soft whoosh of air passed from the infant's mouth as he snuggled against her, already asleep.

Faith held up the pitcher. "Want some?"

"Please." Nancy got to her feet. "I'm going to put Jack in his cradle, and I'll be back to start peeling those potatoes."

Faith had just finished pouring two glasses

of lemonade when Nancy returned to the kitchen.

"Would you pour a third, please? I'm going to take this to Seth. He's resting in the office, and I think it might be just the thing for him."

"It is a rather warm day." Faith poured lemonade into a third glass, then returned the pitcher to the icebox. No doubt they would need to make some more, but for now she was just going to sit down and enjoy a bit of rest.

Nancy came back from seeing her husband, beaming a smile. "He's getting stronger every day. I know he's frustrated at not being able to jump back into his legal work, but it's so hard for him to work for very long because his head starts to hurt. He wants to be able to play with Jack and go places with me, but I'm just delighted that he's alive."

"These kinds of wounds take time to heal. It might be as much as a year or more before Seth is completely healed. He needs to be patient, or it will only slow his healing."

"I'm sure you're right, but I know he also worries about the man or men who did this. He worries they might strike again. He's confident that Lakewood was answering to someone."

Faith nodded. "Worry won't change a

thing. We'll be on our guard, and I know the police check the house regularly."

"I know." Nancy collected her glass of lemonade and brought it to the table. "Want to help me peel potatoes?"

"Sure. Just bring me a knife. Mother always said I was a faster peeler than she was. It took me several years to realize she only said that because my pride would puff up and I'd insist on peeling all the potatoes."

Nancy laughed and brought a huge bowl of potatoes to the table, along with two knives. She poured the spuds out onto the bare wood. "She's a smart one. I'll have to remember that when teaching Jack."

"Are you going to teach him to cook?" Faith picked up one of the knives and a potato.

"I am. My mother always maintained that boys needed to know how to cook as well as girls. At least the fundamentals." Nancy took a long sip of lemonade and then got to work. "Father agrees. He used to have to cook for himself quite often when he was working as a trapper."

"I think it's reasonable to have men learn to cook. Andrew isn't much for it, but the cook on the ship is quite adept."

"When will Andrew and the *Morning Star* return to Portland?"

Faith finished the small spud and deposited it before grabbing another. "In another week. I miss him so much. If I hadn't had those obligations with the college and Connie wasn't returning, I might have gone along with him."

"I certainly would have. You've only been married a couple of weeks, and Connie's been gone seven years. You can wait a few more weeks to see her. I, for one, would rather be in my husband's arms." Nancy gave Faith a conspiratorial smile.

Faith felt her cheeks flush. "I would too."

A knock interrupted their exchange, and Faith got to her feet. "I'll see who it is." She strolled to the door and opened it wide. "Mr. Singleton, if I'm not mistaken." She laughed. "I haven't seen you in years."

Clint Singleton laughed heartily. "It has been a long time, Miss Faith, but you're as pretty as ever."

"I'm an old married lady now. I married steamboat captain Andrew Gratton two weeks ago, so you may call me Mrs. Faith." She laughed. "Actually, just Faith will suffice."

"Congratulations." He dusted off his coat.

"Won't you come in? We knew you'd be showing up one of these days. I know my cousin will be glad for the escort back to the reservation."

"Your aunt Mercy was just telling me the other day that it has been seven years. I hadn't stopped to think of it, but I realized she was right."

Faith led him through the house to the kitchen. "Nancy, Mr. Singleton has come."

Nancy looked up. "Forgive me if I don't rise. Supper must be prepared for the boarders."

"That's quite all right. You don't need to rise for me."

"How was your trip? Did you just arrive?"

He smiled. "It was lengthy but good. And yes, I just got in a few minutes ago on the *Lady Luck*."

"Another paddle-wheeler," Faith said as if explanation was needed. "Well, I'm certain coming by river was easier than the stage."

"But not as fast as the train. We have so many options these days." He chuckled. "Have you heard anything from Miss Constance? I stopped by on my way to my hotel to see if you knew when she planned to arrive."

"We received a telegram from them when they reached San Francisco. They took the train there and plan to sail up the rest of the way. That was over a week ago. We expect to hear from them soon, however. If you don't mind, why don't you have a seat?" Faith motioned for him to take a chair at the kitchen table. "We were just enjoying some cold lemonade. Would you care for a glass?"

"That would hit the spot." Clint sat down and smiled. "It seems the *Lady Luck* gave me some luck after all. I consider myself more than blessed to share such pleasant company."

Faith chuckled as she poured the lemonade. "Well, we're busy, to be sure, so I don't know how much of a blessing we can be." She brought him the drink. "Nancy has a house full of boarders, including me, to keep up with. I do my best to help."

"Will you stay for supper with us, Mr. Singleton, or do you have other plans this evening?" Nancy asked.

"I do have other plans. My father and brother keep me pretty busy."

"That's right, your father is a senator from California and your brother is working with the Bureau of Indian Affairs."

Clint sampled the lemonade and smiled. "Perfect. Both the drink and your summary. That's why I got involved as an agent. My family has always had great passion for righting wrongs, and their desire to see the Indian treated fairly has become a family business."

"Well, we need more people like you," Faith said, once again taking a seat to help Nancy peel. "I suppose you're quite happy to hear about the recording of the culture and tribal history that Connie and Mr. Lowell will be doing."

He frowned. "I can't say that I am. I suppose I'm cautious at best. I worry that it will stir up people's memories of the past and what they once had and lost. It concerns me that in telling their stories, they will be provoked."

"Surely not." Nancy shook her head. "I would think they would proudly share their history and culture."

"Of course they will, but then they will remember that they once roamed free and dressed differently—spoke their own languages and lived their own way."

Faith shook her head and put a peeled potato in Nancy's bowl. "You think they've forgotten that? They know very well what they've lost."

Clint frowned. "I wasn't trying to suggest they had forgotten, but bringing it all front and center again is likely to get people agitated. There are entire generations on the reservation now who don't remember the old life. You can't miss what you've never known."

"I don't know if I agree with that thought." Faith finished another potato. "Sometimes the heart longs for the things it's never known."

"You sound like a poet, Miss Faith."

"Faith is actually a certified doctor and surgeon. She finished her classes this spring."

Nancy put her knife down. "I'm going to go check on Seth and the baby."

She got up and exited the room before either Faith or Clint could acknowledge her. Clint leaned toward Faith. "I heard her husband was nearly killed."

"Yes. Someone attacked him on his way home one night. We weren't sure he would even live, but he's doing much better. He had head and spinal injuries as well as some cracked bones. We take good care of him, however. Much better than the hospital could, so we brought him home early. It's been a little over a month, and he's doing well. Seth is a fighter."

"Did I hear my name mentioned?" Seth stood in the doorway, leaning on his cane.

"Seth, this is Clint Singleton. He's an Indian agent down at Grand Ronde. He works with Aunt Mercy and Uncle Adam."

"Glad to meet you, Mr. Singleton," Seth said, giving a slight nod.

Clint got to his feet. "It's an honor to meet you. I'm glad to hear you're nearly recovered. When I heard what happened to you, I was more than a little angry." He extended his hand in greeting. "I don't know what the world's coming to. I suppose they robbed you blind?"

"No, that was the strange part. It seemed the beating was the only thing they were really interested in." Seth smiled and looked at Nancy, who stepped through the door behind him. "But they didn't count on these two. Nancy and Faith wouldn't even hear of leaving me in the hospital. Once the doctors had me stabilized, they whisked me home to take care of me with the help of all the other ladies who live here, including my sister."

"You are blessed to have so many who care about you," Clint said.

"We were just discussing Connie and Tom's work. Clint is concerned it will stir up warring thoughts amongst the Indians," Faith said.

"I suppose he makes a good point," Seth replied, much to Faith's surprise. "You can never tell how remembering the past will affect a person."

Clint smiled, appearing content that someone finally understood his point of view. "I don't think it has to be a bad thing, but you folks don't live with them like I do. The Indians are always looking for a reason to hate the white man. In fact, they don't even need a reason. They just hate, and that hate eats them up until they want to make someone else suffer for their pain."

Faith shrugged and put a peeled potato aside. "Well, we did rob them of their land and homes, force them to dress and act like us, and make them change their entire way of life. I think they have a right to be angry— even to hate us."

Faith saw a flash of what could only be anger in Clint's eyes. She'd obviously irritated him. "I'm not trying to be contrary." He paused a moment, then continued. "You need to understand the importance of the changes we . . . forced. Those people's only hope is to become like us. No one is going to tolerate them running around half-naked and moving from place to place, trying to live on land they don't own. They don't have the same concept of land ownership we do. They have to change, or they'll never fit in with the white population."

"Maybe they shouldn't have to," Faith replied. "Maybe there's a way we can both live in harmony and still hold on to our heritage and the things that matter to us."

He studied her for a moment and shook his head. "You can't mix oil and water and expect it to blend. It'll separate every time."

Faith nodded. "That's pretty much my point, Clint. You're trying to force them to be oil when they are water."

"That's why we need to find a way to allow for both," Seth interjected. "Maybe we need to focus on being American rather than worrying about the color of our skin."

Jack let out a wail of a cry from down the hall. Nancy smiled and moved past the men. "I believe Jack would like us to refocus our energies on something of a more personal nature—food and a dry diaper."

Seth chuckled. "I just figured he was agreeing with me."

Nancy rolled her gaze heavenward. "I can hardly wait until he's old enough to debate you and tell you exactly what he thinks."

CHAPTER 4

Connie had never been happier to arrive at a place in all her life. She was weary from the long days on the train to San Francisco, then the ship to Astoria, and finally the riverboat to Portland. It was truly a wonder of modern innovation to be able to journey across the country in such a short time. It had been fascinating to see so much of America, but it was exhausting, and Connie was more than ready to settle down.

Each time she started to feel sorry for herself, however, Connie remembered her mother's stories about leaving St. Louis and traveling west on the Oregon Trail. It took months and months of walking and camping in all sorts of weather. Living in fear that sickness or attack would come at any minute.

How very brave she must have been, and yet she was only a child at the time.

"A trip like that makes or destroys your faith," Mama had said.

Connie was glad it had made her mother stronger in spirit and body. How easy it would have been to give up and turn back, especially after the only man in their group died. Of course, Connie also remembered her aunt Grace, who had been married to that man, saying that life got easier after he was gone. What a terrible epitaph. Connie prayed it would never be said of herself.

"Connie!" someone called. She looked up to see her cousins rushing across the dock platform.

"I'm so happy to see you both," Connie said, hugging first Nancy, then Faith, and then both together. "How wonderful to see you again. You both look just as you did seven years ago."

"I seriously doubt that," Faith declared. "Those years have put a few wrinkles on my face."

Connie laughed and touched Faith's cheek. "Mama says they are proof of experience and wisdom."

"She would say that." Faith grinned. "Speaking of your parents, have you let them know you're back in Oregon?"

"I sent a telegram from Astoria. Of course, who can tell when they'll actually get it. I do wish Mama and Papa could have been here to meet us. I'm so anxious to see them again." She pulled back and motioned to a man standing behind her. "I'm being very rude. This is my good friend Thomas Lowell. You can just call him Tom."

Tom raised his hat to the ladies. "I'm pleased to meet you both. I've heard so much about Connie's family."

"We're rather a lot to deal with when we're all gathered in one place," Faith declared. "I'm Faith Gratton. Just call me Faith."

"Faith is the one who recently married a riverboat captain." Connie's explanation brought something else to mind. "I have a gift for you, to celebrate your marriage. I hope you'll like it. I have something for you as well, Nancy."

Tom looked at the other woman. "You must be Mrs. Carpenter."

"I am," Nancy replied. "But please call me Nancy."

"Did Clint arrive?" Connie asked, looking around. She had been both dreading and looking forward to seeing him again. There was a time when she had been madly in love with him.

"He's in town but thought we might like

to meet up with you first. He said he'd join us for supper. That way you'd have time to rest and visit with us." Nancy paused with a shrug. "Of course, at the boardinghouse there isn't a lot of privacy to be had, but we can still catch up."

Connie nodded and looked around. "I don't remember much about Portland before I left, but I know it wasn't anywhere near this big."

"No," Faith agreed. "It's been growing daily. I'd wager to guess that it's doubled in size almost every year these past seven years. It's such a vivacious town, and we have just about any amenity you could want now. Opera, ballet, theater, wonderful restaurants, and so much more. We get some of the best speakers too. I recently invited Helen Hunt Jackson to speak to the town regarding the plight of the Indian Nations, and she said she would come in September. I'm so excited to hear what she has to say."

"That's wonderful," Connie said. "Perhaps we'll all get a chance to attend together."

Faith smiled. "I asked Mr. Singleton to speak too, but he conveyed that the government would not allow it. I thought it might be refreshing to hear his perspective, since he lives with the Indians and tends to their needs."

Tom jumped in at this. "I'm sure he's right. The government wouldn't appreciate the son of a senator and brother of a bureau official spouting off about reservation problems."

"He could focus on other things," Faith protested. "Although I admit mentioning the problems is more likely to raise funds than talking about all the good things." She shrugged. "I just want people to understand what's happening and why the Indians need our support and consideration."

"Well, it's nearly lunchtime, and the ladies of the boardinghouse helped me prepare a wonderful meal. I think you'll enjoy it, as well as meeting all the boarders. They've become like a family to me," Nancy said. "And besides, Seth and our little son, Jack, are there, and you must meet them. After lunch, we'll let you rest. Faith is going to put you up, Tom. And Connie can stay with the ladies at the boardinghouse."

"Are you averse to sleeping on a riverboat?" Faith asked Tom.

"Not at all." He grinned. "Over the last two weeks I've slept on trains and ships. I even dozed on the lovely boat that brought us to Portland. I find that I can sleep anywhere— any port in the storm, so to speak."

Faith smiled. "That's good to hear. Captain Gratton, my husband, will be back with our ship, the *Morning Star*, very soon. We'll give you a room there, since the boardinghouse is women-only, with exception to Nancy's husband and the occasional family member." She turned to Connie. "Did your folks write you about the bad storm we had last January? We lost over half the trees in the city. We're still working toward recovery. The storm hit up and down the coast of Oregon and even the Washington Territory. Your mother wrote to the family that things were bad at Grand Ronde as well."

"I did have a letter from Mama about it." Connie glanced around the area. "But Portland looks quite repaired. They must have worked very hard."

"Yes, the entire city really came together," Nancy said, smiling. "It blessed my heart to see so many people helping out."

"I believe I'll see to our bags," Tom said. "Where will I find you ladies?"

Nancy pointed across the street to a waiting carriage. "I can call a baggageman, if you need help."

"No, I'm sure I can manage. I'll have to make arrangements for the larger crates to be stored here at the docks until we head to Grand Ronde."

Connie laughed. "Aunt Phinny sent every

imaginable thing for Mama and Papa. She sent Papa a dozen new books and so much more, and then there are fabrics and shoes for the Indians."

"I've no doubt. Go ahead and make your arrangements, Tom. We'll wait for you at the carriage." Nancy put her arm around Connie. "Come. We have so much to catch up on."

To Tom, sitting at the boardinghouse table was akin to sitting at a political dinner. Comments were volleyed back and forth, and dishes passed in a whirlwind of constant activity. He hadn't expected so much candor and insight from the ladies, but they were intelligent and full of opinions.

"Mr. Lowell, do you care for candied carrots?" one of the Clifton sisters asked.

Tom couldn't remember which one she was, Bedelia or Cornelia. "Thank you, I do."

She passed him the bowl, then turned her attention immediately to a bowl of potatoes. Tom wasn't sure what else was in the concoction, but it looked as if the potatoes had been diced and mixed with bacon.

"This is a warm potato salad that the Germans make," Miss Clifton explained, passing the bowl to him. "It's quite tasty. Clementine,

Nancy's sister-in-law, learned how to make it from one of her young students' mothers. Of course, she doesn't teach now that she's married to Nancy's brother."

Tom nodded, trying to keep up with all the names and people.

Miss Clifton continued to speak. "We often find it quite satisfying for our main meal. However, since we knew you and Miss Browning were to join us today, we made certain to offer more than just the potato salad. There's sliced honeyed ham and bread as well."

"That was most considerate, Miss Clifton."

"Indeed." Connie joined in the conversation from across the table. "Riverboat food is hardly the best. I was glad Tom thought to pick up apples and cheese in Astoria rather than depend on the boat's fare."

Miss Clifton nodded. "Cheese and apples were a good choice. Quite filling."

Tom met Connie's amused expression and raised his brows, mock-challenging her to suggest otherwise. Instead, she merely nodded.

"Was it a decent trip?" Nancy Carpenter asked Tom.

"Decent enough. There were a couple of delays, but it wasn't bad." Tom sampled the potato concoction and found it quite satisfying. There was a sweet vinegar dressing that surprised his taste buds in a pleasant manner. He'd have to ask for the recipe so that he could have it from time to time. "Train travel is improving all the time," he continued. "I am happy to see that greater care was given to providing a restful sleep for travelers. The trains were equipped with sleeping quarters for men and women."

"I doubt I could sleep amongst strangers," Miss Clifton declared, shaking her head. "It wouldn't be restful at all."

"I am afraid I was so desperate for sleep, at times, that I slept sitting upright in my seat." He leaned a bit closer to the older woman. "I was in good hands, however. Connie watched over me."

"It is important to be able to place trust in one's traveling companions," Miss Clifton declared.

"True," Connie said. "I think I slept better in my seat because I knew Tom was there. But I very much enjoyed the ride, despite it wearing me out. I didn't observe much on my trip to Washington. I suppose my young age kept me from appreciating everything as much as I did on the return trip. It was fascinating to see the changing landscape. There are so many areas of wilderness that just go on and on, as well as huge farms that were cultivated in wheat and corn. The mountains were exceptionally beautiful and still had snow on the highest peaks."

"What a grand journey," Miss Clifton murmured. Tom thought she sounded envious.

He refocused on his food while the conversation went around the table once again, like salvos being fired in a battle, as the women discussed everything from the presidential race to the price of sugar.

About halfway through the meal, a knock sounded on the front door. Nancy excused herself and was gone only a few minutes. "Sorry for the interruption. That was Ruth. She's come to visit with Alma."

They all nodded.

Bedelia leaned close to Tom. "Alma shares a room with Mrs. Weaver. They often take their meals upstairs."

"I see. Well, clearly this house is home to a great many."

Nancy gave him a benevolent smile. "It's a long story, but Alma was once Mrs. Weaver's slave. She was smuggled into Oregon when the Weavers moved here from back East. You might not realize this, but there are laws against black people living in Oregon."

Tom hadn't realized this but nodded as though he had.

"Mrs. Weaver has hidden Alma ever since, but we've been working with Alma to encourage her to get out and about. There is a wonderful black church in the city and several businesses owned by former slaves. We finally managed to get Alma to at least accept visits from Ruth."

"So Alma never leaves the house?" Tom asked.

"Not yet," Nancy replied. "But I'm hopeful that one day she will. However, until then, I must ask that you and Connie keep our secret."

Tom glanced at Connie, and they both nodded. "Of course."

A red-haired man came to the table and took the chair beside Tom. "Sorry for my tardiness. Nancy has a rule about not waking me when I'm sleeping."

"Only until you're completely healed," she replied. "Ladies, be sure to pass the food to Seth."

They did as she asked, never once breaking pace with their various conversations. Seth looked at Tom. "You must be Mr. Lowell."

"Please call me Tom. I presume you're Nancy's husband, Seth Carpenter."

"I am. And you must call me Seth. I hope we'll have some time for conversation after lunch. I don't get many men to visit with, since this is a ladies' boardinghouse. Faith's husband comes when he's in town, but otherwise only a couple of others are brave enough to dare enter this place." Seth winked.

"Oh, pshaw. You'll give Mr. Lowell the wrong impression," Miss Clifton scolded. "The fact is that we cannot have men running about willy-nilly. We ladies need our privacy and comfort, and worrying about a houseful of men would rob us of that joy."

Seth smiled at Tom. "Well, I'm just glad they allow me to run about willy-nilly."

After lunch, Seth showed Tom to his office, which doubled as the boardinghouse library. He sank onto a leather wing-backed chair and sighed. "I'll be so relieved when my energy returns."

Tom closed the door. "I was told you were left for dead."

"I was. I don't remember a great deal about the attack, but thankfully I haven't forgotten much else."

Tom took a seat beside Seth, grateful there was no fire in the hearth. The day was already plenty warm, although the clouds suggested a coming rain.

"This is quite the house." Tom admired the craftsmanship of the room.

"It was built by my wife's first husband. He didn't offer her much in the way of love, but he lavished her with everything else. When he died, she decided to turn the place into a boardinghouse. I wasn't sure at first that it was something she should continue after our marriage, but I'm thankful she did. I haven't been able to work at the law practice since the beating, and the money generated by the boarders has kept us from dipping into savings."

"How many people actually live here?"

Seth considered the question a moment. "Well, there's Nancy, the baby, and myself. The two Misses Clifton, and occasionally Faith is with us when her husband is on a lengthy trip or she's committed to something here in town. We also have Mrs. Bryant. She's a widowed schoolteacher. My sister used to live here, but she's married to Nancy's brother, and they have a little house elsewhere in town. He runs his family's sawmill." He hesitated. "There are two others, but most folks outside of the house only know of one."

Tom remembered the secret Nancy had shared with him. "I heard about them at lunch."

"They are dear women. Mrs. Weaver is far too old to do much work, but Alma likes to help with the housework and laundry to, as she tells it, earn her keep. She's been a great help to Nancy and me. I hate that she's afraid, however. She's so worried someone will find her and force her to leave the state. No one really enforces those laws, but occasionally, you'll hear of someone getting on their high horse and demanding the laws be adhered to, and then a black person is whipped and told to get out of town."

"So she hides?"

Seth nodded. "Nancy didn't even know for quite some time that she lived with Mrs. Weaver. She was moved into the house in a blanket box, and then Mrs. Weaver snuck food upstairs to her and did whatever was necessary to keep her secret hidden from the world. I must ask that you keep this between us. Connie's letter prior to your arrival said you could be trusted."

"Of course. I've already promised your wife I'd say nothing." Tom frowned. "Besides, I have some secrets of my own. I hope you don't mind, but I need to speak frankly with you about one of them."

Seth raised a brow. "With me?"

"Yes." Tom crossed his legs, a habit he was hard-pressed to quit. "I know about your work with the government and the situation with the Indians. I was recruited to come and continue the investigation."

Seth looked surprised. "Well, I must say I wasn't expecting this course of discussion."

"I'm sure. They told me in Washington what had happened to you and that there were still so many unanswered questions. Ever since they started to suspect Connie's folks of being involved, she's wanted to find a way to prove them innocent."

"So she knows too?"

"Not about you. Does your wife know?"

"Yes. She's been knowledgeable about everything for some time."

Tom nodded. "Then I figure once Connie and Nancy have an opportunity to talk, Connie will know about your involvement as well. Mercy and Adam Browning know they're being watched. They know they are suspected of inciting the Indians to war and sneaking weapons and whiskey onto the reservation. Connie has convinced me they aren't guilty, and we've come to prove their innocence, all while working for the Bureau of Ethnology and recording the culture of the various tribes."

"They knew of Connie's connection and still hired her? I find that pretty surprising. I figured they'd think her too close to the matter."

"Yes, well, they don't know she knows. Connie approached me last year, and in turn I put myself in a position to be approached to help the investigation. Connie has been in on it from the start, but she and I have kept her role just between the two of us. I recommended the government hire her on to work with me for the cultural recordings, noting to them that Connie was already known to the Indians and, of course, her parents. I made it clear that I could use her as an asset to gain closer access, and they accepted the idea."

"That was brilliant. However, do you think Connie can be objective? I mean, these are her folks."

"I realize that." Tom uncrossed his legs and stretched them out. "But since you don't know her like I do, I can honestly say I believe she's able to do just that. She's a remarkable woman and wants to see justice win out. If she finds out that her folks are involved, she'll move heaven and earth to convince them to change their minds. And she'd probably be successful. Connie has a way about her."

Seth smiled. "And how long have you been in love with her?"

Tom shrugged. He saw no need to hide his feelings. "About the entire time I've known her, but don't tell her that. She hasn't a clue."

Seth laughed. "They often don't."

They sat in silence for several minutes before Seth spoke again. "If I can help in any way with the things I learned, I will do it. I don't believe Mr. Singleton intends to take you to the reservation before the end of the week. That will give us a few days. Oh, and I'll send an invitation for Major Wells to join us. He's been instrumental in all of this."

"I can't do anything to make it look like I'm here for anything but cultural record-keeping." Tom frowned. "Speaking to Wells would be a big help, however."

"Look, no one needs to be the wiser. The major comes by all the time to check on me. No one will think anything of it, I assure you. I think the opportunity to learn from him would outweigh the risk."

"Very well. I'll trust you to set it up."

CHAPTER 5

Clint hesitated at the corner before approaching the Carpenter house. Constance Browning stood on the porch, laughing with several people. He couldn't help being mesmerized by the way she moved. She appeared to be telling a story about something very active as she twirled and whirled on the porch. Her audience was completely captivated, and no one seemed even the tiniest bit aware that they were being observed.

Connie was certainly no longer the gangly and awkward fifteen-year-old he'd watched leave the reservation. The little girl who was so enraptured with him that she followed him around everywhere like an obedient pup, declaring her feelings for him. No, this was a woman full-grown and quite beautiful.

There was something of the little girl that

remained, however. Something animated and childlike in her delight. He could hear her laughter all the way across the street, and it sounded like music.

He crossed the avenue and gave a wave when Nancy Carpenter caught sight of him. She returned the wave, and the others turned to greet him. Connie stopped at the porch railing but didn't wave or smile. She observed him like a specimen she'd just been introduced to for the first time. Clint thought it almost humorous. She was no longer the lively storyteller. Instead, she looked bored—almost indifferent.

"Mr. Singleton, I see you've returned to join our company," Mrs. Carpenter declared.

"I did indeed. You said to come to supper, and I'm not one to turn down a good meal."

She smiled. "I'm sure you remember everyone." She turned to her cousin. "Of course, this is Connie. It's been what, seven years since you last saw each other?"

He took off his hat and gave her a smile. "It seems like a lifetime ago. Connie, you look quite lovely—all grown up."

She gave a smirk and glanced momentarily heavenward, which only made Clint smile. It would seem she had developed some sass.

"How are you, Mr. Singleton?" she asked.

"I'm quite well—especially now. It seems

like I haven't seen you in forever. I kept thinking you'd make a trip back to the reservation. I know your folks would have liked that."

"Yes, but I was much too busy." She looked beyond him. "Oh good, Faith and Tom are here."

Clint turned to find the couple coming up the walkway. "Is that her husband—the sea captain?" he asked, not really meaning to voice the question.

"Goodness, no. That's Tom. He's my dearest friend and the man I've been working with in Washington. We're going to be working together at the reservation." Connie brushed past Clint and went to where Faith and Tom had stopped. She pressed between them and looped her arms through theirs. "I thought you'd never get here. Supper smells amazing, and Nancy has baked three different kinds of pie."

Faith chuckled. "That certainly has put you in good spirits."

"I'm always in good spirits," Connie said, pulling them along. "Tom, there's someone I want you to meet." She brought him to stand in front of Clint. "This is the man I told you about, Mr. Clinton Singleton. He's been a friend of the family for a long time. He and my father have worked together for years and years."

Clint extended his hand. "Most folks call me Clint." What did she mean, *this is the man I told you about*?

"Thomas Lowell," Tom replied, shaking his hand. "Most folks call me Tom."

"Very nice to meet you." Clint knew that Connie was sizing them up. It was impossible to know what went on inside the head of a woman, but this particular woman almost seemed to be plotting something. "I'm looking forward to getting to know you, Tom. Of course, I already know Connie. We spent a lot of time together before she left for school."

"Yes, back when I was just a little girl," Connie threw out. She looked at Clint with a smile and added, "And Clint was a much older man."

"As I recall, you didn't think the age difference was all that important." Clint returned her smile. The tension grew.

"Yes, but now that I'm more mature," Connie began, "I can see just how silly I was as a child. Goodness, but children come up with some of the most ridiculous notions."

"Like losing your heart to me?" He could see that she was momentarily stunned by his bold words.

All at once she burst into laughter. Everyone was briefly taken aback. Connie let them feel a few moments of discomfort before she sobered. "Exactly like that. Oh my, I'd almost forgotten about that." She looked at Tom and shook her head. "Remember what I told you years ago about there being a man at the reservation I thought myself enamored of? This is him." She looked at the others. "I really was the silliest girl. Of course, living on the reservation probably didn't help. Clint was the only white man besides my father and the occasional soldier. I actually fancied that Clint was like a fairy-tale hero. He used to help my father calm fights and aid those in need." She was completely serious now, and to Clint's surprise, there wasn't a hint of sarcasm. "I know Papa used to say he would suffer Clint's loss like losing his right arm. I was always so grateful for the work you did, Clint, to keep Papa safe."

He narrowed his eyes slightly. What was she about? "Well, it's been a privilege to work with a man as great as your father. Adam Browning is one of the finest men I've ever known."

Connie nodded and looked at Tom. "He really is. Papa would walk twenty miles in the pouring rain to get medicine for someone who needed it. He has never cared about the color of a person's skin or the money in their purse. He just wants to have God's heart when dealing with others. His faith truly guides his choices."

"You can say that again. Your mama is just the same," Clint added. "Fine woman. Their faith has done much to bolster my own."

The conversation seemed to lose its momentum, and Tom took the opportunity to speak. "Connie, you should come down to the riverboat when you get a chance. Faith has fixed it up with a medical examination room. Sort of a floating hospital."

"It was Andrew's idea," Faith replied. "We are often stopping along the river to drop off goods or pick up folks. Andrew suggested we have facilities to help those in physical need. We haven't been called upon very much yet, but hopefully after the word gets out, we'll see more folks."

"Is Andrew coming to supper?" Nancy asked.

"No. He said he'd come by later to pick us up, but he was busy overseeing some repairs and couldn't leave. I promised him we'd save him something."

"Of course."

A baby could be heard fussing somewhere in the house. Nancy smiled. "That would be Jack demanding his supper. I'll see to him, and then we'll plan to eat in about forty minutes or so. Meanwhile, Connie and I made some lemonade, and I'm sure she'd be happy to serve it up."

"I would be very happy." Connie followed Nancy into the house without another word.

Clint could see how Tom watched her leave. The young man clearly felt something for her. Perhaps it was nothing more than a protective brother sort of thing, but Clint didn't think so. It seemed to him there was a definite longing in Tom's eyes.

"I'll help you with the lemonade," Bedelia Clifton said as Connie entered the kitchen. Her thoughts were so muddled by Clint's arrival that all she could do was nod. She'd thought she was prepared to see him again, but she was wrong.

"The lemons have been so abundant and large this year," Miss Clifton said as she retrieved the pitcher from the icebox. "We have truly been blessed. Faith told me that such fresh fruit is one of the best things for the body."

"I suppose she would know." Connie retrieved the glasses and put them on the tray. Bedelia placed the pitcher beside the glasses. "She is a phenomenally intelligent woman." She surveyed the tray. "Do you suppose we should take the sugar as well?"

"Gracious, no. It's plenty sweet, and if the gentlemen don't think so, they can forgo drinking it. I do not believe excess sugar is good for the body. Faith has mentioned that as well, but I had already read several articles about such things. Sugar is known to give you nightmares."

"How interesting." Connie knew she could manage that without the help of sugar. She had been having trouble sleeping ever since they left Washington.

For the most part, she was worried about her mother and father. She fretted about seeing Clint again, and now that it had happened, she wasn't at all sure what she was feeling. He was still handsome, and his smile was still charming. He had a way about him that put folks at ease, but she wasn't allowing his charm to intoxicate her. The last thing she needed was to fall in love with him again.

I must stay focused on the job at hand. Mama and Papa must be found innocent of wrongdoing, and that is my primary purpose and goal.

She lifted the tray and headed for the front door, more than a little aware that Clint waited for her on the porch. Why did he disturb her so much? It wasn't like she fancied him anymore. She could easily say that she wasn't in love with him.

"But I don't know what I do feel for him," she muttered.

"What was that?" Bedelia Clifton asked.

Connie looked up and shook her head. "Nothing important." At least she hoped it wasn't.

That evening, after supper was over and Clint had gone home, Tom and Connie sat on the porch and enjoyed the chilly evening. There was still a bit of light, enough so that Connie could make out Tom's contemplative expression.

"Penny for your thoughts?"

He shifted in his chair. "I was just thinking about Mr. Singleton. He's a part of our investigation."

"Of course." Connie let the rocking chair begin to move. "What did you think of him?"

"I guess I'd rather know what you thought of him." Tom shook his head. "You seemed quite agitated in the beginning and then grew very quiet. Not at all like the Constance Browning I know."

She shrugged. Tom knew her far too well. "I don't know what to think of him. I didn't like being teased by him. It wasn't his place to bring up the past. Not at all a gentlemanly thing to do."

"Are you still in love with him?"

The question was asked so matter-of-factly that Connie answered with equal candor. "I don't know. I don't think so. I can't say that I've given him much consideration these last few years. In fact, I made certain that I didn't think about him. My love for him was that of a child for a heroic figure. It bore little basis in reality."

"Good."

She looked at him. "Good? Why should it matter one way or the other to you?" She got a funny feeling in the pit of her stomach. Tom sounded almost possessive of her.

"Well . . . that is to say . . ." He stumbled over his words. "I wouldn't want it to interfere with our work."

"No." She shook her head and drew a deep breath. "Of course not." For a moment she hadn't been sure where he was taking this conversation, but now she could relax, knowing it was only his concern about work. The last thing she needed was for Tom to fall in love with her.

"This job is much too important, and if you and I don't get to the bottom of it, I fear your parents may bear the brunt of accusation."

"Thank you for your concern for them. It means so much to me that you care." Connie smiled. "This is much too important to me to lose my focus. Mama and Papa are innocent, and I intend to prove it. However, I also want our work to keep a war from taking place."

"As do I."

A hired hack pulled up to the curb across the street. The passenger paid and spoke momentarily to the driver, then gave him a wave and started for the house. It was too dark to get a good look at him, but he definitely knew his way around.

"Captain Gratton," Tom said, getting to his feet. "It's good you could finally join us. I was hard-pressed to leave you any supper—it was the best meal I've had in a long time."

The captain laughed. "Nancy is probably the best cook in Portland, but don't let my cook know I said as much. Where is everyone? Are you all alone out here?"

"I'm here, Captain." Connie got up from the rocker. She had been hidden in the shadows, as very little light was left. "I'm Connie Browning, Faith's cousin."

"I've heard so much about you that I feel I already know you well." He stepped closer. "I'm very glad to meet you."

"Likewise. I can't tell you how wonderful it was when I learned of your marriage to Faith. She's such an amazing person, and if anyone has ever deserved love, it's her."

"I agree and am happy to accommodate," he replied, laughing.

The screen door opened. "I thought I heard your voice," Faith declared, sweeping into her husband's embrace. They kissed tenderly, completely oblivious of Tom and Connie. When Faith pulled away, she took her husband's arm. "Come. I've saved you some of your favorites, including two pieces of pie."

They moved as one into the house without another word to Connie and Tom. Connie found herself feeling a bit envious of their adoration for each other. Laughter rose up from the house, as well as conversation. She liked the feel of this home. It was full of life and love, just as a house should be.

"Now where has your mind gone?" Tom asked.

She couldn't see his face very well and figured he couldn't see hers either. "I was just taking a moment to be happy for Faith. I meant what I said. If anyone deserves love, it's her. She has always been the most giving and loving of all my cousins and family. She has always sacrificed of herself and shown great concern for those around her, and yet she could never expect to marry and felt very alone, I'm sure."

"Why did she not expect to marry?"

"I thought I told you. Faith is half Cayuse. Her mother—my aunt—was one of those at the Whitman Mission massacre. She was sorely abused, and Faith was the result. We don't bring it up because . . . well, for obvious reasons, but I tell you positively everything. I really thought I'd told you about her."

"No, but you can trust me to keep her secret."

"Keep this one too, then. The captain is also part Indian. It was perfectly legal for them to wed."

"Tom," Nancy said, coming outside, "Seth was hoping you might play some chess with him. It helps his mind, you know."

"I'd be happy to. If you ladies will excuse me." He got to his feet. "I'll go and see how badly I can be beaten."

Connie smiled. Tom was an excellent chess player and would no doubt win.

"Jack is finally asleep," Nancy said, leaning against the porch rail. "I love it when he sleeps. I can't help wondering what he's dreaming of."

"Are you certain he dreams? Perhaps babies don't."

Nancy chuckled. "I remember once an old lady told me that babies soar with angels when they sleep. I used to try to remember when I was a baby, to see if I could recall any such trips, but sadly I couldn't."

"People get some strange notions, don't they?"

"That's for sure. Especially with all the nonsense going on at the reservation." Nancy fell abruptly silent.

"What do you know about it?" Connie asked. "Have you heard the rumors about Mama and Papa?"

"I . . . well, yes. I wasn't sure that you had. What do you know?"

"I was just about to ask you the same thing."

"I know they're innocent, Connie. I know Aunt Mercy and Uncle Adam are good people and would never do the things they're accused of. My first husband had a hand in smuggling whiskey and weapons onto the reservation. It floored me to hear your folks accused of being involved." She kept her voice very low. "Did you know that Seth came to Portland to learn the truth?"

"No. I wonder if Tom knows."

"He does. He and Seth had a talk."

"Funny. He never said anything to me." Connie frowned.

"Well, there hasn't exactly been time. You haven't been alone—not really. Maybe it's best not to say anything and let him bring it up. Maybe he didn't want to worry you with it."

"We tell each other everything. It's always been that way in the seven years I've known him. He was one of Uncle Dean's students and spent more time at our house than anywhere else. Of course, his mother died shortly before I arrived, and his father was always preoccupied with business. He had very little time for Tom." She paused to make sure they weren't overheard. "In fact, Tom's father was quite cruel to the family. Uncle Dean was one of Tom's teachers, and he was so supportive and sweet to him. He encouraged him to continue with college and not allow his grief to make his choices. Aunt Phinny mothered him tenderly. Well, she mothers everyone." Connie couldn't help but laugh. "And did so quite well."

Connie remembered those days with bittersweet contemplation. They had been like a little family, and yet she had missed her own family. Her brother, Isaac, had headed off to college prior to her leaving home but returned not long after she'd left. Her mother and father were faithful to write, but it wasn't the same. They all kept thinking there would be time for a trip to bring them all together again, but it never developed, and Connie had been devastated. What if they turned out to be strangers to her? What if home wasn't home any longer?

"Are you two still out here?" Faith held up a lamp as she opened the screen door. "Ah, yes. Room for one more?"

"Of course." Connie put aside her regrets.

"Faith knows plenty herself," Nancy said in a hushed tone.

Connie had not anticipated this, but it was as good a place to start as any. "I think we have a great deal to discuss, then, and we might as well get started. Clint said we'll leave the day after tomorrow."

"The night air is growing damp. Why don't we go back inside? I'll make some tea," Nancy said, moving toward the door without waiting for their response.

"I'll go get your presents." Connie followed. "I keep forgetting to give them to you. I brought them from Washington, since I knew for sure I'd be seeing you. I'll join you in the kitchen momentarily."

She hurried to the room Nancy had given her and opened one of her trunks. Taking up her gifts, she made her way back to join Faith and Nancy. How strange that Nancy should know so much about her real reason for coming to Oregon. Connie couldn't help but wonder what further insight her cousins might provide.

"This is for you, Faith." She placed a paper-wrapped bundle in front of her cousin. "A wedding gift."

Faith untied the string that held the package together. Once the paper was folded back, she gasped. "It's beautiful."

"It's Brussels lace—a tablecloth. I don't know that you'll have any use for it onboard a riverboat, but I thought it was exquisite."

"It is," Faith said, touching it. "I've never seen anything quite so lovely. Thank you. I'll use it for very special occasions."

Nancy came to the table to better see it. She ran her finger along the pattern. "It is beautiful."

"This gift is for you, Nancy. A baby gift."

Nancy took the offered package and opened it. Inside was an intricately fashioned baby quilt. She admired it for a moment, then looked up with a smile. "I love it. How beautiful. Did you make it?"

"Aunt Phinny and I did it together. When Mama wrote to say you were having a baby, I explained to Aunt Phinny how long you had waited for this and how it was a miracle from God. She said we needed to do something to commemorate the event, so we went to work creating this quilt. I went all over Washington, DC, to find just the right materials. You can see the blocks are all samples of various techniques. Aunt Phinny thought the basic colors of red, white, and blue would be patriotic and later make a good lap warmer when the baby grew to adulthood."

"It's perfect. I will cherish it always." Nancy gave her a tight embrace. "Thank you."

Faith got to her feet and joined in the hug. "Yes, thank you, Connie. It's so good to have you home."

CHAPTER 6

Home.

It was a concept that had taken on many forms over Connie's lifetime. She had grown up on the reservation, and it was home. Then the government decided against continuing to allow her folks to be teachers and pastors for the reservation and gave the Catholic Church the job. That was when her family had purchased land just beyond the reservation boundaries, and that had become home. When she moved to Washington, DC, Uncle Dean's house captured the role. Later, the little house in New York had been home when she'd attended college. Seven girls had shared the cottage, along with a house mother who had kept them all accountable. For most of the girls, this was their first time away from the only home they'd known, and they pined and mourned for the familiar.

Connie always felt that home was wherever she determined it to be. Her mother had taught her this. She wasn't one of those people who longed for what had once been, but now, upon returning to the reservation, she felt disappointed.

The reservation wasn't what she remembered. In her memories, she had recalled a lovely place with a pleasant river valley lined by trees. In and around it were hills to climb and open land to farm and log. Spirit Mountain rose like a lone sentinel. Now, however, the place she had once loved looked desolate. Worn down. Lonely.

The storm in January had felled a great many trees, many of which hadn't yet been dealt with. The houses lacked paint and glass windows. Perhaps the latter had been blown out in the storm, for Connie was certain they had once been there. Everything looked run-down and neglected. It wasn't at all as she remembered. But perhaps it was just the difference of seeing with adult eyes.

She couldn't put aside the overwhelming sense of sadness as she continued to look around. The people, what few she saw, appeared weary and depleted of life. It was almost as if their spirits had been taken away.

Their gazes were hollow, striking in Connie a moment of discomfort and fear. Nothing and no one looked familiar.

"Connie!"

She heard her mother's cry and turned to find her parents approaching. Like the land, they too looked tired and old. Mama had some gray to her hair and wrinkles that Connie didn't remember. When had that happened?

"Mama!" She ran to her mother and wrapped her in her arms. "I've missed you so much." To her surprise, Connie's eyes filled with tears as they embraced. Had her mother always been so thin?

"How I've missed you," Mama whispered against her ear.

"What about me?"

Connie pulled away to find her father's smiling face. "What about you?" Her tone was teasing. "I suppose you'll want me to hug you as well." She all but threw herself into his arms, noticing the lines on his face. "Oh, Papa, it's so good to see you again." She let him hold her for a long time. She found herself a young girl once again, her papa dispelling all thought of trouble and harm.

It wasn't long before Mama spoke. "It's good to be together again. Letters do not do justice to an aching heart." She touched Connie's cheek. "Seven years is far too much time to let pass between loved ones."

"Is there room for me to join this party?"

Connie smiled. "That must be Isaac." She let go of her parents and turned to find her older brother grinning from ear to ear. "Just look at you. You're taller still than when you went off to school."

"I think he's finally done growing," Mama commented. "But there for a while we were having to let down the hem of his pants nearly every month."

The siblings embraced. Connie felt a sense of wholeness. Their little family was all together again. Despite the changes in their lives and her worries for the future, Connie couldn't have been happier. She was exactly where she belonged.

"Clint, thanks for bringing her home," her father said, and she pulled away from Isaac.

"I need to introduce you all to my dear friend." She glanced around for Tom and found him standing pretty much where she'd left him. "This is Thomas Lowell, but he goes by Tom."

Mama was the first to reach him. She gave him a warm smile. "I feel, from all I've heard about you over the years, that you're already a part of the family. Welcome."

"Thank you, Mrs. Browning." He smiled. "I feel like I know all of you as well. Connie has told me so much about her family and her life here."

"Well, we're glad you could come. The idea of the government taking a true accounting of the tribes and their culture is a promising thing," Connie's father declared. He extended his hand, and Tom shook it. "I think you're going to find it all very fascinating, although sadly some tribes have already been lost."

"I believe I will enjoy it very much, and hopefully we can still account for those tribes that are now extinct. I think it's important to preserve our history."

"I arranged a room for you in the government house, but Adam tells me that you'll both be staying with them," Clint interrupted.

Connie responded before anyone else could. "My folks live just across the way, and it will be much homier to stay with them."

"Absolutely," her mother said. "I wouldn't rest a wink if Connie weren't staying with us, and there's no need for Tom to feel isolated in a strange place."

Clint shrugged. "Well, if that works for all of you, then I see no harm. I'm sure the government will appreciate not having to pay for their room and board."

"Well, the government can still pay, as far as I'm concerned," Connie declared. "Mama and Papa don't make much money anymore, and they've offered to keep us fed. The government can at least pay for food and Tom's lodging, even if they won't pay for mine."

"I agree," Tom replied. "And I already worked all of that out with them before we came West. The Bureau knows we're going to live with the Brownings, and they were fine with the room and board fee I suggested. Therefore, you needn't worry."

Clint looked momentarily unhappy. Perhaps he was offended at being left out of the decision-making. His dismay didn't last, however, and he smiled. "I'm glad you worked it out before you came. I'll see that the Indians get your things over to the Browning house."

"No need," her father replied. "I believe we four men can manage it."

Connie knew Clint used to abhor manual labor. It appeared he still felt the same way, despite his seeming helpfulness on the trip south.

"I'm sure you're right," Clint replied.

"I nearly forgot. There are several crates of goods for the people." Connie turned to her mother. "Aunt Phinny sent some, and Nancy and the boardinghouse ladies sent others."

"How kind. We can go through it all in the next few days and get it disbursed. There's so much need here that I'm sure none of it will go to waste. Now, why don't you and Tom come on in the house, and we'll have a bite to eat. I'll have it ready in about twenty minutes. Clint, you're welcome to join us as well. We can get the crates after lunch."

"I'd like to, but unfortunately I have some issues that need my immediate attention. Maybe another time." He tipped his hat and looked at Tom. "I'd be happy to show you around the reservation later. It would be good to let the people see you with me."

"Thank you." Tom glanced at Connie.

She decided to volunteer to join them. "I'll come along as well."

Clint seemed surprised by this. "I figured you'd want to spend time with your folks before getting to work. The people know who you are. It's Tom who's a stranger. Your father and I can see that the people get to know him little by little. It should make your job easier to do in the long run."

"We don't have the luxury of taking our time with this project," Connie replied. "The government has a very definite expectation of seeing results immediately. I'm sure you understand how that works. Tom and I have to send in our first report in less than two months." She smiled at Tom. "But I know we can manage."

"I'm going to run over and see the Johnsons," Isaac said. "They have a cow giving birth, and she was having trouble, last I checked. I want to make sure they don't need an extra hand. I'll be at lunch as soon as I can."

"Make sure you clean up before you come to the table," Mama called after him.

"I will!"

Connie looped her arm through her mother's as they walked toward the Browning residence. The house sat outside the reservation boundaries, but not by much. The two-story log home had a small front porch, and there were flower boxes under the windows on either side of the house. Papa had always tended to the needs of the building, and as Isaac had grown up, he learned at their father's side what was important to managing one's property. Mama, on the other hand, had taught Connie sewing and cooking, as well as gardening and the important art of making vinegar. Her family held a strong belief that vinegar could cure most any ailment, as well as wash or purify whatever needed it. Vinegar was every bit as important as water to Connie's family.

She was surprised when Clint spoke up. She hadn't realized he'd followed them.

"I think you should still consider doing things my way," Clint said. "There have been conflicts among some of the tribal members. I wouldn't want either of you to get hurt by wandering around without me. Things aren't the same as they were when you left."

Connie was touched by the concern in his tone. "Perhaps you could take us around the first time. However, Tom and I should be seen together, since we're working together. I have a trust to build with the people as well."

"I suppose you're right. You have been gone for seven years." He looked at her as if really seeing her for the first time. "A lot has changed in that time," he murmured.

Connie felt flushed under his scrutiny. Could it be that she still had feelings for him? For so long she'd pushed such thoughts aside, knowing that he saw her as nothing but a child. Now that she was grown, perhaps his feelings were changing. But did she want them to? She looked at Tom, who was watching her with an odd expression on his face. Maybe he wanted some time alone with Clint. Maybe it would help their case if Tom could get Clint to talk about what he knew— man to man.

"You know, you're probably right." Connie smiled and glanced over at her mother. "We have a lot to catch up on."

"Maybe Clint and Tom could set out after lunch," Mama offered. "Are you sure you won't join us, Clint?"

"No, I have some other things to tend to. I'll find something to eat, don't you worry." He turned to Tom. "Just come on over to the government house after lunch." He pointed at the small building. "I'll be happy to escort you around and introduce you to a few folks."

"Thank you. I'll be there." Tom seemed content with this.

Clint tipped his hat and walked away without another word. Connie couldn't help but watch him go. He was still a very attractive man, and there was something about him that had always captured her attention.

But I'm not in love with him.

"Ready for lunch?" her mother asked, and Connie nodded.

"More than ready."

"Let us pray and give thanks," Connie's father said.

Everyone bowed their heads, and Papa issued a short but heartfelt prayer. "We're so thankful, Lord, that you brought Connie and Tom here safely. Guard and guide them as they set about their work. In Jesus' name, amen."

Connie and her mother murmured *amens,* then reached for the bowls and began to pass the food around the table.

"Connie tells us that you were instrumental in getting her this job, Tom. I have to say it was a real blessing," Mama said.

"Yes, well, she wanted very much to see you proven innocent of the suspicions against you."

"I'm grateful you're both working so hard to see us vindicated," Papa said, taking the bowl of lamb stew. "Although I've been quite confident that God would prove us innocent."

"Since I don't believe in God, I will do what I can to see the matter through to a satisfactory fulfillment," Tom replied.

Connie cringed. She hadn't told her parents that Tom was an atheist. Well, he was more of an agnostic. She didn't really accept that he thought there was no God. It was more that Tom had decided if there was a God, He didn't show the slightest interest in the people of earth, and therefore Tom didn't have the slightest interest in God. It was something she'd worked hard to ignore. Everything else about Tom was practically perfect . . . everything but the most important thing.

"Sorry I'm late," Isaac announced, coming to the table. "The calf was stuck, but we got him out." He turned to his mother and held up his hands. "And I remembered to wash. What did I miss?"

"Tom was just telling us he's an atheist," their mother replied, as if Tom hadn't mentioned anything more exciting than the weather.

"Oh." Isaac nodded. "That could be interesting to hear about." He then appeared to forget about it and started digging into the food around him.

Papa didn't seem remotely shocked. After all, he'd dealt with people who didn't believe in his God for most of his adult life. "That *is* quite interesting, Tom. How did you come to the conclusion that there is no God?"

Tom shrugged and helped himself to a platter of biscuits. "My father suggested it to me, I suppose. Not exactly in words, but certainly in deeds. His underhanded business practices and cruelty to my siblings and me made it clear that if there was a God, He surely didn't care about us. And I found it hard to believe that anyone, even God, wouldn't care about such deception and evil deeds. So I concluded there must not be a God."

"That makes sense," her father said, surprising Connie. "Is it at all possible you might rethink your conclusion if I was able to share insight with you from my own encounters with the Almighty?"

"I'd enjoy the challenge," Tom replied. "People often tiptoe around my beliefs as if I might suddenly grow horns and a tail if they talk to me too long on the matter. But just as I don't believe in a god, I certainly don't believe in a devil."

Connie watched her father as he considered this. He actually smiled. "I'll look forward to our discussions on the matter. Would you be willing to do me the favor of joining us each morning for our family devotionals?"

Tom smiled. "Of course. You are, after all, my gracious host."

"Wonderful. I shall look forward to it. Now, tell me, you mentioned siblings. How many of them do you have?"

And that was all Papa had to say on the matter. Connie was rather stunned. She focused on the meal at hand but couldn't shake the feeling that she'd been deceptive with her mother and father. Of course, Aunt Phinny and Uncle Dean knew about Tom's beliefs, so Connie had just supposed it was common knowledge. She was so used to the idea of Tom's lack of faith that she rarely even thought about it. Perhaps she should have. She was, after all, a Christian, and a big part of being a Christian was sharing the faith. Yet Connie was fairly certain she'd rarely shared her beliefs with anyone. Guilt washed over her. There had been a time when she and Tom openly debated their beliefs, but when that ended, Connie had tried not to think about how different their views were. She hadn't even prayed that he would find the truth about God for himself.

She took a biscuit and tried to put her attention on the food. Her mother's lamb stew was every bit as good as Connie remembered. Her mother cooked in a very simple fashion, using fresh vegetables and meats. She didn't bathe them in creams or sauces to disguise or change their flavors, and Connie found she had missed this plain fare. Even her mother's biscuits, although heavier, were more flavorful.

"I've missed this so much." She forced the words out and pushed ever harder to stuff back her guilt.

"I was afraid you wouldn't find my cooking very satisfying after eating such fancy meals back East," Mama replied. She took her seat after fetching a brown sugar cake. "I hope you still like this." She cut a slice and put it on a small plate. "We don't usually have cake for lunch, but I couldn't resist." She handed the plate to Tom. "This used to be Connie's favorite."

"I'm sure it still is," Connie declared. "Especially if you made your brown sugar butter sauce to go with it."

"Of course she did," her father said, placing a small pitcher on the table. "What's the cake without the sauce?"

"The very thought is indecent," Isaac said.

Connie could almost taste it. What an unexpected delight. Her mother handed her a piece of the cake and then the pitcher of sauce. Connie poured the liquid all over the cake, and then handed the pitcher to Tom. "Make sure you use plenty. It soaks into the cake and is like nothing you've ever had." She waited until he'd copied her actions, then picked up her fork. "Sometimes Mama makes whipped cream to go along with it, but I find it just perfect with the sauce alone." She cut into the cake and popped a piece into her mouth.

The warm, buttery brown sugar hit her tongue in a burst of flavor that made her happy and homesick all at once. She'd never allowed herself to realize just how much she'd missed this place and her parents. Now, sitting here with her family and Tom, Connie thought she had never been happier.

Except for the fact that Tom didn't believe in God.

Tears came unbidden.

"Goodness, I didn't expect to make you cry," her mother said, extending her handkerchief.

Connie took it and dabbed her eyes. She didn't know whether she was crying for Tom or the fact that she'd missed her family. She would choose the latter for the sake of discussion. "I didn't realize just how much I missed you all. I didn't really allow myself to think about it while I was away. I knew I longed for each of you, but the depth of feeling that overwhelms me now was something I didn't let come through. Otherwise I could never have stayed away so long."

Her mother met her gaze and nodded. "I am the same way when thinking of my sisters. I dare not let myself miss them too much."

"Well, I for one think we should eat our cake and be happy," her father declared. He cut his own piece and plopped it unceremoniously on his plate. "Now, please pass me the sauce before Isaac gets a hold of it and uses it all up."

Mama laughed. "There's plenty more. I made sure of it."

When they'd finished with lunch, Connie felt a deep longing for a nap. She was thoroughly spent and crawled atop her old bed without even bothering to undress. She would rest for just a few minutes.

She smiled at the familiar smells and textures, and as she faded off in hazy dreams, she let contentment wash over her. What a peace there was in coming back to where she had once belonged—always belonged.

Tom caught Clint at his desk, sorting through a stack of papers. "Looks like you have more than enough to do."

Clint seemed momentarily surprised. "There's always so much paper work to do. The government is strict about everything being recorded . . . in triplicate. Right now, I'm registering rights of inheritance. The Indian people by law can only transfer property to other Indian peoples. In particular— family. But their families are sometimes so large and extended that figuring out who the direct descendant is can be complicated. We're trying to arrange that ahead of time to make the transfers easier."

"Makes sense to me."

Clint looked past him at the closed door. "So Connie's not coming?"

"You heard her yourself. She could see the reasoning behind us getting to know each other, and besides, she was exhausted. She's napping, and I thought that would give us a chance to get better acquainted. I didn't get a chance to tell you that I spent time with both your father and brother in Washington. They send their regards."

Clint put the papers aside. "Thank you. I hope they were well when you left them."

"Very much so. They were busy with their work for the Native peoples. They are greatly admired."

"Yes." Clint stood and started to reach for his jacket, then stopped. "It's too warm for coats. You might want to discard your own as well."

"So long as it won't make the Indians think less of me," Tom said, shrugging out of his coat.

"I have to tell you . . . they already think less of us. They aren't happy to be under the care of the white man, nor do they wish to be our friends."

"That's sad. We could surely accomplish far more working as friends than as enemies."

Clint shook his head. "They don't really wish to accomplish anything with us. What they want is their freedom."

"And who wouldn't want that? We just fought a war over freeing black people from slavery. Why would we not understand that the Indians desire freedom as well?"

"I believe we understand it perfectly well,"

Clint said, his voice taking on an edge. "It's just not something we can accept."

Tom scratched his chin. "Why do you suppose that is?"

"Simple. The Indians have been warring with us since we arrived on this continent."

"Is that so hard to understand?" Tom asked. "After all, we are the uninvited guests who came in and took over. I would be of a mind to fight, should someone come to take for themselves what I perceived as open to all."

"Well, it's easy to see how you feel about the Indians." Clint smiled and picked up his hat. "Let me show you around a little."

Tom was surprised at the quick dismissal but said nothing. Connie had said that Clint was acting strange and she didn't know why. She had wondered if it had to do with her and the past, or if it was about them coming to do a job of which Clint disapproved. Tom intended to find out.

"As you know, this is the government building. My quarters are in the back. Over there"—Clint pointed across the dirt road—"is the sutler's store. It was originally set up when the army first arrived. The government allows each of the Indian families to have an account there. They can put money on the account from what they earn and then draw on it for their needs. Other things are disbursed to them throughout the year by the government."

Tom nodded and sized up the men standing around outside the store. They were clearly Native Americans, but they were dressed from head to toe in common clothes like his. Not only that, but their hair had been cut short. He remembered the papers he'd read prior to taking on this new job. The government believed that the more the Native people assimilated and took on the white man's ways, the better life would be for all concerned. He couldn't see that it had benefited these men all that much.

"Over there is the Catholic church and school. The Father is very driven to help the Indian children. He speaks Chinook Wawa—the common language between all the tribes—but is working to teach the children English. We've tried hard to get them to speak English only, but despite the rules, many continue to speak their Native language at home."

"What's wrong with that?"

Clint looked at Tom in disbelief. "It only causes irritation and fighting. There are multiple tribes here. They need a common language."

"But you just said they had one."

Clint shook his head. "They need to speak English for their own good. They will never be accepted into the white community—they will never be given white jobs if they can't speak English."

"I wasn't suggesting they not be taught English, but why is it wrong for them to speak their Native tongue at home? Why is it wrong for them to keep their culture alive? After all, that's why I'm here. The government is worried that these cultures will all be lost to the ages."

"You sound like the priest. He encourages them to keep their cultures alive as well. I've told him before—and the nuns as well—that one of these days it'll backfire on them, and we'll have an uprising."

"Maybe you'd find a more peaceful and cooperative people if you worked to incorporate their beliefs and culture into their everyday life. Maybe the children would be more eager to learn if they could share their heritage rather than shun it. I've always known the Indians to be a proud people."

Clint shook his head again. "You've got a lot to learn, Tom. We teeter on the brink of war every day. We dare not give even one of these people a reason to fight, and that includes reminding them of the past. I've been fearful since hearing about your work to catalog the various tribes. Mark my words, this is only going to stir up trouble. The people, once reminded of their old ways, are going to fight to perpetuate their traditions and language. You may well find yourself undoing decades of work, to the detriment of all."

CHAPTER 7

I'm sorry I wasn't able to come see you while Mr. Tom Lowell was still in town," Major Wells told Seth. "I would have appreciated getting to meet him."

"We discussed the situation and the things I'd learned in the past. I told him about our concerns about who was now in charge, since Lakewood and Berkshire are dead." Seth shook his head. "We know there are others involved, but no doubt they are being very cautious."

"No doubt." Major Wells picked up the cup of coffee Nancy had poured him earlier. "Even the local gatherings are being less public with their speaking events."

"Perhaps they realize that they're being watched. I don't trust that Gerome Berkshire kept such things to himself. He might have been spying for us to save himself from jail, but I know he wasn't completely forthcoming with information."

Wells put the cup back on the table with a nod. "It will be good to have a man at one of the reservations."

"And a woman." Seth chuckled. "Nancy's cousin Connie is not easily dismissed. She is angry about her folks being accused. She intends to see them cleared of any supposed guilt. I thought Nancy was stubborn, but Connie is more tenacious than any of them. She's also the adventurous type. She won't back down from a challenge, even if it's dangerous."

"That could cause more trouble than good," Wells replied. "I can't believe the officials brought her in on this."

"They didn't. Connie more or less imposed herself on them. They don't know it, however, and I need your promise that you'll say nothing on the matter."

Wells frowned. "I owe my allegiance to the government of the United States."

"I realize that. I'm only asking that you don't volunteer this information. I'm sharing this with you because I want you to understand how much I believe in this family and their innocence. Please say nothing."

"Very well. I'll remain silent for now.

However, if I see something amiss, I'll have to reconsider." His brow furrowed. "There very well could be unforeseen problems. I've never known women to keep a balanced mind when emotional connections were concerned. I fear that her love of her parents will blind her."

Seth shook his head. "I don't think so. I think she's a very collected and reasonable young woman. I believe she'll be beneficial to everyone concerned."

"And if it turns out her parents are involved? Will she be forthcoming with the truth?"

Seth considered the question. "I believe she will be the first to declare the truth. It won't be easy, and she won't like it, but Connie is staunch in her desire for truth. She would want to see her parents directed toward redemption." Again, he shook his head. "But her parents aren't a part of this. Everyone who knows them refuses to believe they have even the slightest part in stirring the Indians to war. They love those people and have put their lives on the line many times in order to prevent confrontation."

"I hope you're right," Major Wells said, reaching again for his coffee. "I'd hate to see your wife or any of your family have to deal with the situation should it prove their family is involved."

"Just remember your promise to keep Connie's part in this a secret. I know I can trust you, or I would never have told you. I just couldn't help feeling it was right to tell you. I believe it was God's prompting."

"I'll say nothing." The major chuckled. "Although I hardly think God concerns Himself with me."

"Of course He does," Seth countered. "He concerns Himself with all of us, no matter our position or place. I feel confident it's God's Spirit that makes it so evident to me that the Brownings are innocent."

"It must be, because you've convinced me of the Brownings' innocence as well." The major got to his feet. "Hopefully we can soon prove it."

Hours after Wells had departed, Seth sat in the kitchen, relating what they had discussed to Faith and Nancy. The two women wanted to know every detail of the investigation's progress.

"The major said they have a list of men who are watched closely. Most are the laborers who are moving the guns and whiskey. They've taken an inordinate amount of whiskey to the reservations, but it's been allowed to pass through. Wells is afraid that if they intercept the deliveries, it will compromise the rest of the investigation."

"I hate to think of the harm it's doing." Faith looked dismayed. "Alcohol will just cause increasing problems on the reservation."

"I'm sure you're right, but I'm also confident the major's concerns are warranted. We've come too far to give it all away now. Wells said that everything indicates it won't be long until the planned uprising takes place. He would stop it all now, but we don't have the man responsible for planning all of this. Without finding him, we'll only have to deal with him trying this again and again."

"I'm sure you're right," Nancy said, placing her hand atop his. "It's just such a helpless feeling to sit here and not be able to do anything."

"We can pray," Seth said, smiling. "Look what it's done for me—for us." He squeezed her fingers. "God is good. He won't let the innocent be condemned."

"He allowed His only Son to be condemned, and He was innocent," Nancy murmured. "Others have fallen under false accusation to God's glory. You can't say that it won't happen to Uncle Adam and Aunt Mercy. You can't be sure."

"But I am sure of God's righteousness. No matter what happens, we either trust in Him or we don't." He looked at Nancy and then Faith. "The choice is ours, and for me, I believe there is only one choice, and that is to trust. The alternative has no hope for me."

"Nor me," Nancy admitted. "I know Faith feels the same way."

"I do." Faith sighed. "God has already brought me through so much—you two as well. We know we live in a fallen world and that bad things will continue to happen, but we know too that God is faithful. He will deliver us and our family from this mess. He will let the truth be revealed, because Adam and Mercy belong to Jesus, and He is the truth."

"It looks rather hopeless at the moment," Connie's father said in a hushed voice, "but our trust is in God."

Connie had joined her folks at the kitchen table, where many a problem had been discussed over the years. She was sharing with them all that she knew, starting at the beginning. "Tom was given reports on the investigation thus far. Apparently Nancy's first husband was a central figure for a time. He was recruited to buy large quantities of weapons and liquor. He hid these in secret caches and kept separate records regarding what had been purchased. The money for the guns and whiskey was given to him by a group of businessmen in Portland. One of those men was Gerome Berkshire and another was Samuel Lakewood. Berkshire was the contact for Nancy's husband. Berkshire arranged for the contents of the caches to be delivered to the reservations via his various workers. Berkshire, in turn, answered to Lakewood, who answered to someone else. We don't know who that person is or even if that person is the top man, but there is reason to believe he is."

"So the whiskey was brought by Berkshire's men to the reservation, and they got the whiskey and guns from Nancy's first husband, Albert Pritchard," her father repeated, mulling this over. "How long do they believe this has been going on?"

"At least three years," Connie replied. "Probably longer, but they have proof of that long."

"We knew the men here were getting liquor," Mama said, glancing at Connie's father, "but we were never able to figure out how. I mean, to get that much liquor onto the reservation unnoticed would take quite a few people coordinating it."

"And there were. Berkshire had a whole force of workers. At least thirty, at last count."

"But I don't understand why they think

your mother and I are involved." Her father sounded hurt—betrayed.

"They know you were unhappy with the transfer of preaching and teaching to the Catholic Church," Connie offered. "I believe they thought this triggered you to want to get back at the government."

"That transfer took place years ago." Her father's brown eyes darkened to nearly black. "I wasn't happy to lose the job I felt God had called me to, but I wouldn't do anything to harm these people. I've worked closely with Father Croquet over the years to help the Indians and was pleasantly surprised that he was so supportive of the Native people keeping their culture. It's not his fault that the government has enforced rules about westernizing the Indians." He paused. "I love these people, Connie. I would never do anything to hurt them."

"I know. That's why I'm determined to help Tom prove your innocence." Connie reached over and gave her father's arm a pat. "Papa, we know how much you love the people here. Tom and I will do all we can."

Her mother hung her head. "I just can't understand why they would accuse us without even coming to talk to us."

Connie felt bad for them both. They were so secluded and hidden away from the games and nonsense that went on elsewhere. Until recently, they'd had no idea they were at the center of such a large conflict.

"Are other reservations involved?" Papa asked.

"Warm Springs and Siletz are a part of it too. The government thinks there may be others. The thought is that whoever has planned this wanted all the reservations to rise up at once. It will make for massive destruction and many lives lost. The ultimate goal is to cause such damage that the white population will demand the Indians be removed to an even more remote location. There was even talk about sending them to the new lands purchased in the far north."

"Seward's Folly," Papa murmured.

"Yes. There are already Native people there, and it has been suggested that it might be a good place to put all of them."

"Does no one understand or even care that each tribe has its own desired location?" Papa asked. "It's been bad enough to see them separated from their original homelands and forced onto reservations, but the idea of completely removing them to some desolate region that they're ill-prepared to deal with is appalling."

"If we can stop the uprising from happening, there will be no reason to remove them." Connie heard Tom and Clint talking as they came into the house and didn't want to risk being overheard. She put her finger to her lips. "Hopefully Tom and I will get it all figured out. Things will be different."

"Did I hear that something is different?" Clint asked as he and Tom came into the room.

Connie hoped that was all he'd overheard. "Yes. Things are so different here at the reservation. The storm really did a lot of damage. I'm surprised you haven't done more to see it restored."

Clint frowned and sat down at the table uninvited. "A person can only accomplish so much. Your father understands that. The Indian Legislature has done what it can to work with the people to restore the lumber mill, but it was in disrepair, and it will take money to get it working again. Unfortunately, none of the tribal people seem to want to put the time and effort into it."

Connie remembered, years earlier, when the mill had worked perfectly and made a tidy profit. Unfortunately, the Indian agent at the time had violated the agreement and taken the profits. He later apologized, saying it was all a misunderstanding, but the damage was done. Connie was certain the money was never returned. It was little wonder the people had no heart for working the mill.

"It's a pity we aren't closer to Uncle Alex's lumber mills. I'm sure he would help make things right. I wonder if there's someone we can contact about the matter. Someone who actually cares."

"Connie." Her father's disapproving tone let her know she'd crossed a line.

"I'm doing my best," Clint said, looking wounded.

Connie knew she'd hurt him. She didn't know why she felt so harsh toward him. Certainly, part of it was based on the past. Maybe all of it was. She hated the way he'd made fun of her when they'd first met in Portland, and she hated that he'd let her mother and father be blamed for something he knew they had no part in. Of course, there was the possibility that Clint knew nothing of the accusations. After all, she hadn't had time to ask her father what, if anything, he and Clint had discussed about the situation.

It was only then that she realized she was very angry with Clint. She didn't feel at all like showing him grace, and a sense of guilt begin to rise within her. She needed to show kindness—to forgive the past and move forward. Her attitude was completely uncalled for. Just because a godly young man who worked with her father had spurned her romantic notions was no call to be ugly.

"I'm sorry." She barely breathed the words, but at least she meant them. "I'm just frustrated that things look so bad. I suppose it could always be worse, and I know the storm wasn't your fault, Clint."

He met her eyes and smiled. "I probably had it coming. I've been rather discouraged with the way things have gone. You can ask your father. We've talked about it on more than one occasion."

"We have, and no doubt will again," Connie's father declared. He looked at Connie's mother.

"Well, I need to get back to work." Clint smiled and headed for the door.

"Clint, you will join us for supper, won't you?" Connie's mother asked.

He glanced over his shoulder with a smile. "I'd like that, Mrs. Browning."

"Wonderful. We'll sit down at six."

Connie helped her mother with kitchen chores while her father and Tom got better acquainted. Later, while supper simmered on the stove, she made her way outside and filled Tom in on what she'd discussed with her folks. He reciprocated, telling her what he and Clint had discussed. His words seemed guarded, however, and Connie couldn't understand

what was going on with him. They had retired to the small front porch, and Connie
was determined to get to the bottom of whatever was going on.

"What's wrong? You haven't been yourself all day."

Tom shrugged. "I've just stepped into an
investigation that could see your folks im-
prisoned. This area is new to me, and I'm
burdened with the fact that the Indian people
here might never accept me, to name just a
few things."

She leaned against the porch rail. "Is that
all?"

He laughed. "Isn't it enough?"

Connie considered that a moment. "I just
feel like there's a wall between us. Are you
just tired, or have I offended you?"

"I'm not offended. Just curious."

She frowned. "About what?"

"You never told your folks that I was an
atheist."

Connie shrugged. "I figured it was yours
to tell."

"You know we used to have conversations
about God, but then you stopped sharing
your beliefs. Why was that?"

Guilt oozed from the places she'd stuffed
it. "I don't know. I guess I didn't want to hurt
your feelings or destroy our friendship."

"And you thought it would?"

Connie looked away, unable to bear his gaze. "I'm not sure what I thought. I knew you felt the way you did and that I would probably never convince you otherwise. It bothered me so much that you didn't believe in God."

"Then why didn't you just say that?"

She sighed. "I don't know."

"I think you do." His tone was accusing.

Connie had never felt so uncomfortable in her life. She knew exactly why she had stopped talking about God and the Bible— why she hadn't continued to encourage Tom to believe in God.

"Connie?"

She forced herself to look at him. "Some of the things you were saying scared me. My own faith wasn't very strong—in fact, I really hadn't made it my own. I was still relying on my mother and father's faith. I knew I needed to focus on building my own beliefs and knowing God better, or . . ." She stopped, uncertain she could or should explain.

"Or what?" He put his hand on her arm. "Connie, we're too good of friends for you not to know you can be honest with me."

"I know. But this . . . well, it wasn't about you, Tom. It was about me. The things you were saying about why you didn't believe in God were starting to make sense." She paused long enough to swallow the lump in her throat. "I wasn't strong enough in my faith. I stopped talking to you about it because I was afraid that I would start to think like you did. I was already so bitter about what had happened with Clint. Not only that, but I missed my home and family. I was scared, and when I talked to Aunt Phinny, she suggested I not talk to you about issues of faith for a time. And after a while, it just didn't seem that important. We always had other things to talk about."

Tom folded his arms. "I never considered that I was swaying you to forget your own faith."

"But don't you see, it wasn't really my faith. It was what I'd been raised to believe. It was the teachings I'd been given, but I had to come to know God for myself. And I do now."

He smiled ever so slightly. "Does that mean you'll talk to me again about my beliefs? Will you try to get me into heaven?"

She wasn't at all sure what to say. A part of her wanted to beg him to believe in God and the Bible. "I will always be willing to talk to you about what I believe, but I think maybe this time it's more important for you to worry about what you believe and why. I think you should talk to my father. As you've seen, he won't condemn you, and you will probably find it a very interesting conversation."

"I'm sure I will." He looked like he might say something else but didn't. He got to his feet. "I'm heading up to my room for a quick nap before supper. I think everything has caught up with me." He smiled. "Are we still friends?"

She nodded. "You will always be my best friend, Tom. No matter what."

"What about your husband?"

Connie frowned. "What husband?"

Tom chuckled. "What will you do when you finally marry? As a man, I know I wouldn't want my wife calling another man her best friend."

She shrugged. "Then I guess I won't ever get married."

He gave her a look she couldn't interpret, then turned and left without a word.

Connie felt a deep sadness that she couldn't understand. She let Tom go without further prying and took a seat in her mother's favorite rocking chair. Why did all of this with Tom bother her so much?

"Why should it bother me?" she murmured. "Foolish woman, why *shouldn't* it bother you?"

Without Christ as his Savior, Tom would die and be forever separated from God. How could she just ignore that? Just yesterday she had been reading her Bible about the rich man and Lazarus. Chapter sixteen of Luke made it very clear that heaven and hell were real places. The rich man begged for help, first for water and then for Lazarus to be sent to warn his five brothers about hell.

Abraham saith unto him, They have Moses and the prophets; let them hear them. And he said, Nay, father Abraham: but if one went unto them from the dead, they will repent. And he said unto him, If they hear not Moses and the prophets, neither will they be persuaded, though one rose from the dead.

She stared for a moment at the words. Jesus was the One who rose from the dead, and still people denied He could save them from torment and hell. Tom denied it. Tears came to her eyes. He was her dearest friend in all the world, and despite this, she hadn't wanted to upset him with the truth or risk the possibility of losing his friendship.

"But unless he believes in Jesus, he will be lost for all eternity."

CHAPTER 8

Connie awoke early the following morning. Tom was uppermost on her mind as she dressed. He was at the forefront of her thoughts as she helped her mother with breakfast. Then, as they sat down to morning devotions and breakfast, there he was again—this time in the flesh.

Papa opened his Bible and prayed over the meal, then began to discuss Psalm 27. "This passage is one of my favorites," he said. "'The Lord is my light and my salvation; whom shall I fear? The Lord is the strength of my life; of whom shall I be afraid?'" He continued to read, although Connie found it hard to focus. She couldn't help but wonder what Tom was thinking. Did the words make any sense to him? Could he relate even in part?

"'When thou saidst, Seek ye my face; my

heart said unto thee, Thy face, Lord, will I seek. Hide not thy face far from me; put not thy servant away in anger: thou hast been my help; leave me not, neither forsake me, O God of my salvation.'"

Connie wondered why her father had chosen this particular passage. The chapter was actually one of her favorites, but she didn't see it as one to teach someone about the reality of God.

When Papa finished reading, he closed the Bible and smiled at his family. "I've always loved that chapter. We have many fears in life, but we needn't be afraid, for the Lord is our light and salvation—He is the strength of my life. I was especially thinking of the last part." He began to quote it from memory. "'Deliver me not over unto the will of mine enemies: for false witnesses are risen up against me, and such as breathe out cruelty. I had fainted, unless I had believed to see the goodness of the Lord in the land of the living. Wait on the Lord: be of good courage, and he shall strengthen thine heart: wait, I say, on the Lord.' You know, with all those who are plotting against us, I find great comfort in this verse. I am determined to wait on the Lord and be of good courage. I wanted to share this so that you might be of good courage as well. No matter what happens to come our way—accusations or suspicions—I will wait on the Lord. Let's pray."

As her father began to pray, Connie was disappointed. He'd said nothing to Tom about his unbelief. Perhaps he planned to talk to him privately. Maybe he felt it would be too embarrassing to point out Tom's flawed thinking in the company of all.

After breakfast, Tom volunteered to help Mama with the dishes, so Connie decided to go see her old friend Rosy. She knew it probably wasn't the best of ideas to go off alone, but Rosy lived fairly close by.

Rosy had been born with a Shasta Indian name that translated to Flower Blooming in the Summer Sun. When English names had been imposed, Connie's mother had told her that roses typically bloomed in the summer. Because of that, Rosy had taken on the name Rose Johnson, but everyone called her Rosy.

Life for Rosy had never been easy. She had endured the long march from the southern border of Oregon to Grand Ronde in the north with her husband and three children back in the '50s. She had been expecting another baby at the time but lost him on the hard and difficult trail. Two children had also died on the trip. Rosy had been heartbroken, her husband too, but the soldiers wouldn't give them time to perform decent funerals or to grieve. The bodies were hastily buried, and the Indians were moved on ever closer to the reservation.

Rosy had told Connie of how her husband died only a month after reaching Grand Ronde and how her only surviving child—a son—had been shot by soldiers when he attempted to leave the reservation with a group of his friends. They had hoped to reach Canada and a new life without imprisonment. Instead, the five young men had been killed, and Rosy's heartbreak was complete.

Connie couldn't imagine the pain the old woman had suffered. She had often talked with Mama about looking forward to heaven, where she was certain she would see her loved ones again. Life on earth was nothing more than a reminder of loss and pain.

Rosy lived inside the reservation's boundaries but not far from Connie's parents. She had a tiny one-room house with two windows. Both were covered with oilcloth, but once there had been glass. Outside, Connie saw a well-tended garden. She knew Rosy used to sell vegetables to the store, which in turn gave her credit to buy things she couldn't grow. Hopefully that arrangement was still in place.

To the left of the house was a pump. Papa had dug that well for Rosy. Connie had been told the story since she was very little. Shortly after her husband died, Rosy had befriended Mama. When others from her tribe heard about this, they shunned Rosy for having anything to do with white people.

The women brought their water up from the river, but if Rosy tried to go with them, the other women would often pick fights with her, so she would wait and go alone. There was no one for her to talk to. No one to help her if she couldn't manage the pails. Mama told her husband what was going on, and he agreed to single-handedly dig Rosy a well.

Over the years, the shunning ended as Rosy's trust encouraged others to believe that Adam and Mercy were worthy of their friendship. After a time, Rosy and many others came to believe in Christ. The story always reminded Connie of the woman at the well in the gospel of John, chapter four. She too had been outcast, but one day she met Jesus and then invited her people to come meet a man who had told her everything she had ever done. And they came, and many believed.

Connie started to knock on the door of Rosy's house, but she heard someone humming and followed the sound around the side of the house. There she found Rosy bent over a large rosebush.

"Good morning, Rosy."

The old woman straightened and turned to Connie, who grinned from ear to ear.

"Little Connie." Rosy came to where Connie stood. "You are all grown up."

"I am." She laughed. "Finally. I sometimes thought I would never be an adult."

Rosy chuckled. "When you are as old as I am, you will wonder why you were in such a hurry."

They embraced, and Connie found it hard to drop her hold. She'd missed her friend. "How are you doing? I feel like it's been forever since we talked."

"To me it was just yesterday," Rosy replied. "Come inside, and we'll have tea."

Connie followed Rosy into the house. Rosy quickly lit a lamp, then went to the stove to check the metal teakettle.

"I put the water on before I went to check on the roses." She smiled. "I hoped you'd come."

"I wanted to come yesterday, but I was much too tired. Now, after a good night's sleep, I figure we can have a nice long visit without you having to wake me up."

Rosy smiled and poured hot water into a ceramic teapot. Connie glanced around the house. It was a single room. Rosy's bed was in one corner, the kitchen in the other. A small bookcase held various books and basket projects Rosy was making. Connie remembered Rosy telling her stories about weaving baskets with her mother and grandmother. They were precious memories for the woman who had no remaining family.

"Sit, and we will talk as we did when you were young," Rosy declared. "When we were both young."

She brought two cups to the table and then the teapot. There was no other offering, and Connie chided herself for not bringing something. She would remember next time and make something special for Rosy. No doubt the old woman had treats on rare occasions, and Connie wanted to honor her and their many years of friendship.

Rosy poured the tea and took her seat. She hadn't bothered to strain the leaves, so Connie gave them a few minutes to settle. "I've missed you so much, Rosy. I hope you are well."

"I am old, so such things are a matter of perspective." She smiled. "I've lost all but six teeth, and my body aches all the time. Still, I am happy for each breath and happier still for the day I will go to heaven and see my family."

Connie nodded. "It's good to look forward to that day. I'm sorry, though, that you are in pain and have lost your teeth."

"It's of no matter. How are you? Did you learn everything there is to learn, as you hoped?"

Connie had almost forgotten their long-ago conversation where she had told Rosy that was her goal. She smiled. "I learned a great deal, that's for sure. Oh, Rosy, the big city is so much different than growing up here. There is too much noise and so many people. People who are always rushing from one place to another. They are so busy doing things and striving for things that they never seem to put their work aside and just rest."

Rosy chuckled. "When I was a little girl, my mother said I was lazy. If she were here now, she would see how busy I've become and tell me to sit down and enjoy what God has given."

Connie smiled. "Exactly. People are definitely like that in the cities. They work very hard and seldom stop to enjoy life. My aunt and uncle are very busy people. Many people think them wise and constantly seek their counsel. My aunt has a small book in which she writes her various appointments for each day. It is the only way that she can keep track."

Rosy looked appalled. "What a horrible way to live—always bound by those things."

Connie thought about it for a moment.

That had been her life for the last seven years, and while she'd always been occupied, she'd never thought of herself as being bound or chained to those things. When was the last time she'd had nothing to do and spent the day in leisure?

"But now you are home. Will you stay?" Rosy asked.

"At least for a while. I have come with a job to do. The government has hired me to make a list of the tribes here at Grand Ronde. And not just a list—I'm to write an account of the people and their culture. The men in the big cities want to know about the life of the Shasta and the Tututni and the Modoc. They want to know about all the tribes."

"What is it they want to know?" Rosy asked, frowning.

"They realize that some tribes have disappeared. That the great march stole many lives, and that over the years some of the tribes have died away. They want an accounting of those people and all who are left. They want to know what you believe and how you used to live. They want to know about your clothing and way of life. They want to know about your trade goods and hunting, about your houses and ceremonies."

"If they had left us to our lives, they could

easily know those things by observing us," Rosy said with a hint of bitterness.

"Yes. They could have," Connie agreed. "It was wrong of them to take that life from you. Now perhaps some of them are seeing that and want at least to know about that life. I cannot say for certain what is in their hearts, but in my heart, I want to make an accounting that will never allow the people of this vast land to forget the *real people* who were here first." She used the Natives' phrase for the various tribes to remind Rosy of her devotion and respect for the people of Grand Ronde.

Rosy shook her head. "It will not matter. The tribes have lost their heritage—lost their vision. The old ways were taken from us, and all that is left are the stories. Our stories are sacred—they have always been sacred. Why should we share them with the people who have taken away everything else? Should we let them steal our stories too?"

Connie had never seen it that way. She was saddened by the thought that Rosy considered her job to be theft. Connie had thought it good—a way to honor the Indians.

"I have no desire to steal your stories, Rosy. I wanted to come and make a record so that those stories won't be forgotten. So that the people wouldn't be forgotten."

"Our people will not be forgotten. We will tell our children, and they will tell their children."

Connie nodded. "I realize that, but I want everyone to know about your people. Not so they can steal that from you, but so they can learn the truth. I want them to see what they have done—how they have taken those precious things from you."

"Why, Connie? What good will it do?"

For a moment Connie didn't know how to respond. What good *would* it do? Connie and Tom, along with other teams, would chronicle the tribes and their old life, but it wouldn't change anything for these people. Even a record that would ensure the old ways weren't forgotten would never bring the old ways back. It would never give back the *real people*'s way of life. Their history would be recorded and then . . . forgotten.

Still, if even a few refused to forget, wouldn't that be worth the effort?

"The history of your family—your people—is precious to me, just as my own is." Connie chose her words carefully. If she couldn't convince Rosy that this was a good thing, there was no way she would convince anyone else. The women were key to this, and if they wouldn't share what they knew, then Connie and Tom might as well pack up and return to Washington. "Writing it down won't bring back the old ways or those who passed on, but it is a way to honor them. Others should know about the life you lived before the white man came and changed everything. They should be able to see the wrong they did, but more important, they should see the life you lived and how successful it was without their influence. They should know the culture and history of your people and remember it so that it will never be forgotten."

Rosy sipped her tea, and Connie did likewise, hoping her words would encourage Rosy. She wanted so much to tell the story of the various tribes. Though she was here to prove her parents' innocence, she believed in this project as well.

Connie put down her cup. "Rosy, I would never do anything to dishonor you or your people. I only want this new record so that people everywhere will know the truth. Your truth."

Rosy lowered her cup. "That would be good. The white man should know the truth."

Connie nodded. "They must know. Truth is the only thing that matters."

"Your father once told me that Jesus was the truth."

Connie smiled and reached for Rosy's

hand. "Yes. He is. He loves for the truth to be told. God hates lies and loves the truth."

Rosy seemed to think on this for a moment, then gave a nod. "I love the truth, as well. I will speak truth with you about my people and encourage the others to do the same. The truth is my gift to you."

"And I will cherish it, Rosy—Flower Blooming in the Summer Sun."

Rosy smiled at this and covered Connie's hand for a moment with her gnarled fingers.

They finished their tea, and only then did Connie remember the small gift she'd brought Rosy. She reached into her pocket and pulled out a leather bag. "I have something for you." She opened the leather bag and pulled out a wooden cross. "There was a fair in the capital, and I found this and thought of you. It's made from rosewood, which comes from a tree that grows in a land far away." She handed the cross to Rosy.

"It is very beautiful," Rosy said, running her fingers over the polished wood.

"It's made from a single piece of wood and is very strong—like you." Connie smiled. "I wanted you to have it to remind you of Jesus and all that He has done for you."

"I will, and I will remember you and all

you have done for me—all that your parents have done for the people."

Connie walked back to her house after her visit with Rosy, and for the first time since taking the job to make a record of the tribes, she worried that maybe it wasn't going to be the good thing she'd hoped for. Rosy had made her look at the entire project with different eyes. Were they somehow taking the last vestiges of the tribes by recording their stories and their history?

"You look upset," her father said as he joined her on the walk.

"Good morning, Papa. I suppose I am."

"Did something happen? Did someone trouble you? You know you shouldn't wander about alone."

"I just went to see Rosy." She gave her father a smile. "I've missed her very much and hoped we might have a nice talk about old times and why I've returned."

"And?"

Connie frowned and looked away. "I don't think she completely agrees with the job Tom and I have come to do. She saw it as the government stealing their history and stories. I think I helped her understand that by sharing the truth of who the people were and what they treasured, that people everywhere for all time would better know the *real people*. I told her I thought it was important that the truth be remembered."

"And did she accept that?"

"Yes, but it made me start to think that maybe she's right. Are we taking yet one more thing from them?"

Papa put his arm around her. "Being part Cherokee, I want to know my history and the people who went before me. I want to know the old stories that were told—the things the people believed about creation and death. It connects me to my ancestors, and it will connect others as well. I think this is a good thing, and in time, I believe they will see it that way too."

"I hope so. I don't want to cause more suffering. These people have already known far too much. Every day I pray that I might live long enough to see them set free to live among us as equals. I know that's a big prayer, but like you always told me, we serve a God that is bigger than any problem we might bring Him."

Her father laughed and hugged her close. "Indeed, we do, and don't you ever forget it."

"I won't, Papa. I promise." She cherished his embrace and remembered times when she was younger that he had held her like this.

"I've missed you and Mama so much. I tried not to think about it while I was gone, but now that I'm here, I don't ever want to leave again."

"But you will. Not only when the job takes you to other reservations, but one day you'll marry and have a family of your own. I doubt your husband will want to live with his wife's family."

Connie knew he was right, but then Clint came to mind. "He might if he was already acquainted with them and worked alongside them."

"Are you talking about Clint?" her father asked. "Are you still in love with him, as you thought when you were fifteen?" His voice betrayed his concern.

"I don't know. I don't think so, but I'm not sure. My thoughts are all wrapped around this place and what it represents for me. Clint's a part of that, and I think he might be interested in me now."

Her father stopped walking and turned her to face him. "Connie, I think Clint is a good man. He has given a big part of himself to seeing this place made better, and I know his family is strongly supportive of a better life for the Indians. But don't try to make something out of nothing. I wouldn't want you to settle for someone just because you thought it would allow you to remain close to your mother and me."

Connie hadn't considered that she might be trying to conjure up feelings for Clint for such a purpose. In fact, she'd tried her best not to have any feelings at all for him. At least she'd thought she felt nothing for him. But there were times when he came to mind, and she wondered. Oh, it was all so confusing.

"I want you to know real and deep love like your mother and I have known. Nothing is worse than trying to make a romance work where the love isn't true. Pray about your feelings, Connie. God will show you the way."

"I will, Papa. I promise. I honestly don't know what I feel about anything. I put the past aside, and my girlish feelings went with it. At least I thought as much. I've spent seven years trying not to have any thoughts or feelings about Clint Singleton, and I suppose now, being here face-to-face, I can't ignore that I once cared deeply for him. But as everyone points out, I was just a child."

"Don't judge yourself too harshly. The feelings of a child are felt just as strongly. However, tempered by adult judgment and reason, you may well find that such feelings prove false."

Connie thought of Tom and the guilt she

bore. "Papa, can I ask you about something else?"

"You know you can. What is it?"

"It's about Tom." She lowered her head. "I feel guilty for not working harder to teach him about God."

"What do you mean, exactly?"

She sighed. "Tom and I used to have talks all the time about God when I first arrived in Washington, DC. I enjoyed our debates and was confident I would change his mind, but instead I found myself . . . confused and at times very nearly persuaded of his thinking. It scared me so much to realize my faith was more closely tied to you and Mama than to God. I wasn't as strong as I thought. I had to stop talking to Tom about God, because I was afraid that I might be tempted to stop believing in God as he had."

She bit her lower lip for a moment, then continued. "We talked about everything else, but when it came to matters of faith, I avoided any conversation. I sought to strengthen my own walk with God. I talked to Uncle Dean about what I could do, and he suggested reading the Scriptures and studying them deeply to understand the context and meaning of every word. We did some of it together." She smiled at the memory. "My faith has grown stronger, and now it's my own faith. I know why I believe what I believe. I can support and defend my beliefs, and I am not afraid of being tempted away from God. But now I have such guilt. What if I failed Tom in my fear? What if he might have been saved had I just stood strong?"

"You've already admitted you didn't have the strength to stand," her father countered. "You did what was necessary to flee the devil. Tom wasn't the adversary. Satan was and still is. I believe you did the right thing. You didn't cast Tom aside as some would have advised you to do. Instead, you sought God for yourself so that the lies of the world wouldn't sway you. How could you have helped someone when you yourself were going under?"

She nodded and hugged him close. "I just feel so guilty. Since growing stronger, I haven't even tried to save him."

Her father chuckled. "Connie, you can't save Tom. Only God can do that."

"But maybe God wants me to talk to him about salvation."

"Then God will give you the words. Just remember, God is in charge. Not you. Pray about it and ask for His guidance—His wisdom. Remember, the Bible says in James that if you lack wisdom, ask for it, and God will give it."

"I will do exactly that." She stretched up on tiptoe and kissed his cheek. "That makes me feel so much better." She started to walk away, then turned back. "Pray for me."

"I always do," he said, smiling. "More than you know."

CHAPTER 9

Tom sat across from Connie at the breakfast table the next morning with Mr. and Mrs. Browning on either side of him. He was relieved that Singleton hadn't joined them. The agent irritated him. He wasn't happy with the way Clint Singleton seemed to shower Connie with attention. This morning the agent had stopped by, bringing her a large basket of oranges that had just arrived from California. Connie sat, thoroughly delighted, peeling an orange and commenting on how touched she was that he remembered she loved oranges. It was clear to Tom that Clint was trying to woo her. Mercy Browning had invited Singleton to stay for breakfast, but he declined, explaining he had things he needed to see to.

Tom was also relieved that, after reading

the short chapter of Psalm 28, Mr. Browning paused only long enough to pray over the food and then set his Bible aside. Tom wasn't sure why he'd agreed to join the morning devotions. He wasn't going to change his mind about God. That much he felt sure of.

"Tom and I will go around with you later this morning," Connie declared as her mother passed a plate of hotcakes.

"That will be just fine. I'm excited to reintroduce you to old friends," her father said, smiling.

Tom realized he'd missed most of the conversation. He forced himself to focus on what was being said.

Connie took a couple of hotcakes, then passed the plate to her father. "I'm really anxious to get started. Tom and I had plenty of time on the trip out here to talk about what we would do and how we would approach dealing with the people. Rosy promised to talk to some of her friends and help get the word out."

"We've been telling people about it ever since we knew you were coming," Mrs. Browning said. She handed Connie a pitcher of warm maple syrup. "Some of the people are apprehensive. They think anything the government does is suspect. We've had so many problems over the years."

Connie soaked her hotcakes and then passed the syrup to her father. "I know. They have every reason to be suspicious. That's why Tom and I thought that at first we would just spend time with them and explain what we're doing and how it might benefit them in the long run." She lowered her voice. "It might also help us overhear anything strange that's going on—that might lead us to discover who has been bringing the Indians whiskey."

"Clint mentioned something that I hoped you might explain." Tom hoped his introduction of a new topic wouldn't offend anyone.

"Go on. What are you wondering about?" Mr. Browning asked.

"Well, he told me there was some issue with the Indian inheritance situation, especially as it related to property."

"Yes. There has been some trouble. You see, when they established the reservation land, the government set things up so that the Indians could only transfer their property to other Indians, preferably relatives. However, in the case of death, only immediate family could inherit. This created a problem, because in many cases tribal members have chosen to live together under one roof—especially as their people have died off. When they came to live together, they would take on the name of the landowner, so it muddies the water as to who is related and who isn't. Clint has had his hands full trying to figure these things out and make sure that the right people inherit the land. It's just one of many new problems we have to deal with besides the worries of an uprising."

"Since all of the men who headed up their household were entitled to land, why would they give up their property to live with other family members?" Tom asked.

Mr. Browning shrugged. "I suppose because so many tribes have died off. There were thousands of people here at one time, and now only a few hundred remain. As you will learn, many of the tribes are no longer represented. They're all gone."

"Then we will endeavor to speak to those who remember those people and record what we can about their lives. We also intend to make sketches of the Indian heirlooms. Tom is a phenomenal artist," Connie said, smiling at Tom.

When she looked at him with such admiration, Tom felt as if there were nothing he couldn't do. She was always praising him to one person or another, yet she couldn't see how he adored her.

"That's wonderful, Tom," Mrs. Browning said, smiling. "I'm sure that will be a most helpful talent."

"Yes, but don't get your hopes up about seeing too many heirlooms," Connie's father said, shaking his head. "Certain people have come to the reservation with men of power and bartered for or taken what they wanted. You would be appalled at what we've seen over the years. One man in particular, the Reverend Robert Summers, makes frequent visits to the reservation and has for years. He comes and demands the Indians take his money for artifacts and heirlooms. He gives them no choice."

"I can't abide him," Mrs. Browning murmured.

"He treats the Indians with reserved indifference. He sees something he wants and asks how much. When they tell him it's not for sale, he ignores them, thinking this is a game they play in bartering, while in fact the Indians do not wish to part with the things their family has passed down. There's so little left to them after the forced march. What little they have, they hide, and then Summers just comes in and searches until he finds what he wants," Mr. Browning continued.

"That's terrible," Connie said, putting her fork down. "Why is that allowed?"

"It's not against any law, and he makes the trades very lucrative. I believe that, besides being a collector in his own right, he sells off the surplus and nets a tidy sum," Connie's father answered.

"Worse still is the selling of Indian bones," her mother added.

"What are you talking about?" Connie asked. Her expression betrayed her disgust.

"Back in 1868, the US Army Surgeon General instructed the military officers to collect Indian crania. Apparently museums and schools were paying great sums of money for them. Some even wanted full skeletons to study to prove how Indians differed from white people. This spread like wildfire, and soon people all over the world had a morbid fascination with Indian heads and skeletons," Mr. Browning replied.

"That is appalling. I remember your uncle telling our class something about it." It seemed like an eternity since Tom had been in school, but he remembered it as if it were yesterday.

"I'm sure he did," Adam Browning replied. "He was deeply offended as well. People were digging up graves, and with the interest in all things Indians, many people snuck onto the reservations to steal from gravesites and homes. We even dealt with the wife of the agent at the time, who was attempting to fill regular orders for Native pieces. The Indians wised up about her ploys and started telling her they had nothing more. She quickly lost interest. The Reverend Summers, however, forces his way into homes and looks for himself to see what is available."

Tom was ashamed that people thought this was perfectly acceptable behavior. It was terrible to imagine someone forcing their way into homes to take all that was left to these people of their history.

"I remember hearing the story of one Indian chief who had the power of a three-legged coyote," Browning continued.

Connie turned to Tom. "The power of a coyote makes a person mean, but also cunning."

"That's right," her father replied, smiling. "I'm surprised you remember that."

She smiled and pushed back her plate. "I remember plenty."

Browning seemed pleased by her response. "A professor at Willamette University got the body of this particular Indian chief and, shortly after that, became ill with a terrible disease. The Indians said it was the chief's curse."

Tom smiled. "And do you believe in curses?"

Browning nodded. "I do. The Bible says that Jesus became a curse for us. You see, taking on the sins of the world and being nailed to a tree left him cursed, but God resurrecting Him from the dead was a sure sign that God's power was greater than any curse. Believe me when I say that I've seen things happen over the years that leave me little doubt that the evil one has power to cause any number of problems. However, I don't believe God's children have to worry about those kinds of things. Jesus took that on Himself to save us from it. Therefore, I don't believe we can be cursed."

"I just don't believe in curses," Tom said. "It seems like a bunch of superstitious nonsense." He toyed with the last of his flapjacks. He decided to remind Mr. Browning of the tour he'd promised. "Are you still able to take me around your farm and show me your operation?"

Mr. Browning finished his coffee and nodded. "I'd be happy to. Then we'll head over to the store. I can introduce you to whoever is hanging around there. That might give you a leg up when you start your interviews." He got up from the table, then bent to kiss the top of his wife's head. "I'll see you ladies later this afternoon. Are you still having your sewing class this morning?"

"Yes. Same as usual," Mrs. Browning replied, then looked at Tom. "I teach the women and girls to sew our fashions. I show them how to make patterns and cut the materials.

They learn very quickly. I've even done some quilting with them. They really like making the more intricate blocks—they're quite talented."

"I'm sure they are." Tom could imagine the women gathered around the table. "Connie, will you join us?"

"No. I'm going to help Mama clean up so she'll have no delay with her class." She rose and began gathering plates.

Tom watched her for a moment while Mr. Browning went to get his hat. She was so pretty, with the morning sun shining through the window. It made a circling glow around her like a halo. Not only that, but something had changed about her since coming home. She seemed happier, more peaceful.

"You ready, son?" Mr. Browning held his hat in one hand and Tom's hat in the other. He held out the hat with a smile.

"Yes, sir," Tom murmured, wondering if Mr. Browning had any idea how much Tom thought of his daughter.

"It's a beautiful morning," Mr. Browning declared. "I cherish days like this."

Tom gazed out across the open field and a line of trees. The river was just beyond. "I do too. I love the fresh air. The city gets so full of coal soot. I weary of the stench at times."

"I can well imagine. I once lived in a city too. Boston, to be exact."

Tom wondered where they were going but said nothing as Browning walked toward the trees. As silence fell between them, Tom began to feel a little uncomfortable. He'd never been the kind of person who hated silence and had to fill it with conversation, but today he was exactly that person.

"What do you think of the upcoming election?" he asked out of desperation.

"Oh, not much. I've never met either man, so I can't even be sure they actually exist," Browning answered. "We hear very little out here at Grand Ronde and certainly never see the men involved. They could be raving lunatics, for all I know."

"I've met them—both James Garfield and Winfield Hancock. I've heard them speak and know what they are for and against. I'd be happy to bear witness to their platforms for you."

"No offense, son, but why should I believe you?" Browning stopped and looked at Tom with a smile. "I don't know you either. Now, Connie vouches for you, and I've learned a great deal about you through her, so that gives you an edge. When someone I know well passes along information, I feel that I can believe it. Unless, of course, that person is proven to speak falsely."

Tom felt confused by this response. He had asked a simple question about the election, and now Mr. Browning had him questioning his own thoughts.

Browning chuckled. "I'm sorry if I confused you. I just think we can both agree that a lot of the stuff we believe, we've learned from someone we respected. Someone we knew we could trust."

"Of course. And if we choose to believe someone we don't know, it's usually based on the word of other people or personal observation and experience."

"Exactly." Browning began to walk again. "I think the same can be said of God."

Tom cast him a side glance. "God? How did we get from politics to God?"

"Tom, I respect you. Your refusal to believe in God is troubling to me, because I see you as a highly intelligent young man."

"Thank you. I think."

Adam Browning laughed. "I will hang on to the right to change my opinion as we continue our discourse on the Bible and God, but for now, you hold a high place in my esteem."

Tom didn't know what to say, so he said nothing.

Browning continued, "You see, I was taught by people I trusted that the Bible was the Word of God—that it was true and that it was good for teaching others. I read and studied that book from cover to cover, and as I did, I also paid attention to who was reporting the things I was reading. I didn't just take it as truth because my mother and father and grandparents believed it. I worked to prove the validity for myself."

"Yes, but you only spoke to people who believed as you believed."

"Did I? What a presumptive thing to say."

"I apologize, sir. It was indeed presumptive." Tom put his gaze on the far horizon.

"I did talk to people who believed as I believed, but I also spoke to people who didn't believe what I believed. I wanted to know why they thought the way they did. You told me that you weighed your belief on the actions of your father. You decided if God did exist and those actions were sanctioned by Him, then you wanted no part of Him. But you couldn't believe someone to be so cruel, and so you chose to believe He didn't exist at all. Never mind that hundreds of thousands of witnesses come down through the ages to tell you that what was written in the Bible was true—that God not only existed, but came in human form as a babe, grew up and shared His truth, and then died to bring man a way to eternal life. An ultimate sacrifice to meet the blood offering required by God. You easily dismissed the witnesses."

He paused only a moment. "Yet you are about to embark on creating a record of the people on this reservation. You're quite willing to believe what they tell you about their old chiefs and medicine men without ever having met them. You will base your facts solely on the testimony of one man or woman who believes the stories passed down to them. On occasion you will meet someone who actually met the person in question, but those will be few."

"So you think I should believe in the existence of God because of the hundreds of thousands of witnesses who have gone before me to produce the Bible and continue its existence from generation to generation."

"I do. Tom, what are the odds that such a book could be handed down and continue to influence people to this day? There are so few books that can boast that claim, and all of those that have been revered and passed on are books that people chose to believe in with such a passion that they were willing to die for those beliefs. They were willing to give up everything to ensure that others could have a chance to believe as well."

"But the Bible isn't the only book that

has that kind of history." Tom felt like he had the upper hand now. "There are others, especially amongst religions."

"That is true. And those people cling to their books, just as I cling to mine. I don't want to make our conversation about those other books, however. I have studied them, and I believe that those people hold faith in their books, just as I hold faith in what the Bible says. However, I can go beyond that and beyond the witnesses from thousands of years before and speak to my own experiences. I can tell you what God has done in my own life. I can tell you how that book came alive for me and strengthened my convictions. I can point to the prophecies, both fulfilled and yet to be fulfilled, whereas those other books have failed miserably. I only ask that you keep an open mind to what I share with you."

Tom had never heard anyone speak with such zeal regarding the Bible. A chill ran down his spine, and while he wanted to say that he'd changed his mind about discussing the Bible and God, he found himself agreeing to keep an open mind and listen to Adam Browning share about his encounters with God. What had he gotten himself into?

"So tell me about you and Tom," Connie's mother said once the men were gone from the house.

"What do you mean?" Connie brought the last of the breakfast dishes into the kitchen so she could help wash up.

"I just wondered about the two of you. It's obvious you care a great deal about each other."

"We do. We've been good friends almost from my first moments in Washington. He was attending college at Georgetown and had one of Uncle Dean's classes. Uncle was always having his 'boys,' as he called them, home for dinner or an afternoon of additional teaching. Tom loved Uncle Dean's class and would come over all the time, and I got to know him."

"What is his family like?"

"Well, Tom's the youngest of five. His brothers and sister are all married with families and live in various places. His folks have passed on—his grandparents too. Tom is twenty-eight and very smart. I could talk to him for hours about books and politics or history. He's amazing."

Mama looked at her oddly for a moment, then smiled. "I appreciate that he's trying to help us."

"I do too. I'd never have gotten this job if

not for Tom. He came for supper one evening and told us about the job and being posted in Oregon. I'd just had a letter from you regarding the strange things happening around here, including"—she lowered her voice—"that some people think you and Papa are doing underhanded things."

Her mother shook her head. "I just never knew it was as bad as it's turned out to be. I didn't think anyone seriously thought we were involved. Clint brought us the first news of what was being said, but nothing like what you've told us. I still can't believe there are people trying to gather enough evidence to put us on trial. It hurts me deeply. I've spent all of my adult life working for the betterment of the Indians." She shook her head. "Your father and I are both thinking about moving away."

"No, don't do that. Don't you see that if you do, then they win? We'll prove them wrong, Mama. I promise."

"I didn't mean for our conversation to turn back to our problems. Tell me more about you and Tom."

Connie shrugged. "There's nothing really to tell. I feel like we've known each other forever. There's nothing I can't tell him. Well, maybe one thing. I'm not sure about discussing Clint with him."

"Clint? What about him?" Her mother's brows knitted. "You aren't still in love with him, are you?"

"I don't know what I feel for him. It's really the strangest thing." Connie put the dishes in the soapy water her mother had prepared. "Do you want me to wash or dry?"

"Whichever you like."

Connie picked up a dish towel. "I'll dry, then."

Mama nodded and went to the sink. She poured hot water from the stove into the sink and then began washing the dishes. "What makes it the strangest thing?"

"Well, when I left here, I was heartbroken over Clint. I was so sure we were destined to be together. In leaving, however, I was determined to forget him. He'd made it clear he didn't care about me at all. So anytime he came to mind, I forced those thoughts away. I was happier when I didn't think about him, so I knew I must be on the right path. I prayed and prayed for God's insight."

Her mother smiled. "And what did God tell you?"

"About Clint? Very little. But about Himself—quite a bit. I learned so much at seminary regarding the truth of who God is and what we are to Him. I swear I could sit in classes the rest of my life, learning about the Bible and God, and I would never weary of it."

A chuckle escaped her mother. "I've said as much to your father, even though I've never sat in formal Bible classes. Your father, however, is so good to teach me. We have always devoted time every week to study like that."

"Maybe you'll let me join in."

"Of course." She handed Connie a wet plate. "But please continue. How were you able to get over your feelings for Clint?"

"I'm not sure I did. Coming here has confused the issue. I was determined not to care about him. In fact, I've treated him quite poorly just to prove to myself that I don't have romantic feelings for him. But I don't know what I feel. Especially now."

"Why especially now?"

"The way he keeps looking at me makes me wonder if . . . oh, never mind."

"I hope you'll be careful. I've always liked Clint well enough but have never been convinced he was meant for you."

"You never told me that." Connie paused and looked at her mother. "Why, if you felt that way, didn't you say something?"

"I've always been a firm believer in letting love find its own way. I prayed plenty when you were younger and so infatuated with Clint, but I feared that if I spoke negatively, it would only drive you into his arms. And then, if it turned out to be a good thing, you'd always remember that I didn't want you with him."

"Did you actually feel that way? You didn't want us together?"

Her mother went back to washing the dishes. "I prayed so much about it, but it just never felt right. It still doesn't. You and Clint are worlds apart."

"I'm back now to work with the Indians and don't have any intention of leaving again—not even after this job is done. I don't know exactly what God has planned for me, but I know the Indians will be a part of it."

"I'm happy to think of you being close by, but I still feel no better about the idea of you and Clint being a couple. Maybe you should talk to your father about it. He always has sound counsel."

Just then her father and Tom returned from their tour of the farm.

"A good number of the Indian houses collapsed in the high winds in January," Papa was explaining. "They were never well-built. The government sent men to just slap them together. We've been trying to get each family at least some place to live, but they deserve so much better."

Connie grabbed another plate and dried

it quickly. She was still thinking about her mother's comments. Mama had always been wise. She didn't jump quickly to any conclusion but gathered the facts and reviewed them with care. Perhaps if Connie were more like Mama, she wouldn't get into these confusing situations.

"We've saddled the horses, Connie," her father said, smiling. "I thought you and Tom could go with me on my rounds. This way the people will get to know you both."

"I hope many of them remember me."

"I'm sure they will." Her mother bumped her with her hip. "You just go on with your father. I'll get these dishes finished up, and then I'll have my sewing class. I'll be busy until noon."

Connie put the dried dish aside and pulled off her apron. "Let me get my hat, and I'll be ready."

"We'll be waiting for you out front," Papa replied.

She joined them in a matter of minutes. Her broad-brimmed straw hat was good for tucking up her hair. She was just tying it on as she came from the house and nearly tripped. Fortunately, Tom was there to keep her upright.

"You're going to end up on your face if you aren't careful." He helped her mount the horse, folding his hands together for her to step into. Connie grabbed the horn as Tom lifted her upward. She took her seat in the saddle no worse for the wear.

It looked to be a beautiful day. In the east, the sun hung in a cloudless sky, and already its warmth was spreading across the valley. For several hours they rode leisurely through the reservation. Papa stopped from time to time to introduce Tom and Connie. Most remembered Connie and greeted her fondly.

Connie explained from time to time what they'd be doing. She spoke in Chinook Wawa, hoping to put the Indians at ease. Even though the government demanded they speak English, Father Croquet allowed this common Indian language that was spoken among the many tribes.

At one particularly ramshackle home, Papa dismounted as a half-dozen children came running. "Tell us a story!" they squealed. "Tell us about baby Jesus."

Connie was barely dismounted when her father sat down in the dirt, and the children followed suit. She smiled as they began to fish in his pockets and produced peppermint sticks.

"Oh my, how did those get in there?" he said, as if caught by surprise.

The children giggled and again pressed for a story.

"You know Jesus didn't remain a baby. He grew up to be a strong man."

Connie joined her father and the children on the ground. The children looked over at her, and she smiled. She greeted them in Chinook Wawa. "Isn't it a beautiful morning?"

One little boy, his dark eyes wide, gave her a nod.

"Children, do you know who this is?" Papa asked.

Connie knew they wouldn't. She'd been gone longer than they'd been alive. Tom sat on the ground beside her.

"This is my daughter, Connie, and her friend Tom," her father said. The children gave her brief shy smiles and held their peppermint sticks a little closer. Connie might have laughed if not for the very serious way they regarded her. "They have come to learn about you and how your people lived. But first, we're going to talk about Jesus and how He lived."

Connie listened as her father told the story of Jesus feeding the five thousand. The children were mesmerized. They questioned her father as to how this could be. They were used to the fish their parents served. There weren't any fish big enough to feed that many people. Her father explained that Jesus could make the fish big enough that by the time the disciples gave fish and bread to everyone, there were still basketfuls left over.

When he finished, he prayed and blessed the children. Connie felt tears in her eyes and quickly wiped them away while the children still had their heads bowed. She didn't want to upset them by crying, but it touched her so much to see her father sitting there, loving them as if they were family. Of course, in so many ways, they were.

As the noon hour approached, Papa headed them back toward their house. They were all getting hungry, and although several of the Indians had invited them to share their table, her father declined. He told them he would come another time when he could bring something to share, and that Tom and Connie had to attend to important things.

Connie was impressed how Papa knew just the right things to say to keep from insulting the people willing to share their meager fare. Papa was a great diplomat when it came to working with the Indians. If the government would only pay attention to that, they'd know he could never do anything to harm the people.

They stopped at the small sutler's store. Most of the soldiers had been removed from the immediate area, but the store remained and served the reservation. Here the Indian men could get tobacco, and the women purchased sugar. The Indians had developed quite a sweet tooth, and sugar was one of the most-sought-out commodities. Connie remembered how her mother would lay in a supply just before Christmas and make candy for each of the families. It wasn't an easy feat, but she was determined to bless each home with her offering. After a while, Mama's sisters learned of this and started sending big packages of their own homemade treats to share. The Indians looked forward to them each year.

"I'll wait with the horses," Connie told her father and Tom. The men nodded and went into the building.

Connie had seen a group of Indian men gathered beside the store near the well pump. They were speaking quite intently, and she wondered if there were plans afoot. She pretended to water the horses and strained to hear their conversation.

"They will come tonight. We'll be there at the bend to meet them."

She frowned when another of the men replied. She couldn't make out any of his words. She drew closer to the corner of the store.

"Are they bringing whiskey?" one of the other men asked.

". . . and the . . . too much now." The man gave a low laugh. "We will dance."

Connie frowned. That made no sense. She sighed and tried to move closer. At the very end of the building, she leaned back against the wall, trying to look nonchalant. If anyone saw her, Connie wanted them to think she was just resting rather than spying.

"Be there at midnight," the first man instructed.

She heard whiskey mentioned again but didn't know if it had anything to do with their meeting. He might have just been offering to share what he had with his friends, but there was also a possibility they were discussing a contraband shipment. Of course, one of the other men spoke of dancing. She strained to hear more, but the men moved off toward the road.

Not entirely sure what the men had planned, Connie decided not to say anything to her father or Tom. She'd slip out that evening and go to the location they had described. With any luck, she'd learn something valuable. Of course, it could just be that the men wanted to gather and do some sort of power dance. The tribes here believed in the powers that certain spirits could give a person. Some claimed the power of the coyote, which made a man mean and deadly, while others claimed the power of being able to talk to the dead. Some powers entailed mimicking animals or insects for varying purposes. Even the Indians who had accepted Jesus as their Savior still respected the powers that people claimed. They had seen too many things over the years and felt it was important to respect the traditions of their ancestors, so Connie knew it was very possible these men could simply be gathering to do a power dance.

"You ready to head home?" her father asked when they returned with a few things in hand for the house.

"I am." Connie smiled. "I was just enjoying the shade and letting the horses get some water."

Papa nodded and Tom untied their mounts. Once again, he helped Connie mount. "Today would be perfect for a picnic down by the river," Tom said with a grin.

"And a swim," Papa added. "But I know we're all too busy for that. Maybe in a few days."

A swim sounded quite enjoyable, but for the moment, the men's meeting at midnight was all Connie could think of. She prayed her spying would further their cause and help her clear her mother and father of wrongdoing. The sooner they could do that, the sooner she could refocus her attention on the job at hand.

CHAPTER 10

Connie waited until she was certain everyone was asleep before sneaking out of the house to head down to the river. There was a full moon out, which would hamper her plans for secrecy, but she remembered numerous secluded spots along the way, places she had used as a child during games of hide-and-seek.

She knew the reservation like the back of her hand, and years of playing with the Native children had taught her various tricks for sneaking unnoticed through the brush. Connie was quite good at disappearing and staying silent.

Cloud cover was moving in from the west, and with any luck at all, it might eventually hide the full moon. She contemplated waiting a little longer but knew the men had talked about coming together at midnight. Believing it was best to move on, Connie kept to the darkest shadows and heavy brush.

As she drew near the river, the brush grew heavier and the ground less even. There was a steep bank to navigate in this particular spot, and Connie contemplated moving farther downriver to where it was lower. If the men were receiving a delivery, however, they wouldn't be near this steeper bank, and it might give her high ground from which to observe them. She stopped and listened for voices but heard nothing but the river. If the men were there, they were working in silence. She slipped farther down the bank as it narrowed and lowered to meet the water. Hearing voices, she waited in the brush—barely daring to draw breath.

"Keep low," she heard someone say from below.

There were murmurs, and then someone said, "There's the boat. Signal with the lantern."

For just a moment there was light filtering through the bushes. Connie flattened herself against the ground until the light was hidden again.

"They see us now."

There were several hushed replies and the sound of a boat nudging up against the bank.

She heard several men exchange greetings and decided to see if she could get closer. She hadn't gone far, however, when someone grabbed her from behind. A hand closed over her mouth as she tried to scream. She fought, but her captor was too strong.

"Shh. Be still, Connie. It's me, Clint."

She stopped fighting. Her heart was racing so hard that she thought it might burst from her chest. She'd been so afraid that she'd been caught by whoever was smuggling whiskey onto the reservation, and she'd had no idea what they would do to her.

Clint dragged her backward, deeper into the brush and farther away from the river. Connie wasn't sure why he was here, but she went without protest. When they were far enough away, he stopped and turned her to face him. The clouds had moved in to diminish the light, but Connie could just make out his features.

"What are you doing down here? Did you follow me?" she demanded.

Clint didn't answer right away, but when he did, his voice was low and husky. "I did. I was out checking on things, and I saw you leave your folks' place."

"Must have been God's timing," she murmured.

"I agree. Now, what are *you* doing here?"

"I couldn't sleep." She didn't want to lie, but she didn't feel comfortable confiding in Clint. "I was planning a midnight swim. I used to sneak off and do that with some of the other girls when I was younger."

"It's not safe to do that anymore."

"Because of those men at the river? When I saw them, I hid. What were they doing?" She tried to sound as innocent as possible.

"I'm not entirely sure, but there's been a lot of alcohol showing up on the reservation lately, and I was hoping to catch the men red-handed."

"Alcohol?" Connie paused, trying to figure out how best to move forward. She decided to feign ignorance. "Grand Ronde Indians have never been drinkers."

"You've been gone seven years, Connie. That's a long time for things to change."

"I suppose so. How sad. Have they been drinking a lot?"

"Unfortunately, yes. Someone is smuggling it in."

"I want to help. I know my father would never allow such things."

The sound of someone approaching caused Clint to pull Connie deeper into the undergrowth. He held her close with his finger to her lips until the sound faded. It was an intimate moment, but Connie didn't find it at all stirring. She contemplated the past, when she had dreamed about being held by Clint Singleton, but even that didn't stir her heart. Perhaps the danger of the moment made such feelings impossible.

"It's not safe for you to be out here, Connie. You could get yourself killed."

"I'm sorry. I had no idea it was dangerous."

"I couldn't forgive myself if I let something happen to you."

"That's very sweet of you to say, but I'm hardly a child who needs to be watched after." She quickly changed the subject. "Do you know who those men are?"

"No. Some are obviously Natives."

His breath was warm against her ear, and again Connie tried to conjure up some fond feeling. But there was nothing except frustration that she'd been found out—and worry for her parents. Maybe that was blocking her ability to feel love for Clint. Then again, there was always the possibility that she'd been more successful at putting aside her feelings for him than she'd ever thought possible. It would make complete sense to have lost her affection for him over the years. Especially if, as he had once said, her love was nothing more than a childish infatuation.

The men were talking again, and Connie

strained to hear. They were speaking one of the Rogue River dialects. It sounded like the dialect used by the Latgawa people. The man referenced someone named Smith. They were asking where he was. Then someone began to speak in Chinook Jargon again.

"Come on," Clint said, moving away from the men.

"Do you understand what they're saying?" Connie asked. When she was young, Clint hadn't cared to learn the languages of the people. He hadn't even wanted to learn the common language—Chinook Jargon, or Wawa, as it was often called. She knew he understood more of the common language now but didn't believe he was all that good at it, because her father had said Clint often asked for him to translate at official meetings.

"No," he replied. "I never learned that dialect and very little Jargon. Do you know it?"

Connie wasn't sure why, but she didn't want to admit she did. "I heard the name Smith, but while the language sounds familiar, I can't tell you exactly what it is." She hadn't really lied. She wasn't sure which dialect it was. "I'm guessing some Rogue River language." Which could be any number of a dozen languages.

"I'm certain it's regarding the whiskey."

"And someone named Smith. Do you know a man named Smith?"

"There are many people with the name Smith. Shh." He pulled her into a crouch and waited several long seconds. "I thought I heard the sound of glass bottles."

When her legs started to cramp, Connie tried to stand, but Clint refused to let her go.

"Stay down, or they might see us."

Connie did as he commanded, fearful that if she did otherwise, it might completely backfire on her desire to clear her parents' names. She wondered how much Clint knew. There must surely be some way to get him to confide in her.

"You know where it goes," one of the men said in English.

They waited a few more minutes as the sounds of the men faded, and then Clint finally released Connie and helped her stand. Once they were on their feet again, she turned to face him.

"We should follow them and see where they take the crates. We might—"

But before she could say more, Clint pulled her into his arms and kissed her long and hard. His arms tightened around her. Connie had never experienced anything like this kiss, and for a moment she didn't know what to do. Why was he doing this? Then her reasoning returned, and she pushed at his well-muscled chest and stopped just short of slapping him.

"What do you think you're doing?" She could only stare at him as though he'd lost his mind.

"I'm sorry, but I couldn't help myself. I've wanted to do that since you came back."

"Is that your only excuse?" She was angry and startled, not to mention confused. Her feelings were such a mix of emotions that she wasn't sure what to say or do. A part of her wanted to slap him. An equal part wanted to better explore what the kiss implied.

"I'm sorry. I shouldn't have done that, I know. But I keep thinking of all the things you used to say to me—about how much you cared for me, how you loved me. I was selfish and foolish then, and my heart didn't know what it wanted. Not only that, but you were still very young and . . ."

"Too young to tame my own heart."

He grinned. "Well, if you had to tame it so much, it must still have feelings for me. Truth then must surely be truth now. You wanted me to kiss you, didn't you?"

His words only made the situation more confusing, and Connie didn't dare let him continue.

"Who is responsible for bringing the whiskey in?" she asked, changing the subject.

He chuckled. "I don't know. I have my suspicions."

"Who?"

"Well, a lot of folks think it's your mother and father."

"What?" She barely remembered to be surprised. "How can you possibly say that? You know they would never do something like that."

"I didn't say *I* thought they were doing it," Clint replied.

"But you said you had your suspicions."

"I don't suspect your parents. I was only saying what others think. What I've overheard."

"My parents love these people. You know that. You worked with them long before becoming an agent. You know they could never do anything to harm the Indians." Connie was louder than she'd meant to be and lowered her voice. "You know they're innocent."

"I do believe that." Clint took her by the arm and started back through the brush to the main road. "But a lot of folks think they're guilty. They believe your parents are unhappy that they were replaced by the Catholic Church."

"My parents . . . *were* unhappy . . . to have their ministry . . . taken away." She was panting hard as Clint pulled her back up the bank to the road in quick strides. "But they'd never do . . . anything to . . . hurt the Indians."

He continued to move along at a quick

clip until the reservation buildings were in sight. Only then did he stop. "I'll figure this out, Connie, but you need to stay out of it."

"Does my father know about these crates being snuck in?" She continued to play dumb, hoping Clint might give her information she didn't already have.

"Yes. We were together on a night just like this when they brought in another supply. We saw the crates stacked on the banks. Your father wanted to confront them, but I suggested we wait and see if we couldn't learn who was behind it."

"I'm going to talk to my father about this. Together we must learn the truth."

He took hold of her arms. "No. You mustn't say anything about it. Your father doesn't want you or your mother knowing about it. He made me swear to say nothing."

"But now that I know—"

"No!" His tone was harsh. "Look, it's bad enough that you were out there. He'll be livid if he finds out. Just don't say anything. In return for you keeping this between us, I'll tell you whatever I learn. Promise me you'll stay quiet about it."

"Well . . . all right. I promise . . . for now." She wasn't sure what exactly had him so upset. Was he worried that she would cause problems for his own investigation?

Before she could ask, he slipped into the shadows and was gone. He'd left her within ten yards of her house. Connie didn't know what to think or do. She was touched that he was working to see her father cleared, but at the same time she was confused by the kiss. It hadn't filled her with the elation and love she had thought it would. Not that she'd thought it would now, but in the past she had figured it would send her soaring, fill her stomach with the fluttering of butterfly wings, and fill the air with fireworks. It had done none of those things.

"What are you doing out here? It's well past one in the morning."

Connie started at the sound of Tom's voice. "You gave me a fright. I wish you wouldn't sneak up on me."

"I was worried about you. I heard you slip out of the house earlier."

"I'm sorry. I didn't want to bother you. When we were at the store earlier today, I heard a group of men talking about something happening at the river tonight. I went to see what was going on, and it turned out they were smuggling whiskey onto the reservation."

"What? That could have been dangerous! Why didn't you tell me? I could have gone with you."

The moon slid out from behind the clouds, and she could see Tom's worried expression. "I wasn't sure if what I'd overheard meant anything. I certainly didn't expect to see them smuggling whiskey."

"Was that Clint with you? Did you tell him?"

"Yes. I mean, no." She sighed. "Yes, it was Clint, but no, I didn't tell him what I'd heard nor anything else. When I was creeping along the riverbank, Clint caught me and dragged me into the brush to hide. He did tell me he's trying to figure out who's smuggling whiskey onto the reservation. Then I heard one of the men wondering where Smith was."

"Who is Smith?"

"I don't know. I asked Clint, but he didn't seem to know either, and all he wanted to talk about was the kiss."

She hadn't meant to mention that, but since it was Tom and she usually told him everything, Connie wasn't overly concerned.

Tom, however, seemed to see it differently. "Kiss? What kiss?"

"Oh, it was nothing, really. Clint kissed me. I think he's trying to get me to refocus my attention on the past and how I felt for him, but honestly, I don't know what I feel anymore. That kiss didn't make me feel anything but confused. I thought there would be fireworks and butterflies in my stomach, but there was nothing." She started for the house. "We need to figure out who Smith is. Something tells me he's an important part of this. I think we're on to something big."

Tom said nothing, and he didn't follow her toward the house. No doubt he was still upset with her.

"I promise I won't go out again without you," she called over her shoulder. Hopefully that would settle him down.

CHAPTER 11

Tom spent the next few days meeting people either with Clint or Adam Browning. The people seemed apprehensive of him—even hostile at first—but once they'd spent a little time visiting, the Native people seemed more accepting of him. Two weeks after their arrival, he and Connie began their work together as a team. They started with the people who were on good terms with the Brownings. It was generally felt among the Native people that a friend of a friend was worthy of trust until proven unworthy. Of course, not everyone on the reservation considered the Brownings friends.

They started their official recording of Native culture and history with Rose Johnson. Rosy told many stories from her youth, while Tom and Connie took turns writing down every word. Around twelve thirty, Connie opened the basket she'd brought with her and pulled out leftovers from the previous evening's meal. Rosy seemed grateful, especially for the generous slices of cake.

"Rosy, I remember you once told me about the bridewealth. It was a price paid for the bride, but it was also used to reckon certain crimes," Connie commented.

"Yes." Rosy smiled. "If someone murdered one of the wife's family members, it required the killer or his family to make a full payment of restitution equal to the bridewealth—the money her father was originally paid by the groom. The bridewealth also determined what a woman's children would inherit. This made it very important for her father to be paid a good price for his daughter so that the family would gain in importance and wealth."

Tom looked up. "How was the bridewealth determined?" He had finished his meal and took out a journal to make notes.

"It was based on the woman's beauty, moral character, and her rank. The common payment was made in dentalia shells and clamshell disk beads. Woodpecker feather scalps were also required, and one or two deerskins. The more that was paid, the more it increased the woman's value and that of her children. My father received thirty-five long dentalia shells for me and forty woodpecker feather scalps. I don't remember how many clamshell beads, but he was paid four deerskins. I was ranked very high, and my family was highly regarded." Her voice betrayed her pride. "And I was once quite beautiful." She laughed and touched her cheek. "But that beauty has been given to another who is young."

"You are lovely in your old age," Connie told her.

Rosy smiled. "You would have fetched a great price, Connie."

Tom smiled and glanced down at his paper as he continued jotting notes. He thought about what it would be like to pay Connie's father in shells and skins for the right to marry his daughter.

"Could we see your baskets, Rosy?" Connie turned to Tom. "Rosy makes the most beautiful baskets."

Rosy went to her bed, which stood against the wall. She knelt down and pulled several baskets from underneath it. "I must keep them hidden or that awful Reverend Summers will force me to sell them. He once forced his way in here and took many of my old pieces—things my mother and father had given me. So now I keep a few things that do not matter on the shelves over there so that when he comes, he will be content."

"That's terrible, Rosy."

"The government says it is all right, and so nobody cares to stop it. Our police try to stop him, but Reverend Summers always says that he paid for the pieces. And he does, but not all wanted to sell."

She brought the tightly woven baskets to the small table. Connie had already removed the extra food and placed it on Rosy's kitchen counter.

Rosy held up a basket that was about four inches across and the same in height. "This is the first basket that I made completely by myself. When my mother approved it, I was so excited that I ran through the village, declaring the news to anyone who would listen."

Tom began to sketch it.

Rosy continued her explanation. "This shows the four important weaving methods for twining a basket. Here is the solid line. Then the rows that stack." She pointed to the design. "And then you learn the weaving of rows that swirl to the right and then rows that swirl to the left. At the top we finish the basket with a simple weave that we do three times."

"It looks braided," Tom commented as he went back to drawing.

"Yes, but it is not." Rosy put the little basket on the table, then picked up another. This one was bigger—about the size of a small dinner plate.

"I've always loved this one," Connie declared. "Rosy's mother made it for her when she married."

Tom paused again. Where the other basket had been woven in dark and light tones of a dried grass, this one consisted of various dyed grasses in hues of black, red, and even blue. He finished his quick sketch of the first basket, then began drawing the second.

"What kind of grass are these made from?" Tom asked as he drew the basket.

"Bear grass. It's rather wiry and very long," Connie said before Rosy could reply.

"It was taller than me when my mother helped me gather it for the baskets." Rosy laughed. "I sometimes got lost in it. We also used other things. Sometimes we would weave with tulle or cane, and we used all sorts of things for our dyes."

"Tom, I can tell you about those later," Connie interjected. "I helped make dyes when I was a girl. We used flowers and vegetables— fruits too."

Tom enjoyed her excitement over the baskets. It was almost as if she'd forgotten her worries and was transported back in time to her childhood. He remembered the animated fifteen-year-old who had come to live with her aunt and uncle and wondered what she must have been like as a very young girl.

By the time they finished with Rosy, Tom felt he had a great overview of the history of the Shasta people. Rosy said most of them now lived on the Siletz Reservation near the ocean. It would be some time before Tom and Connie made their way there, but for now, Rosy's detailed memories of her life as a girl would make for a great outline of life in the Shasta villages.

"She's a very nice woman. I can see why you consider her a good friend."

Connie carried the empty food basket. "Rosy was good to my mother even when the others were still so angry."

"You can hardly blame them for being angry. They were uprooted from all they knew, forced to leave behind so much that was precious to them and march for hundreds of miles."

"And they watched many of their loved ones die and were then forced to live on a reservation with their enemies." Connie shook her head.

It was nearly three o'clock, but Connie said they could still talk with another family.

They stopped at the poorly structured, unpainted house of the Sheridans.

"The Sheridans are Modoc. The Modoc were enemies of the Shasta at one time. Joseph Sheridan and my father, however, were good friends. They knew each other before the move to the reservation," Connie told him. She knocked on the frame where a blanket hung instead of a door. "I hope they'll speak with us."

An older woman appeared. She seemed surprised by Tom and Connie and called over her shoulder in Modoc. Tom had no idea what she had said, but she disappeared behind the blanket, and two large men appeared.

"Mr. Sheridan, do you remember me?" Connie asked. "I'm Adam Browning's daughter, Connie."

"I heard you had returned," the older of the two men said. "You frightened my wife. Why have you come?" He had a long scar on the side of his neck, and his face was weathered and wrinkled. Tom wondered about the stories he could tell.

Connie explained why they had come. "It's a good thing that the government has finally seen the importance of remembering the *real people*, don't you think?"

"No. I don't," the younger man spat. "The less the government knows about us, the better. Then maybe they will forget about us and let us live our lives as God intended." He crossed his arms and glared at Connie. Despite his anger, Connie seemed undaunted.

"We are your friends, but you treat us like enemies, not even inviting us in."

"We are no longer friends," the younger of the two declared. "Your father would not help my father when he came to him many years ago."

"Your father came to my father for help in leaving the reservation," Connie countered. "It was illegal, and your family would have been killed."

"I lost my wife and daughters," the old man said, his voice low. "We died just the same."

Connie shook her head. "I was sorry for your loss. I loved your wife. She was like an aunt to me—teaching me Modoc cooking and speaking. Now we've come to make sure that those things are not forgotten. That the *Moatokni maklaks*—the Modoc people—are remembered."

"The *Moatokni maklaks* do not need your help," the younger man declared, puffing himself up to tower over Connie.

Tom stepped forward at this. "We come in peace, but you act as though we are at war."

"You are not our friend. You are a white

man. You have stolen our land and ways of life. You force us to dress like you—to speak like you—to live as you do. We have no friendship."

Connie frowned. "I'm sorry you don't want to be our friend anymore. But even though it hurts me, I don't wish you ill. My heart still cares for you, and I will still call you my friend. I will also pray for you and ask God to heal the pain in your heart."

The younger man shook his head and walked away. He said something in Chinook Jargon that Tom couldn't understand, then disappeared behind the blanket and back into the house, where the sound of children could be heard.

Joseph looked hard at Connie. "There is war coming between our people. My son Samson will always feel hate for the deaths of his mother and sisters. Do not come back here. We will not speak with you again." He returned to his house, leaving Tom and Connie to stare at each other in silence.

"That was rather uncalled for," Tom said.

"No." Connie shook her head as they walked away. "Joseph blames my father for the deaths of his wife and daughters. He wanted to sneak off the reservation with his entire family—sons, daughters, and their spouses—and make their way to Canada. He went to my father for money and told him what he would do. Papa wouldn't help him because it was against the law and the soldiers were everywhere. He told Joseph he would be killed, but Joseph felt certain they could make it. He told my father if they stayed, he knew it would turn out badly, but of course Papa couldn't do it. He knew Joseph and his family would be caught or more likely killed."

They walked slowly back to Connie's home.

"Joseph told my father he knew that if they stayed, his family would suffer, and they did. His wife died two weeks later, and his two daughters died not long after that. One in childbirth and one from typhoid. They left behind little ones who also died a few years later." Her expression betrayed her sorrow. "Rosy has always said there are more graves holding children than cradles on this reservation."

"That is terribly sad." Tom wanted to offer comfort but knew there was none to be had. "Who was the other man—the younger one?"

"Samson, Joseph's son. I think he'd be about thirty-three now."

"What did he say there at the last? I couldn't understand him."

Connie stopped and shook her head. "He

said war is coming and he will do everything he can to kill all of the white people."

Adam Browning sat on the other side of Clint's desk. He seemed troubled and had come to Clint for advice. Clint had always liked the way Adam treated him like an equal even though he was years younger than Adam.

"It's just so perplexing. Why have the people gotten so interested in liquor? I talked to the priest, and he's just as baffled. The Grand Ronde Indians have never been given to drunkenness. Now we seem to have an epidemic."

"I know, and I'm trying my best to get to the bottom of it, just like you are. Every time there's a rumor, I check it out, but so far I haven't learned anything."

"There has to be an answer. Someone must know more than they're saying. I hate to sound demeaning, but the tribes here don't have the connections to pull this off themselves. There are white men involved in this."

"I agree, but proving it will be difficult." Clint moved a stack of papers and pulled out a letter he'd just received. "That brings up another issue. The clerk at the sutler's store sent me this note. Apparently he's frustrated by your family handing out goods for free."

"My sister and others send crates of clothes, blankets, kitchen goods, and so forth. Mercy has been coordinating the distribution."

"Yes, well, besides the store missing out on sales, there is some concern that you might also be giving away guns."

Adam rolled his gaze heavenward. "Who is saying that? I'll go speak to them."

"I already did. I know you aren't handing out weapons, but I wanted you to know there were concerns."

"You already know what they're saying about us. It's ridiculous."

The store clerk burst into the office. "You've got to stop them."

"Stop who?" Adam asked.

"The Indians. They think I've poisoned them, and they're threatening to string me up."

Clint got up and threw on his coat. "What are you talking about, Jeb?"

"A bunch of folks got sick, and they think it was from the flour I sold them. They think it's poisoned. I need you to calm them down. Otherwise we're going to have a riot."

Clint and Adam made their way to the group milling outside the small mercantile, where Clint called everyone to attention. "I understand many of you think you've gotten sick from the flour Jeb sold you. Even if this is true, I assure you that no one here is seeking to poison you."

"It must be poison. My family is sick. They can't keep anything down," one man declared.

"Neither can mine," another yelled, and soon everyone was protesting their situation.

Clint waved his hands and called to them. "I can't help you if everyone talks at once." One by one, the people fell silent. "Thank you. Look, a lot of things can happen to flour barrels during transport. I can't tell you why your people are ill, but I will look into this. In the meantime, bring back the flour you think is bad. We'll send for a new batch, and while you wait, I'll see that your returned flour is credited to your account. As for the sick, if your own healers are overwhelmed, let me know, and I'll get the reservation doctor to come." He paused and looked at Adam. "Or I'm sure Mrs. Browning will be more than willing to help nurse the sick."

"Absolutely," Adam agreed. "You know that we care deeply for the people here. We will do whatever we can to get you what you need."

There was a great deal of murmuring and muttering, but the people finally began to disperse.

Clint looked at Adam and shrugged. "I

hope that means they've accepted my offering." He heaved a sigh.

"I hope so too. I'll let Mercy know what's going on, so if someone does want her help, she won't be caught off guard."

"Good. That way she can have her things ready." Clint smiled. "Maybe make a new batch of vinegar."

Adam smiled. "You joke, but my wife swears on it. Says it will cure a great many ailments."

"Yes, well, she can put her faith in vinegar. For the time being, however, I've got to figure out what was done to this barrel of flour and get a replacement in here immediately."

Tom sat on the Brownings' small porch and thought about everything that had happened since he'd come to Oregon. His main purpose had been to see Connie's folks cleared of suspicion so Connie could stop worrying about them and maybe, just maybe, put her attention on him.

He'd been in love with Connie almost from the first moment he'd met her, despite their six-year age difference. Connie had always been mature for her age. She found Washington politics fascinating but took just as much interest in her uncle's work on the ancient world. Tom remembered one year when her uncle and aunt had taken Connie with them to the Holy Land. She had long given up talking to him about Jesus by then, but upon her return, she was reenergized in her passion for learning everything she could about the Bible. She even tried her hand at learning Greek.

Tom thought about his conversation with Connie's father. Mr. Browning had never once tried to force his religion on Tom. The things he said were very different from those Tom had grown up hearing in his father's church.

He frowned. The very thought of his father put him in a foul mood. His father had only cared about his success in business and making sure his friends and family seemed perfect. There was never any room for error, and when one was made, Tom's father was thoroughly condemning. During one particularly severe whipping, Tom's father had declared that God Himself had instructed that he punish Tom. Maybe that was where Tom's dismissal of God had its origins.

An owl hooted somewhere off to his left. Tom wondered at the species and wished he'd studied harder to learn more about birds. There were a good number of them he wasn't familiar with.

"I thought I might find you out here," Adam Browning said, joining Tom on the porch. He sank into his wife's rocker and smiled. "I can see why she loves this chair so much. I may have to find another one for myself."

Tom looked at Connie's father, although the darkness obscured his features. "I was just thinking of the time your sister and her husband took Connie to the Middle East. They invited me to go along, but I couldn't manage the time away. Connie came back so excited about everything she'd seen and heard. She was already strong in her faith, but that trip seemed to further stimulate her desire to learn."

"That was about three years ago, wasn't it?" Mr. Browning asked.

"Yes." Tom nodded. "She was just nineteen, and I was twenty-five. I was working for the Bureau of Indian Affairs as a lowly office clerk, and it was impossible to leave because I was in line for a promotion. I knew that taking off on a pleasure trip would have spelled doom for me."

"I'm sorry. I wish you could have gone. Perhaps you would have had more of your questions answered."

"What do you mean?"

"Well, I remember the first time I went to

Washington, DC. I walked around the city, thinking about the men who had walked there before me. I imagined men like Lincoln walking the same streets as he considered the Civil War. I thought of Andrew Jackson, the president responsible for driving the Indians into the West. Men like Jefferson who penned the Declaration of Independence. It made them more real to me than any history book ever could."

"And you think if I'd gone to the Middle East, the existence of Jesus would have become real to me?"

"I like to think it would have. I mean, with such a great abundance of history surrounding you with proof, even the writings of those who weren't of the faith but still encountered Jesus, I believe you would have come to see the truth of Him for yourself."

"Why do you believe? I've told you why I don't believe, so now I'd like to know why you do."

Adam was silent for several moments. Tom heard him draw in a deep breath and let it out slowly. "My mother. She taught me through her actions how important her faith was to her. It impressed me that when people scorned her, she baked them bread. When they taunted her, she made them cookies. My mother forgave when it would have been so easy to hate. I asked her how she could possibly forgive such ugliness, and she told me she forgave because that was what the Lord asked her to do. It was what He had done on the cross when people scorned and ridiculed Him."

"But, if as you say, He was God—why should that impress me?"

"Because He was also a man. I know it's a mystery that goes beyond our ability to understand, but Jesus was both man and God."

"That makes little sense to me. Why would He go through the sufferings He did if He was indeed God? He could have stopped the torment at any time. He could have prevented the cross altogether and still gotten His point across."

"Yes, He could have, which makes the cross all the more precious to me. Jesus went willingly for the sake of sinners just like me. He knew that without the cross, there would be no reconciliation between God and man."

"But God can do anything. Surely there could have been another way of reconciliation."

Adam chuckled. "Careful there, Tom. You're starting to sound as though you believe God really exists."

CHAPTER 12

C onnie sent a letter," Faith declared, bringing the mail to the dining room table, where Nancy and Seth were enjoying a leisurely lunch. Mrs. Weaver and Alma had just retired for a nap, while the Clifton sisters and Mimi Bryant had borrowed Nancy and Seth's carriage and gone shopping.

"Why don't you sit down, and I'll read it." Nancy pushed her dishes back a bit to make room for the letter.

Faith handed the envelope to her cousin, then took her seat.

Nancy opened the letter and unfolded the pages. "'Dear all,'" she began. "'Life at Grand Ronde is much depressed since last I was here. The storm destroyed many of the trees, and most of the buildings suffered damage. Still, I think this area is some of the prettiest in the state. I had forgotten just how much I love it.

"'Father and Mother are well and send their love. I thought them to have aged far more than seven years would normally allow for, but given their worries over all that is going on, it isn't surprising to find gray in their hair.

"'Tom likes the family very much and enjoys working with the Native people too. We've been hard at work taking down information from every person who will speak to us about their culture and history. The Fourth of July is soon upon us, and the priest and nuns are planning a celebration where the Native children will put on a play. I think I shall look forward to that. The children are so precious. I wish they could remain as loving and kind as they are now. Sadly, I know that the bitterness of their families will spoil their current outlook. How could it not? Hatred is so strong. I pray for them daily, but evil is strong too. The church hopes to resolve the problem by forcing the children to board at school for the year, but they go home on occasion, and the anger is reinforced. I fear we are doing more harm than good.'"

"That wouldn't surprise me," Faith commented. "Hate is like a disease that quickly spreads."

Nancy looked up. "Hate is found on both sides, sadly. I wish there were better ways to make people understand the destructiveness of hatred."

Seth shrugged and rubbed his neck. "No matter how strong the hate and bitterness, God's love is stronger. There is nothing God can't do to change hearts."

"I know, but it's just so heartbreaking to see how people hurt each other." Nancy glanced down at the letter and began to read again. "'We are trying to encourage the people to repair the sawmill and get the lumber business going again. The people are very discouraged from the first time around. They worked hard, only to have their profits stolen by the agent in charge at the time. I thought it might be wonderful if Gabe or Uncle Alex could come and help them get it up and running again, but I don't think Clint would appreciate our interference. The Indians probably wouldn't either. Hopefully the Indian Legislature will stir the people to make repairs and once again earn a profit. There are all the storm-felled trees to cut, and I'm certain the railroad would buy the wood—especially if it were cut for ties.'"

Nancy looked up again. "Maybe we can encourage Gabe and Clementine to take a little trip to visit Uncle Adam and Aunt Mercy. Surely that couldn't be frowned upon."

"I find that anything, even the best of intentions, can and will be frowned upon by people who are bitter," Faith countered. "But I suppose we could talk to them about it."

"Just remember, it's usually best not to interfere." Seth smiled. "Even when that interference is done in love."

Nancy returned to the letter. "'Many of the people want nothing to do with either Tom or myself. They don't want the government keeping a record of their people. They fear the government is only doing this to gather information that can later be used to destroy them. I find it sad, because their history will be lost if we fail to keep a record.

"'As for our other problems, we are no closer to understanding who controls things. We are making it our priority alongside the Bureau's work, but no one seems to know anything. I talked at length with my parents, but they have no idea—no direction in which to point us. We will continue to do what we can and pray that God will open our eyes to the truth before it's too late.'" Nancy refolded the letter. "She signs off with love to all."

"Well, we didn't expect them to learn the truth overnight," Seth said, rubbing his neck again.

"Are you in pain, sweetheart?" Nancy put the letter aside and got up to massage her husband's shoulders.

"I'm pretty stiff, and it has given me a headache. I think maybe a storm is coming. You know how that always seems to bring on pain."

Faith frowned. "I could give you some laudanum."

"I think I'll try resting first. If that doesn't help, I may let you." He drew Nancy's hand to his lips. "I believe I'll go lie down for a while." He kissed her fingertips.

"I'll come check on you after I get the dishes washed. Don't forget that Jack's sleeping."

He nodded and got to his feet. Nancy worried for her husband. He'd been so wounded by the beating he received only a couple of months earlier. And even though he was healing quickly, there remained issues that Faith said were quite normal. Headaches and body aches, restless sleep. How Nancy wished she could make it all go away. She prayed that, in time, God would take the pain from Seth and give him back a normal life. She gathered the dishes and took them to the kitchen.

"You're worried about him, aren't you?" Faith asked, following her with the remaining food.

"I am. I can't help but worry. I hate that he ever got involved with this. I feel like it's all my fault, since he was investigating my late husband."

"It's a job he chose to take, Nancy. You won't do either of you any good in placing blame. If it's any comfort at all, his recovery has been remarkable. This is all very normal, including the fatigue. The body is expending all its energy on healing, and that takes a toll. Resting is the very best thing for him. I think in another few months, you'll be surprised at just how much better he'll be."

Nancy nodded but wasn't all that convinced. After reading Connie's letter, she wondered if the next few months would hold anything but pain and sorrow.

"We're leaving now," Mrs. Weaver said from the arched doorway. Behind her stood Alma and their new friend, Ruth. Ruth and Alma had become the best of friends. Their pasts were very similar. Both had been slaves from the time of birth, and both had been set free with no place to go. Their former owners had been merciful, but in Ruth's case, her owner had died shortly after moving to Oregon from California.

Nancy went to Alma and took her hand. "I'm so proud of you for leaving the house and going to this fellowship."

"I'm scared," she admitted, "but we prayed, and I know the Lord will be with us." She looked to Mrs. Weaver and then Ruth.

"She'll be very safe and welcomed," Ruth declared. "Come on now, Alma. We'd best go, or we'll be late."

"Are the Clifton sisters still meeting you, Mrs. Weaver?" Alma asked. It had earlier been determined that Mrs. Weaver would walk with Ruth and Alma to the church, and then the Misses Clifton would pick her up in the carriage to go shopping for fabric.

"They are, bless them." Mrs. Weaver looked at her longtime companion. "I'll be praying the whole time. I couldn't bear it if someone hurt you."

Alma smiled. "The Lord is with us, and we've got nothin' to fear."

Connie kept thinking about Reverend Summers forcing the Indians to sell their artifacts. One woman had told Connie that she faced him at the gate to her yard and told him she had nothing for him to buy. The reverend had pushed her aside and gone into her house uninvited. There he had gathered up the things he wanted and given her what he thought they were worth. It angered Connie to no end, and she thought it was time to confront Clint about it.

Her father had offered to take Tom on a ride to the far side of the reservation, so Connie saw it as the perfect time. She marched over to Clint's office and pounded on the door. Clint showed up within seconds.

"To what do I owe this pleasure?" He grinned. "And my, don't you look pretty today."

She was wearing a forest-green calico with hints of yellow and orange. It wasn't anything special. "Thank you, but getting compliments isn't why I came here today."

"Well, why don't you come into my office and tell me why you did come?" Clint stepped back to give her room to pass.

She made her way in and stood waiting at the corner of his desk, hands on her hips. "What are you going to do about Reverend Summers?"

"What are you talking about?" Clint sat down. "Why don't you sit and tell me what has you so upset?"

Connie shook her head. "I'll stand, thank you. I'm talking about the way Reverend Summers comes here and forces people to sell their artifacts and heirlooms. It's wrong, Clint, and you know it."

"I'm not happy about it either, but there's nothing I can do about it. He's good friends with the governor. He also sells those artifacts to some wealthy and powerful collectors. You aren't going to get much support to stop him."

"We've taken everything else from these people, and now you're taking away their family history. It's wrong to let this go on." He watched her with great interest. Connie felt as if he was dismissing the entire situation and focusing on her appearance. "Clint, are you even listening to me?"

He grinned. "Well, it is hard to listen when you're standing there being so delightfully pretty."

She rolled her gaze to the ceiling and huffed. "You are no help at all."

"After that kiss the other day, I've had a hard time thinking of anything else."

"Oh, for grief's sake. That kiss meant nothing." And she realized the truth of it the moment she spoke the words. "I don't want to start anything with you, Clint. Those childish infatuations have been buried with the past."

She felt a sense of peace flow over her. Clint was just a friend from the past. She neither regretted nor esteemed him. He simply . . . was.

He was frowning as she continued. "I

might have had feelings for you when I was fifteen, but that's long gone. You were wise to refuse my nonsense, and for that I thank you, but that still isn't why I'm here. You are failing these people by allowing Summers to do as he pleases."

Clint looked past her to the window. "I've spoken to him about it and asked him to stop. I've spoken to my father and brother about it. There's nothing else to be done."

Connie fumed. "There has to be something. He and others like him come in and steal the people blind. They're even raiding their burial places. They're digging up bodies. Disturbing the dead so that they can take skulls and even full skeletons for museums. It's positively scandalous, and even the soldiers are guilty of it."

"Look, I told you that I've tried to deal with it. There's nothing more to discuss on the matter. What I want to return to is us. You can't just show up after all these years and not give me a chance. I know Tom fancies himself in love with you, but you clearly don't love him."

Connie was stunned by this comment. It wasn't the first time someone had suggested that Tom cared for her, but for Clint to do it seemed completely out of line. "My relationship with Tom is none of your business. I care very deeply for Tom."

"I just want a chance to woo you—to show you that the feelings you once had for me aren't dead. They only need to be revived."

She shook her head. "I'm not interested. I'm here to record Indian culture and tribal information. I'm also here to see that they're treated right. You can't let their graves be disturbed."

"I can hardly set up guards night and day."

"Why not?"

Clint seemed momentarily stunned by the question. "It's the Indians' responsibility. If they want guards at the cemetery, then they need to put them in place. It's completely up to them."

"And what is your responsibility, Clint? It seems to me that as an Indian agent, you have been tasked with watching over the tribes and ensuring their well-being. You're the only one they have to fight for them."

"I wouldn't say that. You're doing a good job of it yourself." He crossed his arms. "Honestly, Connie, you can't save the world. You can't even save half of it."

She frowned. "Maybe not, but I can fight for this little piece of it. I'm going to send a letter to my uncle Dean in Washington. Maybe he can get together with your father and brother and come to a different conclusion."

She headed for the door, but before she could reach it, Clint had come around his desk and closed the distance between them.

"Leave my father and brother out of this," he growled, taking hold of her.

Connie had never seen him look so angry. For a moment she felt afraid, but then she pushed her fear and Clint aside. "Stop trying to intimidate me."

"I'm doing my job," he continued, sounding less angry. "I'm doing the best I can with what the government gives and the laws allow. I don't like a lot of it any better than you do, but some of the men responsible have powerful friends. Friends who would just as soon replace me and put one of their cronies in my place. You think it's bad now? That would spell disaster for your friends."

Connie considered his words for a moment. Maybe he was right. She knew how the various political groups scratched one another's backs. It could prove disastrous if they replaced Clint with someone who truly didn't care about the welfare of the Indians.

"I'm sorry, Clint. I just get angry when I think of soldiers digging up graves. It's heartless and cruel."

"I know, Connie." He moved closer. "You need to understand that I've wrestled with this for a long time. It's been going on for decades and probably will continue. I promise, however, that I will keep trying to find a way to put an end to it."

She heard the sincerity in his voice. "Thank you, Clint. I appreciate your heart." She shook her head. "I'm sorry if I offended you."

"You didn't. I've always appreciated your passion for righting wrongs." He touched her cheek. "In fact, I greatly admire your passion."

Connie backed away. "I'm sorry, Clint. I just don't have those feelings for you anymore."

She was already halfway out the door when he spoke.

"Tom's a lucky man."

She knew better than to respond. If she told him she wasn't in love with Tom either—that they were just friends—it might only encourage his affections. Connie just kept walking. She wondered if she should tell Tom about the encounter but decided against it. The last thing she needed was Tom being angry at Clint and Clint being jealous of Tom.

Lord, I need some direction on this. I don't know how to handle what's going on. I thought I would always love Clint—at least I did when I was fifteen. Now that I'm grown, I can see our differences would never have allowed us to have a good marriage.

She thought for a moment, searching her heart in case there was some motive in her for revenge. Was she just rejecting Clint because he had rejected her? No. She didn't feel anything toward him at all. No desire for revenge or reckoning. No need for him to be hurt because he'd hurt her. She didn't even completely blame him for what was happening on the reservation. After all, the Catholic Church and the army also played roles in the past and present. Not to mention the government as a whole.

She changed her mind about going home and decided instead to visit Rosy. Maybe she could help Connie figure out a solution to put a stop to the grave robbing.

She knocked on the door and waited for an answer. Nobody came. Connie waited a moment and was about to leave when she heard moaning and the barely audible words, "Help me."

Connie tried the door and found it unlocked. She opened it and called out. "Rosy?"

"Help."

Spurred on by the frail sound, Connie entered the house and saw Rosy lying on the floor near the table in her kitchen.

"Rosy, what happened?"

"I'm sick."

Connie felt her head. It didn't feel feverish.

She couldn't see any reason for the ailment. "Let me help you up. I'll get you into your bed and then fetch Mama. She'll know what to do."

The old woman couldn't have weighed more than ninety pounds, but it was still difficult for Connie to get her off the floor. Thankfully they only needed to go a few feet. Once she had Rosy in bed, Connie rushed for her parents' house.

"Mama! Mama!" she called before even stepping through the door.

"What is all the ruckus?" her mother asked, descending the steps.

Connie stopped to catch her breath. "It's Rosy. I found her collapsed. She's sick."

Her mother nodded and went to the kitchen for what Connie called her healing bag. Mama and her two sisters, as well as Faith, all had them.

"Does she show any symptoms?" her mother asked.

"I found her on the floor. She's terribly weak and told me she was sick."

"Come on. Let's see what's going on."

Together they hurried back to Rosy's place.

"So many have been sick," her mother said. "They're convinced the flour was poisoned. I don't know that I believe that. I think perhaps it's something else. Bad meat, maybe. The heat makes it spoil so quickly. Your father and I rarely eat meat in the summer unless it's freshly killed chicken or fish."

They entered Rosy's house, and Mama immediately went to her bed. "Rosy, what seems to be wrong? Connie, bring me a chair, please."

Connie brought a wooden chair for her mother to sit on. Her mother began to check Rosy's eyes and ears and mouth. She felt Rosy's forehead and then checked her neck and arms for rash or any sign of injury.

"What have you had to eat?"

"Bread and fish." Rosy closed her eyes, but a strange smile appeared on her lips. "And cake. The cake Connie brought."

"That's odd. None of us got sick from the cake," Connie's mother told Rosy as she continued her examination. "Perhaps it was the bread, though I would more easily believe there's been bad meat shared around. Did you have any meat?"

Rosy said nothing for a moment, then nodded. "Fish stew. Adela brought it yesterday."

Mama turned to Connie. "Go see if Adela and her family are ill."

Connie nodded and headed out, only to run full-speed into Tom.

He steadied her. "What's going on? I

saw you and your mom practically running here."

"Rosy's sick, and Mama is trying to figure out what's wrong. Come with me. We need to do a little investigating."

Tom went with Connie to the house of Adela and Howard Riggs, nearly a mile away. Connie seemed relieved to find them all healthy and thriving. Adela gave Connie a detailed list of what had gone into her soup, as well as her certainty that it couldn't possibly have made Rosy sick.

"I hope they can figure out if it's really the flour, and if so, why it's making people ill," Connie said as they left the house. "We really don't need one more issue to deal with."

"No. That's true enough. But I'm not sure we'll ever really know." Tom shook his head and shrugged. "If it was poisoned, no one is going to admit to doing it. The excess flour has been confiscated, and folks were told to turn in any flour they'd purchased from this shipment. Hopefully that will be the end of it."

"Yes, but that doesn't mean it won't happen again. I honestly don't understand the heartlessness of people. Their hate is so intense."

"Have you heard anything more from Clint about the shipments?" Tom asked, changing the subject.

"No. I was talking to him earlier about my disgust at artifacts being all but stolen from the Indians, as well as the grave robbing that goes on, and all he wanted to talk about was his feelings for me."

Tom could well imagine. It seemed Clint was always watching Connie. "I know it probably doesn't make sense to you, but I don't trust him."

"Why not?" She looked at him but continued to walk. "Just because he thinks he's in love with me doesn't make him untrustworthy."

"I don't know. I guess it's just a feeling. He often has meetings with the Indians that no one else is invited to attend."

"He's the Indian agent. I would hope he has meetings with them."

"In the middle of the night?"

"How do you know he's doing that?" This time she stopped and waited for his response.

"You wanted us to prove your parents' innocence, and that's what I'm trying to do. I've been getting up in the night and watching him. He often has meetings with as many as ten men."

"That is rather strange." Connie frowned. "Have you any idea what he's up to?"

"No. I can never get close enough to the house. They always post lookouts. Whatever they're discussing, they don't want anyone to know about it."

CHAPTER 13

The Fourth of July passed without much ado. The Indian children performed a play about the birth of America, but Connie doubted they did it by choice. Independence Day meant very little to a people who weren't free.

Rosy's health improved, but Connie's mother reminded her that Rosy was up in years and probably didn't have much more time. The Indians had suffered such malnutrition and endured so many struggles that it had taken a big toll on their life expectancy. It troubled Connie. Why had a government who held life, liberty, and the pursuit of happiness so dear believed themselves justified in treating the Indians so poorly?

Near the middle of the month, Isaac left for Oregon City in order to bring back a small herd of sheep he'd purchased from their aunt Hope and uncle Lance. On August first, he returned, and with him came Hope and Lance Kenner and Connie's cousin Faith. Just their presence managed to cheer everyone.

"I can't believe you're here," Connie's mother said, hugging Hope tightly. "How I've missed you."

"I've missed you too. It's hard not having you and Adam close by." The sisters pulled away and just looked at each other for a moment. There were many untold secrets between them after all they'd gone through together. Especially when they'd been held hostage at the Whitman Mission.

"How is Grace doing?" Mama asked.

Hope smiled. "She's doing very well. She sent a few gifts and told me to tell you that she's almost convinced Alex and Gabe to come for a visit as well."

"That would be wonderful," Connie interjected. "Maybe they could advise the Indians on the best way to get the mill back up and running."

"I'm sure they would," Aunt Hope said, turning to Connie. "It's hard to believe you're all grown up."

"I hardly recognized her when she showed up at Nancy's," Faith said, laughing. "I suppose we all have to accept that time will never stand still."

"Speaking of Nancy," Mama asked, "how is she? How is poor Seth?"

"He's recovering well," Faith replied. "They're both doing quite well, and little Jack is growing so fast. He's a little cherub."

Connie looked around. "Where did Isaac get off to?"

"The men are moving the sheep into one of the fenced pastures. After the sheep are secured, Isaac and your father hope to convince the others to help them put up fencing for another pasture so the sheep can be moved around." Her mother turned to Aunt Hope. "I tell you, Isaac has worked hard to make those pastures perfect. He walked every inch, planted good grass seed, and got rid of any poisonous vegetation."

"That's the workings of a good shepherd," Faith offered.

"He plans to get a good sheepdog too. We have promised him the pick of the litter when Dilly has her pups," Aunt Hope announced. "But that won't help in the immediate future. Hopefully we'll be able to locate one already trained. We've advertised in several newspapers. Even the one in Salem, since it's closer than Portland and Oregon City."

"It'll be nice to have a dog around the place. When our old spaniel died, we just never got around to getting another. There are so many dogs on the reservation as it is."

"Well, a good sheepdog is worth his weight in gold. He'll keep the sheep contained and safe. Hopefully we can find one soon." Hope looked at Connie. "I understand you're here to record information about the various tribes."

"I am. Tom and I were hired by the Bureau of Ethnology to document all of the Indians on the reservations here in Oregon. For the time being, we're assigned to the Grand Ronde, Warm Springs, and Siletz Reservations. We chose to start here so that I could be near my family." She didn't know how much she could say about her personal investigation. The fewer people who knew, the better, but at the same time she was pretty confident the family was already well aware of what her mother and father were being accused of.

"It sounds like quite the task."

Connie knew Aunt Hope had gone through terrible things at the hands of the Cayuse Indians when they had massacred the men and one woman at the Whitman Mission back in 1847. Connie had heard the story from her mother only once, and then it was never mentioned again. She often wondered what Aunt Hope thought of Mama's devotion to the Indians. After all, her mother had been at the mission as well but hadn't suffered the things Aunt Hope suffered. Aunt Grace had once told Connie that her mother had more mercy and forgiveness than she or Hope put together and that neither were surprised when Mercy made the announcement that she wanted to work with the Indians. Connie could only imagine the things her mother and aunts had seen in the past thirty-some years. How the world had changed since the 1840s.

"You seem lost in thought, Connie."

She shook off her thoughts. "Sorry about that. I didn't mean to be rude."

"No harm done." Aunt Hope gave her a smile. "We can talk about your mission after lunch. You wrote and said that there was a problem with sickness on the reservation. Has that passed now?" she asked her sister.

"Did you ever figure out what the sickness was?" Faith asked.

Mama shook her head. "Not exactly. The agent had to send for the reservation doctor— not that the people wanted to use him, but so many were ill that Clint worried it was an epidemic of some sort. The people thought they'd been poisoned by bad flour, but the doctor assured them it wasn't the fault of the food. I'm not convinced. It could have been a summer malady. Those things happen all the time. However, it really did act more like food poisoning. Even the doctor was hard-pressed to give it a name. Everyone is doing better now, so at least no one is calling to kill anyone."

"What are you talking about?" Hope asked.

Mama waved to the living room. "Why don't we sit? I have stew simmering on the stove and bread warming. When the guys come back, we can eat."

Connie followed her mother and aunt to the front room and explained, "The Indians often kill the medicine people if they fail to heal. I suppose it ensures that the healers do their best."

Her mother took a seat. "It's true. You must remember that was part of the problem at the Whitman Mission."

Hope gave a solemn nod. "I had forgotten, but now I remember. The chief's children died from measles, and he blamed Dr. Whitman."

She and Connie's mother exchanged a glance, and in that moment, they were connected in a way that excluded Connie and Faith.

"So many Cayuse were sick," Mama declared. "It was a bad time for everyone. Grace even went to the Cayuse village to do what she could. It didn't sit well with Dr. Whitman, but Grace didn't care."

"I can imagine." Connie had heard all sorts of stories about Aunt Grace, and all of them involved her strong will and determination to heal the sick.

"Will your Indian agent be joining us for the meal?" Aunt Hope asked, seeming anxious to change the subject.

Mama shook her head. "He's gone to Portland on business."

"He has?" Connie asked before thinking it through. She didn't want anyone thinking she cared one way or another.

"Yes. He said he had officials to meet with and reservation business to tend to."

"I thought that usually took place in Salem."

"It does, but two men who work with his brother in Washington were in Portland and had no plans to be in Salem. I really don't know all the details, but Clint said he'd be gone for a week."

"Perhaps he'll call on Nancy and Seth, since he met them on his last visit," Connie said. "He seemed to really like Seth."

"Everyone likes Seth," Faith countered.

"That's why his beating came as such a surprise."

"Yes, but didn't you say it was because Seth stepped on the toes of the smugglers?" Hope put her hand to her mouth.

"It's all right. Connie knows all about it. In fact, she partially got this job so that she could work to clear our names," Mama replied.

Hope lowered her hand. "And have you found out anything new?"

Connie shook her head. "Not really. I know that whiskey is being smuggled onto the reservation." She thought about mentioning what she'd seen at the river, but Clint had told her to remain silent on the matter. "And I know there are some very angry men on the reservation who would probably do whatever they could to kill white people."

"Did someone say something?" Mama asked.

"I spoke with the Sheridan men early on, and they were very hostile. If anyone is planning an uprising, I bet they're involved. I've not spoken with them since."

Her mother sighed. "They still blame your father for not helping them escape the reservation. It's so sad, because Joe used to be such good friends with your father. And Faith's friend Ann-Red Deer is stepmother to Samson Sheridan's wife, Ruth."

"Ann is here?" Faith asked, excited. "I thought she was on the Siletz Reservation."

Mama nodded. "She was, but she remarried to Will Orleans, and they settled here to raise Will's three children. Ruth is the youngest."

"Oh, I'm so happy. I want to see Ann as soon as possible."

"Tom and I plan to interview her this week. Maybe you and I could go over there first, and you could introduce us. Maybe then she won't be afraid of us."

Her mother's expression turned sad. "I think the people here are afraid of anything the government does. Even something as positive as recording their history. Adam told me that there has been great interest in this area, and white settlers are seeking to drive the Indians off this land. He believes firmly that this is the reason for the whiskey and rifles. Powerful white men want to cause the Indians to start a war so the army can sweep in, kill as many Indians as possible, and round up the rest to put away elsewhere. Connie said there was even thought of moving all of them north to the Department of Alaska."

"That frozen void?" Hope asked. "I heard a lecture on that place. It sounds absolutely terrible, and there are already quite a few Natives living there."

"Exactly," Connie said. "The thought is that they will round up all the Native people and put them in one place. They'll put guards on the borders and naval ships to keep the harbors closed to all but government ships, and then they'll leave the Natives to figure it all out for themselves."

"That would be terrible," her mother said. "I can't believe anyone with even a lick of sense would think that to be sound reasoning."

"I doubt they care," Faith said, shaking her head. "They only want to be rid of the Indians and probably hope that they'll kill each other off. But when it comes to organizing an uprising, the Indians aren't doing this by themselves. And furthermore, getting rid of everyone who is Indian or even part-Indian won't solve the issue of hatred that lives in the hearts of those people responsible."

The conversation fell silent. Connie knew they were most likely considering the fact that Faith, the result of her mother's rape at the Whitman Mission, was half Cayuse. If they sent the reservation Indians away, would they insist on sending all Indians away? Even Connie and her father and brother were part Cherokee, and while their percentage might not be considered all that much, there were those who said that even a drop of Indian blood was too much.

The world was going mad. Their country had abolished slavery, but there were still so many who hated the former slaves that secret organizations had formed for the sole purpose of killing them. The government had rounded up all the Indians—at least they were attempting to do so—and now was considering options for getting rid of them altogether. There were anti-Chinese leagues and people who had no tolerance of anyone whose skin color was different. Grief, there were even those who felt that anyone who spoke a language other than English should be forced out. It was madness.

"Where are my favorite girls?" Connie's father called as the men returned to the house through the back door.

"We're in the front room, waiting for you fellas to return so we can eat," Mama replied, getting to her feet. "Come along, ladies."

"I'm sure you're happy to see your aunt and uncle again," Tom said as he and Connie worked on their notes that evening. Connie was rewriting what they'd learned for the official report.

"Yes, I love my family. They're all so

good to one another. I've seen and heard of other families fighting and purposely harming each other, but that has never occurred in our family. Since I was quite young, all I've ever known from them is love. Of course, they have their disagreements, and once in a while someone gets their feelings hurt, but they always make up."

Tom nodded. "My brothers and sister fought all the time as children and still fight to this day. They neither seek each other's company nor enjoy it when they're together. My father died over ten years ago, and they're still fighting over the estate. I think I've fallen in love with your family."

Connie laughed. "They are a good bunch. I tell you what—we'll just adopt you and make you a part of our family. There's always room for one more."

Tom let his gaze settle on her for a long moment. She had no idea how much he wanted to be a part of her family, but not for the reasons she might think. Working with Connie and living so near her, Tom couldn't deny his heart. The question was, how could he make her see his feelings? Should he just tell her how he felt and see how she responded?

"Your drawings are so good, Tom. I know this will be a special part of our report. I only wish I could draw as you do."

"Maybe I could show you some techniques sometime," he offered.

Connie smiled. "That could be fun." She paused, and her expression changed. "By the way, did you know that Clint is in Portland?"

"I knew he hasn't been around."

"Mama said he had business with some of his brother's associates. I wonder if it has anything to do with the whiskey smuggling."

Tom had wondered how much Clint knew about the smuggling himself. "Has he talked to your father about it?"

"I don't know how much, but he has in the past. He told me that Papa observed one of the deliveries. He told me not to tell my father what I saw that night at the river because he'd be upset."

"How well do you really know Clint Singleton?"

Connie considered this for a moment. "He's always been good help for my father. He came here and worked with Papa long before he was assigned as an agent. His father wanted him to join their cause to see the Indians properly treated. So even when he wasn't getting paid, Clint worked with my father. I think his own father paid him a stipend.

"Clint has always been eager to please his father. As far back as I can remember, he's talked about how important that is to him. His family has always cared deeply about the Indian cause. They are strong believers in seeing the Native peoples given citizenship and treated as equals."

"What about Clint's spiritual feelings?"

Connie shrugged. "He always shows up for church. We never talked about it before I left home, and now that I'm back, all he wants to talk about is giving him a chance to prove he's worthy of my love."

Tom looked at her. "He said that?"

She chuckled. "Yes, but he said a lot of things. He even had some opinions of you and your feelings for me."

Tom wondered if this was a chance to share his heart with Connie. He opened his mouth to speak, but just then Isaac called to him.

"Hey, Tom, do you have time to lend me a hand?" He came into the dining room, where Tom and Connie had been working. "I'd like to get some fence up before dark."

"I'd be happy to help." Tom knew his declaration of love would have to wait for another time. He looked at Connie. "Sorry to leave you to work on this alone."

"It's no matter. Mama and the others will be back soon, and then there will be no time for it. I promised that when they returned with the berries, I'd help prepare them for making jelly and jam tomorrow. I guess we each have our promises to keep."

Tom nodded. He followed Isaac out to the pasture, but he left his heart with Connie.

CHAPTER 14

"Are you certain everything is ready on your end?" Mr. Smith asked Elias Carter.

The squat, fat man mopped his perspiring brow. "We're ready when you are. The men are more than anxious to see this thing started and finished. As soon as word comes of the uprising, we will do our part and storm Salem with our demands."

Smith smiled. "Good. I'm glad to hear everyone is being so cooperative. I was rather concerned that some of our men were less than committed."

"No, no. Everyone is of like mind. We all want to see the Indians removed."

Smith could see the poor man was nearly ready to have a heart attack. "Look, Carter, it might suit you to have a few drinks. You look nervous." Only then did it dawn on Smith that perhaps Carter was anxious for another reason. "You haven't chosen to abandon our side, have you?"

The fat man's eyes widened. "No. No, sir. These things just always make me a little nervous. Are you sure we'll be safe enough in Portland? No need to send my family east for a time?"

Smith studied him for a moment, then shook his head. "No, they'll be quite safe here, I can assure you. Besides, if you were to do that, it might start a panic amongst the others. We wouldn't want that to happen when we're so close to victory, would we?"

Carter shook his head and swallowed hard. "No, sir."

"Good." Smith picked up his walking stick. "I'm counting on you, Elias."

Smith made his way from the building and hailed a cab. The driver opened the carriage for him. "Where to, sir?"

"The Grand Hotel." Smith settled back into the worn leather seats of the hired conveyance. It wasn't the quality he preferred, but it would get him where he needed to go.

He thought about the meetings he'd had and wondered if he'd covered every possibility. He was determined that nothing go wrong. He'd worked too long and hard to see this thing to fruition. Now they were heading into the final days, and the thrill of the game was driving him forward in a frenzy of excitement. Once it was all said and done, a new world would dawn in Oregon. A world in which they would finally be rid of the Indians.

Smith smiled and began to hum a tune he'd heard at the opera the night before. Life was good, and it was about to get so much better.

"I thought I might never see you again," Faith declared as she embraced her old friend Red Deer. The Tututni woman, who was now called Ann, was the mother of Mary, Faith's playmate when she lived on the Rogue River. "I didn't know you were here. I looked for you once when I came to spend the summer with my aunt and uncle, but they said you were at the Siletz Reservation."

Ann cupped Faith's cheeks with a fond smile, then dropped her hands. "I was. After my husband died, I went to live with Mary and her family."

Faith shook her head. "It's so hard to imagine Mary grown with children of her own."

"She has four and is expecting another.

She's been blessed that their health has been so good."

"I married a few months ago and am hoping to have children of my own one day," Faith said. "Family is everything to me."

"Mary feels that way too. She is quite happy, even living on the reservation. Her husband is a hardworking man who has learned to farm."

"I want to hear all about them, but first let me introduce someone." Faith stepped back. "Do you know my cousin Connie? She is Mercy and Adam Browning's daughter."

Ann looked at Connie and smiled. "I heard about her coming home. I knew her when she was a very small child, but then I went to Siletz to live. I'm pleased to meet you again, Connie."

"I'm glad to meet you too, Ann—Red Deer."

"Connie is working with a young man to write about the culture and heritage of the various tribes. The government doesn't want your history to be lost."

"I heard about that. The people are very guarded and uncertain about why the government wants this."

"I think it's probably a good thing," Faith said, looking thoughtful. "The tribes need to ensure that future people will know all about what went on in the past. I think telling the history will help the tribes to remain a part of the future."

Ann nodded. "I hope that is true and that it is a good thing."

"I would never do anything to harm the *real people*," Connie declared. "They are like family to me."

Ann nodded again and patted Connie's arm. "Come in and rest. I have fresh apple cider and warm bread. We can talk more."

Connie followed Faith into the well-kept house. She was more than a little impressed with how nicely arranged the house was. There was a large open living area with three doors on the far wall. "You have a lovely home."

"Thank you. We are blessed."

Faith nodded. "Tell us how it has been with you all these years."

"It is good. After my husband died, I married Will Orleans—a Yamhill man with a good reputation. He has four sons and a daughter. I helped to raise them, especially his daughter, Ruth. The boys are all married with their own family. Ruth is married and expecting her first baby. She'll be stopping by soon so that we can work on baby clothes."

Faith seemed so happy. "I'm only here for

a short time with my mother and father. We came to visit my aunt and uncle. If you'd allow me to help, I'd love to stay. Then we could really catch up on all the years."

"I would like that. And you, Connie? Would you like to stay and help?"

"For a little while, if you don't mind." Connie smiled. "You should know that Faith is very good at stitching. She's now a certified surgeon."

Ann frowned. "A surgeon?"

"I am a doctor who can perform surgeries," Faith explained. "When someone is injured inside their body, I can cut into them and fix the problem, then sew them back up."

Ann nodded. "A surgeon," she tried the word again. "That is wonderful. I'm sure you save many people. Sit at my table, please."

Connie and Faith sat down just as a light knock sounded and the door opened again to admit a young woman heavy with child. She looked at Connie and Faith with great apprehension.

Ann brought a plate of freshly sliced bread and a bowl of butter to the table. "Ruth, come in. I was just telling my old friends about you."

The shy young woman stepped up to the table. She wore her hair in braids but pinned up. Her dark eyes searched the room and then her stepmother's face.

"This is Faith," Ann said. "I knew her when we lived on the Rogue River before the great march. And this is Connie, her cousin. Connie's parents are Adam and Mercy Browning."

Ruth smiled and gave a slight nod.

"They are going to help us make baby clothes and talk about the old days."

Seeing her stepmother so at ease, Ruth seemed to relax. She eased onto a chair and sighed.

"Ruth is due anytime," Ann explained. "I am so happy for her to have a baby of her own. She will be such a good mother."

Connie smiled. "I'm sure you will be a great mother."

"And you are blessed to have Ann as your stepmother. She taught me so much," Faith said. "Her daughter Mary was my very best friend when we lived with the Tututni."

Ruth looked surprised. "You lived with the Indians?"

"Yes, and it was wonderful. Oh, how I sometimes long for those days. We swam in the river and played in the forest. We were so carefree. It wasn't like the way the government has made the reservations. We were a part of the Tututni village."

Ann's eyes were edged with tears. "It was a good life."

Faith reached out and touched Ann's arm. "I am so sorry for all that was lost. It should never have happened."

"So many people died on the march here," Ann remembered. "There was so much pain. The government did not care how the soldiers hurt us. We did not want war, but now I fear we will have it again."

"Why do you say that?" Connie asked.

Ann and Ruth exchanged a look. "There is so much unrest," Ann finally said. "The men—they are not happy. I fear it will lead to war."

Ruth nodded. "I fear for my child." She put her hand to her stomach.

"Is there talk of war?" Connie pressed. "I have heard rumors."

"There is always talk of war. Each time the men hear of someone standing up to the white man, they get ideas."

"Sam says we will defeat the white man," Ruth said, her voice a whisper. "But I am afraid for what it will mean for us."

Connie shook her head. "Is Sam your husband?"

"Yes. Samson Sheridan."

Now she understood. "I met your husband. The Sheridans were once good friends to my mother and father."

Ruth nodded. "I know. Now there is only

bitterness between my husband's family and yours."

"There is no bitterness in my family. My father misses his friendship with Joseph. Do your husband and father-in-law not realize they would have been killed like so many others? If they had left the reservation, the soldiers would have hunted them down and killed them. They didn't even care about returning runaways to the reservation. It was too much trouble. They just shot them and left them to rot. It shames me deeply to think of our soldiers acting that way, but it was how they did things and probably still is."

"Sam has so much hate," Ruth said, shaking her head.

Ann sighed. "It is true. I knew his mother. Of all her children, he was the happiest. But not anymore . . . I fear for him."

"I do too," Ruth said, wiping tears from her eyes. "I fear soon I will be a widow with a child, dependent upon others for my well-being."

"Why do you say 'soon'?" Connie asked. "Do you know of something specific that is being planned?"

Ruth looked upset. She turned to Ann, a look of questioning in her eyes. Ann nodded, and Ruth turned back to Connie. "There is talk of a war coming."

Ann held her stepdaughter's hand. "We hope it is nothing more than talk, but the men are making plans. They've been working with someone outside of the reservation, but I do not know who. It must be a white man, however. Who else could bring them guns?"

"Someone is bringing the men guns? Have you ever told my parents or Agent Singleton?"

"No. If word got back that we had, we would be shunned forever," Ann replied. "We are so afraid for what might happen. If our men kill the white settlers, the soldiers will come and kill all of us."

Faith scooted her chair closer to Ann's and put her arm around her old friend. "If you know anything about it, you must tell us. We won't say where the information came from, but we must stop a war if we can. You are right that there are so many white people who want only to see the *real people* dead. We cannot let them win."

"Why do you care so much about what happens to us?" Ruth asked.

Faith looked around. "Can you keep a secret? Would you swear an oath to me to say nothing of what I tell you?"

Ann smiled. "Of course. You are my friend—like a daughter to me."

Ruth gave a reluctant nod. "If my step-mother says it, then so do I."

"I am part Indian. If they work to kill all of the Indians, they will probably want to kill me too."

Connie wasn't comfortable enough to include herself in that statement as well, but she nodded to confirm that what Faith said was true. She didn't know if the women believed Faith, but Faith didn't seem to think they would question her.

"My mother was forced by a Cayuse brave, and I was born," Faith explained.

"You do not look Indian," Ruth said, staring hard at Faith's face.

"No. I don't. My mother said that was God's blessing for me, because I lived with white people. But I also lived with Native people, and I love both. I know people can live as one and love the other—if they allow God to control their hearts."

"We believe in the one God," Ruth replied. "My mother taught me." She looked at Ann and smiled. The smile faded as she continued, "But my husband does not believe in God. He did once, as did his father, but now he wants no part of it. He's angry at God."

"You can't be angry at God if you don't believe in Him," Faith declared. "I think your husband is just angry. He probably feels that

God has let him down—hasn't treated him fairly. God can work on his heart. You must pray for him."

"We will pray for him too," Connie said, remembering how angry Samson Sheridan had been when she and Tom tried to talk to him. Only love could quell anger. Perhaps the love she showed to Ruth would be a start. She smiled and rubbed her hands together. "I'm looking forward to helping you with the baby clothes. I helped sew a baby quilt just a few months back. I'm also very good at embroidering. Perhaps I could embroider some of your family's basket patterns on the gowns."

"You can do that?" Ruth asked in awe.

"I believe I can." Connie gave her a smile. "I can do this for my new friend."

"But they didn't have a date for when this war would begin?" Tom asked as Connie explained what they'd learned at Ann's house.

"No, but they felt it would be soon. Ann told me that if she heard when the men would next be at the river to receive guns and whiskey, she would tell me."

Tom glanced toward the sky. It would soon be dark. He'd convinced Connie to take a walk with him, but there had been plenty of light then. "I think we should get back to the house." He looked around. They were farther from the house than he'd intended.

Connie followed suit, scanning their surroundings. "Are you worried something will happen to us?"

"I can't rule it out. It would be foolish to remain out here, just the two of us." Without thought to what he was doing, he took Connie's hand. "Come on."

She looked at him oddly but said nothing. In fact, she was strangely silent until they reached her parents' house. She was trembling by the time he let go of her hand.

"I didn't mean to scare you," he said. Connie crossed her arms over her chest, and he continued. "I know it won't sit well with you, but I think you shouldn't travel away from the house alone. In fact, I think we should probably start carrying a gun with us when we go around the reservation."

Still she said nothing.

Tom took a small step closer to her. "Don't worry. You should pray too. You once told me that God brought us here for a reason. If that's true, I don't think it was for us to die in a massacre."

"Have you changed your mind about God? You sound almost as if you believe He exists."

"I have to admit your father is very persuasive. I think I convinced myself there was no God because so many people were suffering. I couldn't understand how there could be a good God who would stand by and allow such evil in the world. If God can do anything—then why not offer unconditional protection to those who choose to serve Him?"

"I've never heard you even allow for the possibility that God exists, much less consider His actions."

He smiled. "Like I said, your father is very persuasive and learned. I can't say that I'm ready to accept all that you believe, but I'm spending a lot of time reading Scriptures and trying to be open-minded."

"I'm amazed by that and, well, happy. I don't want you to go to hell. It bothers me a lot to think that someone I care for would be lost."

Her words touched him. "Well, maybe from time to time you can start talking to me again about all that stuff you used to tell me when you were just a child. I remember quite vividly that you always quoted one verse in particular."

She nodded. "Romans ten. 'That if thou shalt confess with thy mouth the Lord Jesus, and shalt believe in thine heart that God hath raised him from the dead, thou shalt be saved.' I remember it well. I remember your response too."

"I'm afraid to imagine what it was." Tom tried his best to remember.

"'If it was that simple, Connie, everyone would do it . . . everyone who was willing to believe the fairy tale that God really exists.'" She shook her head. "You used to frustrate me so much. I prayed for you all the time—that God would open your eyes before it was too late."

"But you stopped?"

"Stopped what?"

"Stopped praying for me." He suddenly felt very alone.

"Of course not." Connie sounded disturbed that he would even think such a thing. "I still pray for you. I pray for you every night as I fall asleep."

Tom wanted to pull her into his arms to kiss her and thank her. He knew her beliefs— knew how important she thought it was to pray. That she spent time praying for him made him love her all the more.

"Oh, there you two are." Connie's father came out of the house. "Isaac suggested we play our Bible game tonight."

"Bible game?" Tom asked.

Connie smiled and nodded. "Papa made

us a Bible game with questions about the Bible. We answer them, and the person who gets the most right in a certain amount of time wins the game. It's a lot of fun."

Tom shrugged. "I don't know how good I'll be at something like that, but it sounds like fun."

"Maybe we could have teams, rather than playing individually. You and Connie could be on one team, and Isaac and Mother on the other," Mr. Browning suggested.

Connie looped her arm through her father's. "I think that idea is perfect. I hope Mama has dessert for us too. The game isn't nearly as much fun without dessert."

Her father laughed as they disappeared into the house.

Tom stared after them for a moment. Maybe it was time to talk to Connie's father and tell him how he felt. Maybe Mr. Browning could offer some advice on how to court Connie.

Court Connie.

The thought made him smile despite the fact that he felt as if he'd been courting Connie for the last seven years. He glanced heavenward. "If you really are up there, then maybe you'll help me." He had to laugh to himself. He had just prayed—well, after a fashion. He had prayed to a God he still wasn't completely convinced existed.

"Tom, are you going to join the family?" Connie called from the house.

He chuckled and murmured to himself, "If I have any say about it, I am."

CHAPTER 15

Days later, Connie was surprised when Ann showed up at her parents' house with a request.

"Can you and Faith come to my home? Ruth has been feeling ill. She has been staying with me because her time is close. I wondered if Faith would use her skills as a doctor and help her. If you would both come, we could just tell others that you are going to sew with us."

Faith joined them. "I heard my name mentioned." She grinned. "What's going on?"

Connie turned to her. "Ruth isn't feeling well, and Ann wondered if we could come to the house."

"Is she in labor?" Faith asked, sobering.

"No. She has chills and wants only to sleep."

"Could be the ague," Faith said. "Let me get my bag."

"You mustn't let it be seen," Ann said, shaking her head. "Please hurry." She left Connie and Faith and rushed toward the trees.

"What do you suggest we do?" Faith asked.

"Ann suggested that if anyone asks why we're going to her house, we'll tell them we're going to sew together. Mother has some burlap sacks. Let's take Ann a few things. We'll hide your bag in the bottom."

They went inside and told her mother and Aunt Hope what was going on. Mama came up with several things that hid the medical bag perfectly.

"I put in two yards of white flannel for diapers over and around the bag. On top of that I have several other pieces of cloth, some jars of jam, and a small sack of cookies. That should convince anyone nosy enough to look that it's just that and nothing more."

Faith took the sack. "It's like carrying around books again."

She and Connie headed out the door and began the long walk to Ann's house. Connie couldn't help but contemplate everything going on. "Do you suppose we can get to the bottom of all this nonsense before someone starts a war?"

"I hope so. I don't want anyone to die." Faith shook her head. "It's been a heavy weight on me these past few years. Being half Indian, I bore a sense of guilt for not being honest about my heritage, but also for what was being done to the Indians by white people. I'm both . . . so how can I choose a side?"

"I know. I may only be an eighth Cherokee, but I've had some of those same thoughts." Connie glanced over as Faith shifted the bag. "Are you sure you don't want me to carry that?"

"I'm fine. Do you and Tom have any suspicions about who might be in charge among the Indians?"

"Obviously Samson Sheridan is involved, but as young as he is, I doubt he's in charge. I keep trying to figure out who would be obvious. Joseph Sheridan was eager to leave the reservation, but so were others. Rosy's son tried to escape, and he was shot and killed by soldiers. Many other families endured the same thing. Maybe I could ask Clint who on the reservation has been the biggest trouble-maker. I could ask on the pretense of wanting to stay away from those people until he could go with Tom and me to interview them."

"That might work. At least to narrow it down to the most likely to start a war. I wish you could come back to Portland with me next week. Helen Hunt Jackson is coming to speak there. It's a brief stop, as she's winding her way down to California. I've been corresponding with her and am just so happy that she's agreed to do this. I'd love for you to hear her ideas. She's amazing."

"Where are you bound to, ladies?" Clint asked as they passed the government office. He happened to be outside smoking a cigar.

"We're going over to our friend's house to sew baby clothes. Want to come?" Connie smiled, knowing it was the last place he'd want to be.

"Wish I could—just for the pleasure of your company—but alas, I have too much work to do. I have to meet with the Indian Legislature in five minutes. I just figured I'd catch a few puffs on a cigar before the meeting began."

"I hope it's a positive meeting. Have you found what's needed to restart the mill?"

"I got some idea of the cost when I was in Portland. I talked to a man I believe is related to you both. Gabe Armistead."

"Yes, he's our cousin. We hoped he and our uncle Alex would be willing to help."

"Mr. Armistead assured me they are. Even more amazing, they don't expect anything in return. They're going to send down parts and a man to help make repairs. Now I just need to motivate the men here to work the mill again. They can already start work bringing the downed trees to the mill. There's lots of other preparatory work too." He sighed. "But motivating lazy people is never easy."

Faith frowned, and Connie hoped she wouldn't say anything. The last thing they needed was to fight with Clint and draw attention to themselves.

"Well, good luck. We have to get going." Connie tugged on Faith's arm. "Don't we?"

Faith nodded and allowed Connie to pull her forward. Once they were out of earshot, Faith gave a growl. "I hate it when people talk like that. You'd think he'd know better, having lived with the Indians all these years."

"I know, Faith, but it wasn't going to serve any good purpose to argue with him. Not when Ruth needs our help right now. Tell me more about Helen . . . what was her name?"

"Helen Hunt Jackson. Though she just calls herself Helen Jackson now. She was married to an army captain named Edward Hunt. He died in a military accident. She had two sons who also died not too long afterward. Very tragic and sad."

"Why did she take up the Indian cause?"

"She heard a lecture by Chief Standing Bear of the Ponca Indians. He spoke of his tribe's forced removal from their lands in Nebraska and of the woes they endured at the hands of the soldiers. It moved her so much that she immediately began to research the matter, as well as other similar events. She got involved in writing and speaking in order to raise money to help the Indians. She's working on a book about various tribes and the atrocities done to them."

"She sounds fascinating. I would very much like to hear her. Maybe I can convince Tom that we need to go to Portland and hear her as part of our work."

"Speaking of Tom—what's going on with the two of you?"

Connie glanced at Faith. "I'm not sure I understand."

"You and Tom. Are you just working together, or is it something more? It seems to be so much more."

"So everyone says, but Tom is just a friend. A very good friend, I'll give you that much. There's nothing I wouldn't tell him. I would do just about anything for him, and I believe he feels the same way about me."

"I believe he feels a great many things for you."

Connie frowned. "You aren't the only one to say that. Everyone seems to think Tom has some sort of romantic feelings for me, but he's never said anything about it. I can't believe he is in love with me, because he would say as much if he were. We don't keep secrets from each other."

"Maybe it isn't a secret so much as a desire to find the right time and place."

Connie considered this for a moment. "I don't know. A few times Tom has mentioned wanting to talk to me about something, but he's never brought up the idea of being in love."

"How do you feel about him?"

"I don't know. I care a great deal about him. He's been my best friend for such a long time. But as for love, well, I've just never considered it. After all, he's an atheist. Or at least was. I think Papa has just about worn that thought out of his head."

"Well, maybe it's time to consider how Tom fits into the scheme of things. I think you need to spend some time thinking it through. You seem ideal for each other, and friendship is the very best foundation for marriage. I see Tom's lack of belief to be the only true obstacle."

Connie said nothing. That obstacle was insurmountable unless God moved it. Perhaps that was why she had never considered the possibility of Tom loving her. She didn't want to face the tremendous disappointment of loving someone she knew she could never have.

They had reached Ann's place, so Connie felt no need to respond. She knocked on the front door.

"Come in," Ann said, glancing behind Connie and Faith to see who might be watching.

"We brought some materials and other things to hide Faith's medical bag," Connie said once they were inside.

Faith placed the burlap sack on the floor and opened it. She pulled out the jars of jelly first and handed them to Connie. Then she took out the sack of cookies and the first stack of material, and finally she pulled out the flannel.

"My mother sent all of this for you." Connie waited as Faith produced her bag. "Where is Ruth?"

"I had her lie down. She said she has pain in her back."

Faith nodded. "Which room?"

Ann took her to the room and opened the door. "Faith is here, Ruth. I asked her to come and see if she could help you."

Ruth looked pale and small. "I'm so afraid."

Faith smiled. "Don't be. First babies often cause women a lot of fear, but everything will be all right." She looked over her shoulder at Ann and Connie. "Give us a few minutes alone."

Ann closed the door and looked at Connie. "I'm worried about her."

"Then maybe we should sit down together and pray. I find that always helps."

"You remind me of Faith's mother, Eletta Browning. Your aunt, I believe."

"Yes, she was married to my father's brother. I never met her, but people tell me she was an amazing woman."

Ann nodded. "She was. She showed such great love. We were good friends. She always said prayer would change everything."

"It does. I've been so busy lately that I might have temporarily forgotten that, but now it's uppermost in my mind."

Ann took Connie's hand. "There is much we need to pray about. I fear for my people and for Ruth."

Connie squeezed the older woman's hand. "I understand, but more importantly, God understands. Let's just give it to Him."

The day was fairly warm. In fact, if Tom was honest, it was downright hot. It wasn't as bad as Washington, DC, however. The humid days of summer there were unbearable at times. There were days when he could feel heat permeate from everything around him, and often he felt he was slowly being cooked alive.

To alleviate the warmth, Tom went to the pump behind the government house and wetted his handkerchief. The cold water felt so good as he wiped his face and neck that he wetted the cloth again. As he made his way around the house, Tom caught the sound of voices through the open windows. Clint was talking to someone about the mill and processing the fallen trees. Tom was glad to hear the agent was finally doing something to help get the mill up and running. If the Indians could produce lumber, it would be a good way for them to make money and better the reservation.

On his way back to the Browning house, he remembered that he needed pencils and turned to head to the little store. Inside, the dim light made it hard to find things, but he supposed most folks relied on memory. He found the pencils and took five of them to the clerk at the counter. The clerk seemed almost put out at having to deal with Tom's cash rather than credit.

"You could set up an account like everybody else," he suggested. "Makes it easier."

"I prefer cash, but if that's the way you

want to do things, I suppose I can set up an account."

The clerk shrugged. "Doubt you'll be here that long anyway." He gave Tom change for his dollar.

"I intend to be here for a long time. My job will take a while. We're supposed to interview all of the Indians who live on Grand Ronde."

The clerk gave a huff and turned back to his dusting. "Might not be anyone to interview."

Tom wondered what he meant by that. Did he know something about the uprising? Tom started to ask, but two Indian women walked into the store, talking in a language Tom couldn't understand. The clerk turned back around and spoke to them.

There was nothing to do but leave. If Tom stayed, the clerk might think it curious, and if he flat-out asked what the man knew about the uprising, it could give away his other reason for being at the reservation.

As he walked past the government house once more, Tom heard raised voices.

"We'll do it my way or not at all," Clint was all but yelling.

Several men replied in lower voices. The Indians seemed unhappy about something. Tom caught the gist of it having to do with completing their plans. Clint responded by telling them that they needed to trust him with this decision.

Tom tried to make himself as inconspicuous as possible, but there was no place to hide. Needing an excuse to tarry, he let the pencils scatter on the ground. He knelt to pick them up, being slow and careful in his retrieval.

"I know you're anxious and everything is pretty much in place," Clint declared. "We just need to wait for the shipment. You know as well as I do that without the proper tools, we can do nothing. The shipment should be here next Thursday. We can act after that."

Tom felt an icy finger go up his spine. Suspicions began to dance in his head. Was Clint talking about guns? Or was he working on seeing the mill put back together? Tom knew Connie's family planned to help. The mill had been damaged long ago and then again in the storm. There was much required repair.

"Now, I want you to go home and wait for my instructions. As soon as I know more, I'll be in touch."

Tom quickly made his way toward the trees. He drew a deep breath and tried to settle his thoughts. He watched as the men left the house. These men were not members of the Legislature. It suddenly dawned on Tom that Clint might very well be the connection they were looking for. Someone who was white and familiar with the reservation was most likely to be heading up the planned uprising. There was no doubt someone at Warm Springs and Siletz would be involved, as well. From what Tom understood after talking to Seth Carpenter, there was an organized group of men from around the state—wealthy men who could afford to buy mercenaries as well as organizers.

"But Clint's family has always worked to improve conditions for the Indians." Tom barely whispered the words. It didn't make sense that Clint would be planning an uprising. Or did it? Perhaps he didn't feel as devoted to helping the Indians as his father and brother did.

By the time he reached the house, Tom had considered any number of possibilities, but all of them eventually pointed back to Clint Singleton. It was time to have a talk with Connie's father. He knew Clint better than anyone else. If Clint was capable of such thinking, Adam Browning would surely know.

"Will she be all right?" Ann asked as Faith came out of the back room.

"She's running a fever," Faith admitted. "I think she's caught some sort of sickness, but I can't figure out what it is since it's at such an early stage. Make sure she gets plenty of liquids—maybe try a little honeyed tea. Keep her here. Tell Sam you'll take care of her, that her time is very near. I'll slip back this evening."

Ann looked frightened. "Is the baby all right?"

Faith put her hand on the older woman's shoulder. "So far everything is fine. Just make sure she stays in bed and drinks plenty."

Connie followed Faith to the door. Faith put her bag back into the burlap sack. "I'll be back after dark," Faith promised.

Outside, the two girls walked back to the Browning house. Faith kept her voice a hushed whisper. "Ruth told me about a house where Sam goes every day."

"What about it?" Connie kept watch around them. Ever since her evening walk with Tom, she'd been rather spooked. She had known Tom was afraid that night, and the thought filled her with worry. Were any of them really safe if a war was about to start?

Faith's voice was barely a whisper. "She said it's full of guns—rifles."

Connie looked at Faith. "Was she certain?"

"Oh yes. She said Sam is always talking

about the war he's going to help start. He wants to kill as many white men as possible. He believes once the Native peoples rise up, the government will have no choice but to set them free. Ruth said she had to tell us because she doesn't want anyone to be hurt."

"We need to talk to my father. And Tom too." Connie scanned the area, more worried than ever before.

When they cleared the trees, Connie had to fight to keep from running across the clearing. She felt a great sense of dread. What was going to happen and when? Should they leave the area? Should they call for the army?

"Where's Papa?" she asked as they came through the back door into the kitchen. "I need to speak to him and Tom."

Her mother and Hope had been working at the stove, canning more jelly. "What's the matter? What's going on?" her mother asked.

"There's going to be trouble." Connie moved from the kitchen into the dining room. "Papa, where are you?"

"We're in the front room," he answered.

When she and Faith entered the room, Connie was relieved to find that Uncle Lance and Tom were with her father. What she didn't like was the worry in their expressions.

"Connie says there's going to be trouble," Mama said from behind her.

It was only then that Connie realized her mother and aunt had followed her and Faith into the living room.

"What do you know?" Tom asked.

"Faith was tending Sam Sheridan's wife, over at Ann's house. I'll let her explain."

They all looked at Faith.

"Ruth said there's a house where Sam goes every day. She said it's full of rifles for the war that's being planned. The war to kill all white people."

CHAPTER 16

It was hard to know what to do. No one had any idea where this house might be. Papa suggested the women pack up and return to Portland, but no one knew how that could be accomplished without arousing suspicion.

"It's clear we can't do anything drastic without causing people to wonder why," Uncle Lance said. "Maybe we could spread the word that we're leaving. That our visit is over, and we're heading home and taking Mercy and Connie with us to see the rest of the family. That would make total sense."

Papa nodded. "It would. I like that idea. Especially since you planned to leave in a couple of days anyway."

"Meanwhile, we can just go about our business," Mama suggested. "Faith can go with Hope and me to gather herbs. That will give us an opportunity to search areas that aren't well traveled."

"I used to be a fairly decent tracker," Lance added. "I'll go along and keep an eye out for signs of foot traffic. No one will think it strange for me to be there to guard the women."

Papa nodded. "That sounds good. Connie and Tom can move about doing interviews. There's one couple, the Menards, who live not far from the river to the east. They're past the other landholdings, so you'll need to ride. Maybe take the wagon. James Menard is a good friend. Tell him we need information— that I have asked. See if he knows about any strange things going on. Ask if he knows about a house where weapons are being kept, and tell him it must remain a secret between us. He can be trusted."

"I could go visit them alone," Tom suggested.

Connie could see he was concerned about her. "I know the place. It's not easy to find. I need to go with you."

Tom shrugged. "If I look lost, no one will suspect that I'm doing anything untoward. That might well work to our benefit by giving me the chance to look around."

"I'm not going to sit here doing nothing.

I'm going to the Menards', and that's that."
Connie went to get her satchel. "With or
without you."

Her mother chuckled. "Let me get a loaf
of fresh bread for you to take to them."

Connie and Tom arrived at Christine and
James Menard's house after a roundabout
journey. They had chosen to ride on horseback since horses could travel where there
were no roads, unlike a wagon. They'd hardly
spoken on the road, and Connie worried that
she'd upset Tom.

They dismounted and secured their horses,
but before approaching the house, Connie
took hold of Tom's arm. "I'm sorry if I made
you angry."

"What?" He shook his head. "I'm not
angry."

"Oh. I thought perhaps I'd upset you by
insisting I come along."

"No, not really." The edges of his lips rose
slightly. "I'm used to your bossiness."

"I just want to get to the truth as soon
as possible, and I think we must all work together."

"Hello there," a man said, coming around
the side of the house. "Can I help you?"

Connie stepped forward. "Do you remember me, Mr. Menard? I'm Adam and
Mercy Browning's daughter, Connie. I've

returned after being gone for seven years. My friend Tom and I have been hired to make a record of the Indians at Grand Ronde."

"I heard about that." He smiled and ushered them into the house. "Welcome to our home. Your father is my good friend," he told Connie. "He mentioned last week that you'd be coming to see us sometime. You can call me James."

A beautiful Indian woman appeared from a back room. She had a small boy clinging to her apron.

"This is my wife, Christine, and our son, Ned."

Connie soon learned that Christine and James were Clackamas Indians in their forties. Their house on the far east side of the reservation came with several hundred acres that they put up in hay each year, along with a small amount of wheat. They had three children—two were girls in their teens, and the boy was just three.

"Our girls are helping the nuns today," James explained.

"My mother sent this bread," Connie said, remembering to take the loaf from her satchel.

Christine took the bread. "You must thank her for me."

Connie nodded. Her mind was ever on the rifles. "Are there any other houses nearby? I didn't see any as we approached."

"The Monadas are fairly close. They are Kalapuya. And there are other Clackamas, but not too close," James explained.

"No other houses? Maybe something small that hasn't been around long?" Tom asked.

James shook his head. "No. I'd know if there were."

Connie liked the couple from the start. They remembered life before the tribes were moved to Grand Ronde and were eager to tell what they remembered. They had just married in 1856 and lived near the Willamette River when their tribe was forced to leave, but unlike many of the other Indians, they bore little bitterness.

"We love your mother and father, Connie," Christine told her. "They were so good to us. When we had no food and everyone was starving, your father did what he could to bring in supplies. He didn't ask for money either. He gave to the people without charging. The agent told him not to do that—that the government would provide." She shook her head. "But they only sent flour and salt. No meat. Your people brought us cattle and sheep."

"And chickens," her husband said, smiling. "I like your mother's fried chicken very much."

Connie laughed and nodded with great enthusiasm. "So do I."

"But my favorite is salmon," James added. "Your father brought us baskets full of salmon. He saw us through in those early years."

"The salmon were everything to us," Christine explained. "When we lived on the Willamette River not far from the falls, my father was one of the best fishermen. He would lash long poles together and secured them under the large rocks. This let him go out over the falls at different levels, where he could catch fish with his net." Her voice was filled with pride as she continued. "There was only one better fisherman, and that was my husband. He and my father had contests to see who could catch more salmon." She smiled at James, and Connie smiled at Tom.

She hadn't expected to catch him watching her, but his blue eyes captured her with such intensity that for a moment she couldn't look away. What was he thinking? Was he worried?

"We were happy then." Christine shifted her son as his eyes grew heavy. He put his head on her shoulder.

The sound of Christine's voice drew Connie back into the conversation. "I understand you made wonderful canoes." She looked down at her journal, pencil poised to write. "Tell us about those."

James picked up the conversation. "We made many good canoes, and not just for the river. They were used as coffins too. When a person died, we would put them in a canoe and lash them in with their favorite things, and then put the canoe up in the trees along the falls on either side of the river."

"How did you make the canoes?" Tom asked. "Describe them to me."

"We would find a large cedar log," James replied. "We would strip the bark, then sand the wood until it was smooth. Woodworkers used fire to hollow them out. It made it much easier to carve. The front of the canoe had a shovel-nose." He held out his hand to Tom for the journal and pencil. Tom handed both over. "They were twenty to twenty-five feet long. You could put hundreds of pounds in a canoe—even a dozen or more men. And some were carved with the most amazing patterns." He drew quickly on the journal page, then handed it back to Tom.

Connie leaned over to see what James had drawn. It was quite good and easy to see that it was a canoe.

"Thank you," Tom said, smiling. "This is very good."

James seemed pleased. He was far and away one of the more friendly men they had encountered.

"Did your mothers and fathers make the march to Grand Ronde?" she asked.

Christine shook her head. "No. There was much sickness. They died in 1855. That year the Clackamas people signed a paper that deeded our lands to the white man. They promised to pay our people two thousand five hundred dollars a year for ten years." She shook her head and looked down at her lap. "But they never did."

Connie nodded, not knowing what else to say. There were stories of such failed arrangements among many of the tribespeople. Apparently the government was poor at keeping its word. No wonder the tribes at Grand Ronde were considering war as an option.

"Thank you for your time," Tom said, getting to his feet. "It's getting late, and we need to return home. Could we come again another time?"

James nodded. "It is good to tell old stories and remember the days when we were still a free people. You can come again tomorrow."

Connie gathered her things and put them in the satchel she had taken to carrying when they made their rounds. Christine stood and placed the now-sleeping Ned on a pallet of blankets.

"I must leave now," James said. He glanced at Christine. "I will be back later after I help Paul with his hay." He nodded to Tom and then Connie. "You are always welcome, and I will tell the others good things about you."

With that, he left, and Connie wondered if he was really going out to hay. Shame immediately hit her. She had become so suspicious of everyone. Papa had said James could be trusted and had even encouraged her to ask him about the weapons house. She'd gotten so caught up in his stories that she'd forgotten.

She smiled at Christine as they headed out of the house. She looked around for James, but he was already gone.

"Does James always help others with their hay?" Connie asked, hoping it wouldn't be too prying.

"The men help each other. Paul helped James harvest earlier. The land is very bad, and it is hard to bring in crops for people. It's better to plant food for horses and cattle and sheep. It was hard to make a farmer out of a fisherman, but my James is good at both." Christine chuckled. "He can do most anything. Next week James and Paul will fish together. We will dry a lot of fish for the winter."

"He seems to be a very good man," Connie declared.

Christine glanced toward Tom, who was retrieving the horses. "Your man is good too. I can tell."

Connie didn't know what to do or say, and at the sound of someone approaching on horseback, she gratefully turned to see who it was. The last person she expected was a uniformed soldier. The man dismounted and strode toward them like he was in charge and they were his minions.

"I want your tribal pieces," he said to Christine. "I've come to buy them all."

"I have none to sell," Christine replied. Fear filled her eyes, and Connie stepped closer and put her arm around Christine's shoulders.

"I doubt that's true," the soldier said. "I believe I'll have a look around your house."

"She said she had none to sell," Tom said, putting himself between the women and the soldier.

"I didn't ask you. If you're smart, you'll stay out of this. I have permission to be here and the right to search for artifacts."

"By whose authority?" Connie asked before Tom could speak.

"By the authority of the US Army," the soldier replied. "And the right of a white man to take whatever he wants from an Indian. Now, move aside."

"I don't think so." Tom took a step toward the soldier, and without warning, the man drew his pistol and smashed the butt into Tom's head.

It all happened so fast, Connie could hardly believe what he'd done. Tom fell to the ground unconscious, and Connie let out a scream as blood began to stream from his head.

This only irritated the soldier. In two steps he reached Connie and slapped her hard across the face, putting her on the ground not far from Tom.

"I can't abide screamin' women. Shut up."

Connie struggled to get back on her feet, but the soldier kicked her. Thankfully her satchel took the brunt of the blow.

The soldier gave a holler and swore. "What do you have in that bag of yours, rocks?"

Connie tried to get up, but her legs were caught in the skirt of her gown. She fought frantically to free herself. At least Christine had been smart enough to go back into her house. With any luck, maybe she could slip out the back with her son and get to safety.

The soldier seemed to forget about his pain as Connie struggled to get on her feet.

He looked at her in disbelief. "You're a stubborn one, but if you know what's good for you, you'll stay down. Otherwise, I'm gonna give you a beatin' you won't soon forget."

"Then you'll have to do it after you've bested me."

Connie looked up at the new voice to see Clint pull his wagon to a halt just before their horses. She'd never been so happy to see someone.

The soldier turned and eyed Clint as he climbed down from the wagon. "Stay out of this, mister." He flipped the pistol into the right position for shooting.

"Watch out, Clint, he has a gun," Connie yelled.

"So do I, but I'm not going to need it to get the edge on this fool."

In one fluid motion, Clint was on top of the soldier, who didn't even know what hit him. His gun went flying, and he swung at Clint, managing to connect with the side of his head. It didn't matter, though. Clint hit him back, and the cracking sound seemed to echo around them. The soldier went down and stayed there.

Clint picked up the fallen pistol. "Now he'll have a broken jaw to deal with. Maybe that'll keep him from molesting Indians and abusing white women."

Tom had begun to moan, and Connie untangled herself from her skirt and rushed to his side.

"Tom? Tom, can you hear me?" She drew him up in her arms. There was blood where the gun had struck him. "Oh, Tom, please be all right." She gently wiped his head with the hem of her skirt. The wound was bleeding something fierce. Connie pressed down on the cut, then looked up at Clint. "We need to get him to my parents' house. My cousin Faith is a doctor and can take care of him."

"I'll put him in the wagon," Clint said, frowning. "I was just out this way delivering grain. Menard's was my last delivery. Let me unload the wagon, and I'll be back."

He took off, leaving the unconscious soldier there. Connie couldn't help but worry. What if he regained consciousness? Then it dawned on her. She and Tom had been carrying a pistol with them wherever they went these days. It was in her satchel and was probably what the soldier managed to kick. She worked to hold pressure to Tom's head while she retrieved the gun. If the soldier came to before Clint returned, she wasn't sure what she'd do, but at least she had the means to protect herself if there was no other choice.

"Are you all right?" Christine asked as

she and her husband came running. "I went to get James."

"I'm fine, but Tom is hurt."

Christine nodded. "James can carry him to your mother's house."

"No, Agent Singleton is bringing up the grain wagon." Connie sighed. "I wish he'd hurry. I don't know how to help."

Tom's eyes opened. He blinked a moment, then closed his eyes again. "You all right, Connie?"

"I'm fine, Tom. You're bleeding, so lie still." He didn't reply, and Connie's eyes filled with tears. "Tom?" He was unconscious again. "Please hurry, Clint." Her voice was hushed. "Please, God, help us."

Clint made short work of getting Tom loaded and the horses tied to the wagon. He started the wagon for the Browning house and every so often glanced over his shoulder to see what was going on. Connie fussed over the barely conscious young man and murmured prayers. Clint had been wrong about her. He'd thought Tom's feelings were unreturned, but it was clear now that she was in love with him. She hadn't even thanked Clint or asked how he was feeling. He might as well not even have existed.

He drove in silence, thinking back on the girl who used to follow him around, begging for his attention. Connie had thought he hung the sun and the moon. She had once told him he was the most admirable man she knew. The thought almost made him laugh. If only she knew.

"What . . . happened?" Tom asked.

"Lie still. That soldier back at the Menard house hit you with his gun. Christine went to get her husband, so they're safe. Clint showed up in the nick of time and knocked that hoodlum out. He told James to bind him and deliver him to the government house so he can't hurt anyone else."

Clint glanced over his shoulder from the driver's seat. "We're nearly to the Browning house. Try not to bleed to death in the meantime."

Tom squeezed his eyes shut and then reopened them. "I'll do my best." Clint saw Connie smile at this. Tom continued in a whisper, "Hurts like the dickens, though."

"Of course, it does. Faith will stitch you back up, however. She'll know exactly what to do."

"What were you two doing out this far?" Clint asked.

"Interviewing the Menards. My folks are good friends with them and thought it would be a nice, easy encounter for us. I have to admit it was nice not to deal with hostility."

"You're prying into their lives. I can't blame them for being hostile," Clint said, snapping the lines to encourage the team to pick up the pace. "I wouldn't want anyone prying into my life—recording the details about me and my kin."

"It might be interesting to know all about you and your kin, Clint," Connie retorted. "It might answer a lot of questions."

He laughed. "I didn't know you had any about me. With our lengthy history, it seems you would have already found answers for all of your questions."

She said nothing in response.

After delivering Tom to Faith, Clint joined Connie in the Brownings' living room. Connie's mother and aunt were busy helping Faith and had forbidden a very pale Connie to join them.

"Are you doing all right?" he asked her. "You look a little green."

Connie had been gazing down at the blood on her dress. "Mama says I'm pale, and you say I'm green. Stop worrying about me. It's Tom who needs our prayers."

"Did that soldier hit you?" he asked, although he already knew the answer. There was a clear handprint on her face.

"Yes." She put her hand to her cheek. "Goodness, I must be a sight."

He frowned. "Did he hurt you otherwise?"

Connie looked confused. "What?"

"That fool of a soldier. Did he do anything else to you?"

"He kicked me, but my satchel took the brunt of it." She pulled the strap of the bag over her head and set it aside. "I'm sore, but I'll be all right."

"Well, that's more than I can say for that idiot." Clint got to his feet. "Which reminds me—I have business to tend to. Let me know how Tom makes out. He's a lucky man."

Connie's confusion did nothing to convince him that she wasn't in love with Tom. Her concern over Tom's wound and worry over his recovery was enough evidence to convince Clint that she had definitely put away her childish infatuation. He'd kind of hoped that by having her on his side, he might be able to accomplish even more than he'd planned.

He made his way out to his wagon and started to climb up.

"Clint!"

He turned to find Connie racing after him. He smiled and stepped down. "Yes?"

She surprised him by giving him a hug.

"Thank you for what you did for Tom. I think he might have bled to death if you hadn't come along."

"I think you're the one who might have faced a worse time of it," he said as she stepped back. "I'm glad I could keep you from such a fate."

Connie blushed and looked away. "I appreciate all that you did. I just wanted you to know. My father will no doubt extend his thanks as well, as soon as he hears what happened."

Clint chuckled and climbed back up onto the driver's seat. "Your hug was all the thanks I needed. That and our kiss will keep me happy for some time to come."

She looked at him without speaking. Apparently he'd shocked her into silence. Well, good. Just let her think on that awhile. Maybe she'd start to believe that his feelings for her went deep. At least deep enough to serve his greater purpose and perhaps compete with the wounded Mr. Lowell.

CHAPTER 17

Clint stopped by to check on Tom two days later. He'd already heard from Adam that Tom was nearly ready to be back on his feet and that he and Connie would visit with some of the Molala people the following day.

Mercy Browning welcomed him at the door and pointed him upstairs. "Faith and Connie are up there with him. Go on up. First door to the right."

Clint thanked her and made his way up the small, steep stairs. He heard Connie speaking in a hushed tone and paused outside the open door of a bedroom.

"We're praying the truth will come out, and we're doing what we can to find that truth."

"Yes," Tom answered, "but there are

folks fighting equally hard to keep the truth buried."

"Well, we have to figure it out before it's too late," Faith said.

Clint frowned. What were they talking about?

"I, for one, didn't come all this way to stop now." Connie spoke with determination. "This is too important to me."

The trio fell silent, and Clint knew he couldn't hide his arrival much longer. He stepped into the room. "I hope I'm not intruding. Mrs. Browning sent me right up."

Connie was on one side of the iron-framed bed, and Faith was on the other, changing the bandage on Tom's wound. Both women looked surprised—even upset. Clint decided to keep talking and hoped they wouldn't worry about what he might have overheard.

"Well, it certainly looks like you have the best of it, Tom." Clint smiled.

"I have a great nurse and an excellent doctor," Tom replied. "And I understand I have you to thank for saving Connie and me from something much worse."

Clint shook his head. "Rogue soldiers are always trouble. That man was absent without leave, so he's now facing a court martial. But enough about him. How are you feeling?"

"Pretty good. I plan to get back to work

tomorrow. Mrs. Browning and these two said I could do that if I promised to stay in bed for two days, and I've honored that commitment, so they must honor their part."

"We only wanted to make sure his brain didn't swell," Faith said, finishing her work.

Clint glanced at Connie. She seemed attentive but not overly so. Maybe the attention she'd given Tom after the attack was simply due to her fears and nothing else. He knew Tom was in love with her, but until the attack Clint hadn't seen anything to suggest she returned the feelings. Maybe Clint had conjured romantic motivations where none actually existed.

He frowned at Connie. "Your cheek is bruised."

She nodded. "Yes, I've been told that more than once. It's not a problem. Just a little sore."

"I wish I'd taken the opportunity to give that soldier a good beating."

"That would hardly have made my cheek feel any better," Connie said with a smile.

"Maybe not, but it would have made him think twice before assaulting someone I care about." He saw the look Tom gave him and added, "Seeing you two on the ground like that, with Tom bleeding, well . . . it didn't sit well."

"I feel just fine, though," Tom continued. "A little headache still, but I think I'd forget all about it if I was actually able to work."

"Faith agreed to let you work on preparing our first report to be sent in," Connie reminded.

"That's true, but while the bed is comfortable for sleeping, it's not very good for working."

"I can well imagine," Clint said. "Still, you have two of the prettiest ladies to attend you. I wouldn't complain too much."

Tom grinned. "Yes, but one is married to a well-muscled riverboat captain, and the other is married to her job. It does me little good in either case."

Clint laughed. "Well, I wouldn't want it said that I encouraged breaking up marriages."

Tom joined him in laughter.

"Oh, honestly," Connie said, shaking her head. "You two are ridiculous."

That only made the men chuckle all the more.

"Well, I hope you'll soon feel completely well, with no more headaches. In the meantime, I need to get back to my office." Clint headed for the bedroom door, but neither Connie nor Faith offered to see him out.

As he made his way downstairs, Clint

wondered what the trio was up to. Maybe he hadn't paid enough attention to them. He frowned, remembering that Connie had been down at the river the night the Indians were bringing in smuggled goods. She'd said she was just out for a walk, but now Clint had his doubts. What had she really been up to?

He made his way back to his office and found a telegram waiting for him. It was from his father. Clint read through it and frowned. His father was coming for a visit. Apparently he was headed home to California to encourage votes, since it was an election year. Four years earlier, the election had been hotly contested. Electoral votes in several states were disputed, and a special Electoral Commission was formed to decide the outcome. Rutherford B. Hayes, the Republican, had been chosen as the winner, pledging, because of the controversy, that he would not run for a second term. He had stuck to that pledge, leaving both parties to come up with brand-new candidates. James A. Garfield was running for the Republicans, and Winfield Scott Hancock, a Civil War general, was the Democratic choice. It was clear who Clint's Republican father wanted.

Clint crumpled the telegram. He didn't

need his father here right now. The senator had a way of disturbing even the most peaceful setting, and Grand Ronde was far from that. Clint took off his coat and hung it over the back of the chair. He was just going to have to make the best of it.

He had just sat down and gotten to work, still pondering what he could do that would be most beneficial to his own plans, when a knock sounded on the outer door. At one time, Clint had a secretary who handled visitors, but the government had cut back on staff.

"Come in!" he called.

To his surprise, Connie entered, with Faith close behind her. "Mama insisted we bring you this piece of chocolate cake. She meant to send it with you, but you got past her somehow." She put the plate down in front of him.

"Is that her famous berry compote on the side?" he asked.

Connie chuckled. "It is."

"I'll be hard-pressed not to dig in." He smiled up at Connie. "Thanks for bringing it by."

"That's quite all right," she answered. "We're on our way to Ann's. Ruth is about to have a baby. She fell ill, though, and Faith has been trying to help. Of course, don't say anything to Ruth's husband. He and his father seem to hate all white people. They don't want anything to do with our help."

"Samson Sheridan and his father and brothers have been at odds with us since your father refused to help them run away to Canada."

Connie nodded. "All the same, there's no anger toward them on our part. My father misses his old friend and still tries from time to time to make amends."

"I know he does. I've tried to repair the relationship as well." Clint shook his head. "The Indians act like spoiled children."

"Not all act that way," Faith countered. "No more than white people do. I'd say this is more of a personal feud."

"Nevertheless, there is a growing hatred among the Indians, and I fear it's going to explode and destroy everyone and everything. Now, if you don't mind, I have work to do. A lot of work."

"We have our duties as well." Connie headed for the front door. "Enjoy your cake, and don't forget to bring back Mama's dish."

"I won't."

Clint looked at the cake and then at the work he had to manage. Supplies needed to be ordered.

He dipped his little finger in the compote and then licked it off. Supplies could wait. He picked up the plate and headed to the kitchen to find a fork.

"The baby isn't moving much," Ann told Faith. Ruth gave a weak nod.

Connie took Ruth's hand. Ruth tried to squeeze Connie's fingers, but it was a poor attempt. Whatever had been wrong was still hanging on, and she wasn't very strong.

Faith felt Ruth's abdomen. She pressed the baby first one way and then another. She frowned. "When did you last feel him move?"

Ruth shook her head. "I'm not sure. I've mostly been sleeping."

"Which is good for you both." Faith straightened. "You rest. I'm going to speak with your stepmother." She motioned to Connie and Ann. Once in the main living area, Faith wasted no time. "Do you know when the baby was last moving?"

"Just before she got sick. I think that was Friday. I remember her laughing about how he was sure to break her ribs with his kicking." Ann grabbed Faith's arm. "Please. What is wrong with her?"

"I'm not sure. It could be one of a number of maladies. What concerns me is that I couldn't get any reaction out of the baby. I'm going to go back and examine her further, but I'm worried."

Ann looked at Connie with tears in her eyes. "My poor girl. She's talked of nothing but this baby for months. Why would God take him from her now? Have we angered God?"

Connie put her arm around Ann and led her to the table. Together they sat. Connie finally worked up the nerve to speak. "Bad things sometimes happen, Ann, but this isn't about God being angry. I'm certain of that. I'm sure Mama could explain it better than I can. She lost a couple of babies and nearly died when I was born."

Ann shook her head. "Sam is looking forward to being a father. He's already so angry, and I fear he won't be able to bear this. I just don't know what to do."

"We can pray about it," Connie said. "We can pray right now." She took Ann's hand. "Oh, Father, you know how hard this is. We want so much for Ruth and the baby to be all right. Please touch them both and give Faith wisdom as to what she can do to help. Father, this is such a difficult time for Ann. Give her strength and understanding to help Sam through this as well. We don't always know why these things happen, Lord, but we know that you have promised to be with us always."

Faith came out of the bedroom. "I can't tell if the baby is still alive. I must get him delivered. I'm going back to the house to have Aunt Mercy mix us up a special tea that will bring on Ruth's labor."

Without warning, the front door burst open, and a very angry Sam came into the house. "Where is Ruth?"

"She's ill, as I told you," Ann said, getting to her feet. "She's just in there." She pointed to the bedroom. "She would be pleased to see you."

Sam looked at Connie and Faith. "Why are you here?"

"We're friends with Ann and your wife," Faith replied. "Ann and I were very close when I lived among the Rogue River Tututni. Are you Ruth's husband, Sam?" She smiled. "I've heard so many good things about you."

He glared. "Get out of here. You have no right to be here."

"They are my friends, Sam," Ann protested. "They're good people. They helped us make baby clothes."

"We don't need help from white women. There are plenty of good sewers among our people."

"Of course there are," Ann countered. "But my friends wanted to do this out of love."

"The white man knows nothing of love except for himself." He pointed to the door. "Get out of here and don't come back."

"Sam—"

"If they don't go, I'll take Ruth somewhere else to deliver our child. You may be her mother, but I will not honor that if you allow these two to remain."

"There's no need to fight." Connie took Faith's arm and prayed Sam wouldn't notice her medical bag. "We're going. But, Sam, there's something I want you to know. I care for your wife and Ann. I want to do good things for them and help them in any way I can. You too. I'd like for us to be friends. I remember when our fathers were best friends. Like brothers. I'd like to see that happen again. I want our families to be one."

"No. That will never happen. Your father betrayed my father, and because of that, my mother died. We will never be one. Now, go!"

The rage in his expression was evident, and for the first time Connie feared he might kill them. "Good night, Ann." She kissed the older woman's cheek and whispered, "We'll find a way to come back."

Faith hugged Ann and appeared to say something as well.

Connie moved to the door. "We'll be praying for all of you."

They had barely stepped out of the house when they heard Sam yell at Ann.

"This won't bode well for Ruth," Faith said. "She's not doing well. I think there's something wrong with the baby or else there's something wrong with Ruth that's causing problems for the baby. I fear that if she doesn't have the baby soon, they might both die."

"Is she strong enough to deliver?" Connie feared she already knew the answer.

"I can't be sure. She might require surgery."

Connie shook her head. "Sam would never allow that."

Faith shrugged. "He doesn't have to know. Maybe Clint or your father could keep him occupied elsewhere."

"Maybe, but he hates them as much as anyone. I would almost be afraid to ask them to do that. Sam might well kill us all."

"But if we don't risk it, Ruth will die and the baby with her." Faith paused. "There's something else. Ruth said more about the house with rifles. She said it's just north of where the big bend in the river starts. It's hidden in the woods, and they always have guards."

CHAPTER 18

In the middle of the night, the entire Browning household was awakened by pounding on the back door.

Connie came out of her room in her nightgown, her hair hanging to her waist. This kind of thing had happened often when she was younger. Someone would come to them in the middle of the night for any number of reasons.

She threw her mother and father a look of questioning as they joined her in the hallway. They were soon followed by her aunt and uncle and Faith. Then a shirtless Tom came from his room near the stairs, and Connie's eyes widened. She met his gaze in the dim light of her mother's lamp. There was a look in his eyes that she couldn't quite understand.

"Here, you might need this," Faith said, handing Connie her robe.

Connie had forgotten all about her modesty. "Thank you." She quickly donned the robe and tied the belt. Maybe that was why Tom had such an odd look in his eyes. She felt her face grow hot. She dared to look at him, but he was busy wrestling on his shirt.

There were voices coming from downstairs. Apparently Isaac had beaten them all to the door. Her father went down the steps first, with Uncle Lance and Tom following close behind. Connie saw that Papa and Uncle Lance both had revolvers. It was only then that she grew afraid. Had the time for the uprising come?

Isaac met them all at the bottom of the steps. "Ann is here. Something is wrong with Ruth. I sent her back home and told her I'd bring Faith right over."

"I'm going too," Connie declared. "She might need me."

"We could come as well," her mother offered.

"No, it's probably best only Faith and Connie go. They're younger and can run faster if the need arises," Papa said. "With Sam making his anger clear, I don't wish to let any of you go, but I know we must help."

"I'll get dressed," Faith said and started for the stairs.

Connie followed her into the room they

shared. "Do you think you'll have to operate?"

"It's hard to tell at this point. If the baby is already on its way, we may only have to help with the delivery. Have you ever done anything like that?"

Connie shook her head. "I went with Mama a couple of times when she helped local women, but only to watch."

"Just follow my instructions, and we'll be fine."

Connie kept thinking about Faith's comment an hour later. It was already light, and she had no idea if Sam would stop by to see his wife. It worried her to think he might come and catch them there.

Ruth was doing her best to give birth to her child, but it was rough going. At one point the poor girl fainted, scaring Connie half to death. Faith handled the situation without batting an eye. She was so capable and qualified. She seemed at ease and without worry as she talked to Ruth after she regained consciousness.

"Just try to rest between the waves of pain," Faith told her.

Connie looked at Ann. "Sam won't stop by now that it's morning, will he?"

Ann shook her head. "He's helping his father and brothers round up horses. He told me yesterday that he'd be gone for a couple of days."

"Good. That's very good." Connie looked at Faith. "We should be all right."

Faith motioned for Ann and Connie to follow her out of the room. "If she doesn't make progress soon, I may have to operate. She's much too weak, and I'm afraid this could kill her—not to mention the baby. Her sickness has already made her fragile. I don't think she can take much more."

Ann nodded. "You do whatever you have to, Faith. Try your best to save them both."

Faith did what she could, but the progress remained slow. Ruth struggled to push, but there was no fight left in her, and Faith decided to give her a tea that would help expel the baby.

"I need you to go to your mother and ask for more of the tea we used to quicken Ruth's labor."

Connie nodded. "I'll be back as quickly as I can."

She made her way via the shortcut, worrying about what would happen if Ruth died. Sam was already so angry. He would probably start a war all on his own if he lost his wife and child.

Her mother was in the garden when Connie reached their house. She was cutting stalks of rhubarb and humming to herself. Aunt Hope was at the other end of the garden, picking herbs. She glanced up and saw Connie approaching.

"Mercy, Connie's back."

Connie hurried to her mother's side. "Faith asked me to get more of the tea that quickens labor. Ruth isn't doing well, and she's making such little progress that Faith is worried."

Her mother nodded. "Follow me."

They went into the house and to the small room where Connie's mother cured herbs and created her healing concoctions. She reached up and took down a jar of crushed leaves. Then she selected a bottle of liquid.

"This is a strong tincture of the same herbs that are in the tea. I've had great success with it, getting labor to progress. Tell Faith this might be easier to use than the tea. Especially if Ruth is very weak. She might not be up to drinking much. A few drops of this will do the trick."

Connie nodded. "I think Faith is pretty worried. You might pray."

"We've been doing that since you left. Has Sam tried to stop by?"

"No, he's off gathering horses. He won't be back until late tomorrow."

Mama looked relieved. "I'm glad. That alone is answered prayer."

"I'd better get back." Connie kissed her mother's cheek, then made a mad dash for the back door.

By the time she reached Ann's house, Connie realized she'd seen nothing of Tom or the other men in her family. She wondered what they were up to. Hopefully they were figuring out where the weapons were hidden. If they could only find the house with the cache of guns, then the Indians wouldn't have the weapons needed to start a war.

"I'm back," Connie said, hurrying into the house.

Faith came out of the bedroom. She looked quite worried, and Connie couldn't help fearing the worst. "Is she . . . dead?"

"No. But I fear she will be if that baby doesn't come soon."

Connie held up the bottle and jar. "Mama said this tincture would work faster and be stronger than the tea."

Faith took the bottle. "Good. We'll give it a try."

Around three o'clock that afternoon, the baby was delivered. A stillborn son. Faith wrapped him carefully in a blanket provided by Ann. "I'm so sorry," she said as she placed the baby beside Ruth.

"My baby. My baby," Ruth murmured and wept.

He was perfectly formed and looked like he was sleeping. Was Faith certain he was dead?

"We wanted to call him Joseph—after Sam's father and my mother's son who died. Now he walks with them." Ruth pulled the baby close and washed his face with her tears.

"I'm so sorry, Ruth. I know you're devastated," Faith told her. "But you are very weak. We need you to fight to live."

Ann took a seat on the bed beside her stepdaughter. She used a damp washcloth to wipe Ruth's forehead. "Don't leave me, daughter. Do not go after your son. Stay with us."

"A baby needs his mother." Ruth's words were barely audible.

Connie could barely stand it. The grief of Ann and Ruth was so painful to bear, and yet Faith managed it stoically. Perhaps that was what made her a good doctor.

After about thirty minutes, Ann got up and took the baby. "I'll wash him." She and Ruth had said very little, but words seemed unimportant. The love between them was their strength and consolation.

By suppertime, Faith told Connie they'd done all they could and should probably slip away—hopefully unnoticed. They made their way home, keeping to the forested path rather than the main roads.

Connie wanted to talk about what she'd experienced but didn't know what to say. How could a person speak of such a sad thing and make any sense of it? But still she wanted very much to understand.

"Why did the baby die?"

Faith turned to her. "I don't know. It happens sometimes, and we don't always understand why. Ruth was sick—some sort of ague. Apparently, it made the baby sick as well. Or perhaps the baby was sick and made Ruth ill. I just don't know. It's one of the most frustrating things about being a doctor. We do what we can to understand, but it isn't always possible to have answers. Sometimes babies just die, and sometimes both mother and child die. It's still possible Ruth may pass away, especially if she's lost the will to live."

They walked in silence the rest of the way home. Faith immediately went inside while Connie lingered outside. She heard Faith explaining what had happened, and tears came to her eyes. She could never be as strong as Faith. She could never be as strong as Mama or Aunt Hope. She sat down by the back steps and buried her face in her hands.

"Are you all right?" Tom asked, his voice gentle and soothing.

Connie looked up and shook her head. Tom sat beside her and put his arm around her. Connie slumped against him, grateful for his support.

"Ruth's baby died. Faith couldn't save him. Ruth may die too."

"I'm so sorry. That must have been hard for everyone."

She nodded. "I so admire Faith. She was so strong and brave. I could never have that kind of strength."

"You're strong in other ways. Everyone has their strengths."

"I just don't understand why the baby had to die." She sniffed back tears. "Faith didn't either. She said sometimes there just isn't an answer. But that's not good enough for me. There's always an answer. We just don't know what it is. But we should."

"Maybe so, but knowing won't change things."

She loved the sound of his voice. She pressed her ear against his chest and listened to the steady beat of his heart. *Thump-thump. Thump-thump. Thump-thump.* That soldier could have killed him, and the thought of this made Connie cry all the more. Tom didn't seem to mind. He held her tight and never tried to hurry her grieving.

What a great friend Tom was to her. No one cared about her like he did. No one . . . loved her as he did. She thought about his supposed feelings for her. Was he truly in love with her? Could she love him in return? She already did love him, in a way. He was her dear friend and always managed to see her through bad times. There was no one in the world whose company she would rather have.

She eased away from his hold. "I'm sorry for being so weepy. I've never had to deal with something like this." She studied his face for a moment, then gave him a hint of a smile. "Thank you. I should go and make sure Faith is all right. I'm sure she is, but I should check."

"Of course," he said in a hushed voice.

Connie hurried inside and found her mother and Aunt Hope cleaning up after dinner.

"Are you all right?" Mama asked.

"I think so. I don't know how Faith does it. She's so strong, and no matter how bad things got, she managed without fear. I wish I could be more like her." Connie moved toward the stairs. "I'm going to go lie down. I'm just so tired."

"You have a nice long rest. We'll bring you up something to eat," her mother said. "Don't worry about anything."

Connie nodded. She heard her uncle and father in the living room. It sounded like they were playing chess, so she didn't bother to greet them and instead made her way upstairs. Each step seemed to take more effort than the one before. She went to the bedroom she was sharing with Faith and quietly pushed the door open. Faith was curled up on her bed, her face buried in her pillow, weeping softly.

Maybe Faith wasn't able to deny her feelings as well as Connie had thought. She guessed doctors were just as human as everyone else.

The next morning, as Tom helped Adam Browning care for his livestock, he couldn't help but think of Connie. She had felt so right in his arms. All he wanted was to tell her how much he loved her—how he wanted to spend his life with her.

"Tom, check the leg wound on the bay, would you?"

"Sure thing, Mr. Browning." Tom inspected the wound. "It's healing nicely."

"Thanks. Would you mind turning him out in the pen?"

Tom led the bay to the outdoor pen and removed the lead and bridle. Besides thinking of Connie, he thought of the transformation that had happened in his own life. Connie's father had helped him see that God did exist. It hadn't happened in one stellar moment, but rather in a long presentation of truth. Adam Browning had used the Bible, but also had proven God in nature and by the word of his own testimony. His patience and kindness toward Tom had struck a deep chord. If his own father had been a godly man, Tom might never have doubted God's existence.

He turned at the sound of someone approaching and saw a worried-looking Isaac entering the barn. Tom made his way back inside and found Isaac whispering something to his father.

"What's wrong?" he asked.

They both looked at Tom. Isaac glanced around, then spoke in a whisper. "We should get inside. There's trouble brewing."

They headed into the house. "Mother?" Isaac moved through the kitchen into the dining room. The aroma of sausage gravy and biscuits filled the air.

Mrs. Browning and Mrs. Kenner sat in the front room, reading the Bible. They smiled when they looked up, and Mrs. Browning asked, "Ready for breakfast?"

"There's going to be trouble," Isaac answered. "Where's Uncle Lance?"

"Upstairs," his mother replied. "Why?" She frowned. "What's wrong?"

"Ruth Sheridan died. One of Sam's friends learned of it and has gone to find Sam. Worse yet, he knows Faith had something to do with the delivery."

Mrs. Kenner gasped and put her hand to her throat.

Mrs. Browning sighed. "We knew it was a possibility. The tribes all believe that if the doctor can't save the patient, they too should die. Hope and I were just talking about that yesterday."

"We should get them out of here. Faith isn't safe, and Connie might not be either."

Mrs. Browning nodded. "How long do we have?"

"Not long. Sam was in the north gathering horses, but he'll leave that in a heartbeat when he hears the news."

"Then we haven't much time," Mr. Browning declared.

A hard knock pounded on the front door. Tom was closest and went to see who it was.

Clint Singleton came inside without invitation, pushing past Tom. "We've got trouble."

"We know," Adam Browning replied.

Singleton frowned. "You know about the soldiers?"

"What soldiers?" Tom asked before Mr. Browning could.

"There are several companies of soldiers coming our way. No one knows why, but word has spread among the Indians that they're coming here to kill everyone."

"The soldiers may actually be to our benefit," Mercy Browning said. "Faith and Connie helped Sam Sheridan's wife, Ruth, yesterday. She was in labor, and the baby didn't make it. Isaac just told us that neither did Ruth. Sam's friend has gone to find him. He will no doubt demand a blood price."

"You're right. The soldiers may well be our salvation," Clint said. "Where are Faith and Connie now?"

"Upstairs. They had such a rough time of it yesterday that we let them sleep in."

"You should get them out of here. Maybe you should all go," Clint said, shaking his head. "I don't think any of this is going to calm down so long as you're here."

Mrs. Browning turned to her sister. Mrs. Kenner was positively white. "Hope, you should pack your things. We'll get you an escort and get you out of here before Sam can harm Faith."

"Take Connie with you. If she was a part of this, she won't be safe either," Adam declared.

Tom wasn't sure what part he should play. He wanted to make sure Connie stayed safe, however. "I can help them get away," he offered.

"Thank you, Tom," Mr. Browning said.

Mrs. Browning headed for the stairs. "I'll go wake the girls and get them packing."

"I'll get our things packed," Mrs. Kenner said, hurrying away.

"I'm serious," Clint said, looking at the men, "you should probably all go."

Mrs. Browning stopped at this and came back. "I won't leave, Adam."

Mr. Browning shook his head. "I don't believe they'll hurt Mercy or me, but anyone who is a stranger might be a problem. How far out is the army?"

"Only about ten miles," Clint answered. "I'm going to go speak with the Indian Legislature. I sent word for them to come to my office."

Browning nodded. "Lance, get your things ready, and when the army arrives, I'll go immediately and request an escort to at least get you and the others to the train. For now, though, I'm going back to Clint's office with him. We'll try to head things off with the tribes."

"Are you sure you won't be in danger as well?" Tom asked.

"These people know me. They know I am not the enemy, and I mean to prove it by staying to face them. It won't be the first time we've had trouble." Mr. Browning moved to the door, then turned back. "But frankly, it might be good for you to go with them, Mercy. I won't have time to worry about you, and I may need Isaac's help."

"I don't want to leave without you," Mrs. Browning said.

"I know, but do this for me."

They both fell silent for a moment, and finally the gravity of the situation seemed clear. Mrs. Browning nodded.

"Let's go," Browning said to Clint.

Once they were gone, Mrs. Browning went upstairs, and Isaac went to move his sheep into the pen rather than the far pasture.

Tom didn't like the situation at all. Once they left the protection of the house, the Indians would have the advantage. They could lie in wait and ambush the entire lot. He needed to talk to Connie.

He made a dash up the stairs, hoping he could have a minute alone with her while her mother helped her sister and niece pack. He saw Connie huddled with her female family members in the bedroom. It was obvious they were praying.

Tom had only just come to believe God existed. Would God listen to him if he prayed? He was a sinner. Wasn't there a verse in John that said God didn't listen to the prayers of sinners?

"Oh good, Tom, you can help us," Mrs. Browning said as she caught sight of him standing in the doorway. "We need to hurry."

By the time the army arrived, it had been decided that Tom would remain at the reservation while Connie and her family would head to Portland. Isaac insisted on staying to care for the livestock so their father would be free to do whatever he could to maintain peace.

Connie didn't want to leave, but everyone insisted. Even Tom and Clint wanted her out of the way. She knew there was still the matter of figuring out who was responsible for inciting the Indians to war. She hadn't had a chance to speak to Tom about the additional details Faith had learned about the location of the Indians' gun house. She knew she needed to tell him before they forced her from the reservation. Unfortunately, he'd been busy helping Isaac with his sheep.

That evening they ate in shifts and tried to keep an eye out for anyone approaching the house. Connie had never seen her father so upset, and in turn, that upset everyone else. Adam Browning was known for being calm and collected, and the fact that he was agitated and afraid was unusual.

"Connie." She turned to find Tom. "I was hoping to talk to you."

"I wanted to talk to you too." She pulled him into the kitchen, where they could be alone. "What did you want to say?"

"You go first."

Connie felt momentarily lost in his gaze. He really did have the most beautiful blue eyes. "I . . . uh, Ruth said something about the place where Sam goes. The house filled with rifles. I don't know where it is exactly, but it's not far from the big bend in the river. Near where I saw them unloading crates."

"The night Clint kissed you?" Tom asked.

Connie nodded, ignoring the fact that he sounded jealous. "Exactly. Ruth said it's in the woods to the north of the river. Get your journal, and I'll sketch it out as best I can." He started to go, but Connie stopped him. "Wait, I almost forgot. Ruth said there are always guards around the house."

"That makes sense. If your entire future depended on the contents, you'd have guards there too." Tom turned to go, but heavy pounding on the front door drew their attention. "It sounds like someone is trying to beat the door down."

Connie started for the front room, but Tom held her back.

"What if it's the Indians?"

"Papa and Uncle Lance would never let anyone get the drop on us." She pushed past him, and Tom had no choice but to follow her.

Two soldiers stood just inside the living room with another dozen or so outside the door. Maybe they'd come to stand guard.

"I'm afraid I don't understand," her father was saying to the captain.

Connie froze in place. She could feel the tension. Something wasn't right.

"You're under arrest," the captain said. "We're taking you back to Portland to try you for the murders of Gerome Berkshire and Samuel Lakewood."

CHAPTER 19

It's the order of Major Wells, ma'am," the
captain told Connie's mother. "All of you
women are to leave the reservation, including the Sisters at St. Michael's."

"But we're not on the reservation," Mama
protested.

"Sorry, ma'am. That's the way it's going
to be." The dark-haired captain refused to
be moved. "We'll have a wagon arranged for
all of you to ride in."

"I don't want to leave my husband." Mama
had been fit to be tied since the soldiers marched
Papa away hours earlier.

"He'll accompany us under guard. Now,
if you'll excuse me, I must arrange your transport." The captain gave her a curt bow and
exited the house.

Mama looked at Connie and then at Aunt

Hope and Faith. "This can't be happening. Why do they think Adam killed anyone? He hasn't even been away from the reservation for some time."

"Don't worry. Lance will figure it out," Aunt Hope said, putting her arm around her younger sister.

Connie could see that her mother was trying to be strong. "Poor Adam. He loves these people so much," Mama said.

"Which is partially why they believe he killed Mr. Berkshire and Mr. Lakewood," Faith reminded them. "We know he isn't capable of it, but they don't. I'm sure once we're able to speak to Major Wells, everything will be sorted out. Major Wells has always been fair, at least from what Seth has said. The few times I've met him, he's seemed very friendly and reasonable."

"I hope you're right."

"We'd better finish packing. The captain said his men would be coming for us soon."

Mama nodded. "I'll get my things together."

Aunt Hope gave her sister's shoulder a squeeze. "I'll put together food for the trip. I know the army will have their own, but just to be on the safe side, I'll make sure we have what we need."

Her mother looked to be in such a state of

shock that Connie could hardly bear it. "I'll help you, Mama." She followed her mother upstairs while Aunt Hope went to the kitchen to pack food. She couldn't imagine the pain her mother was feeling. "Try not to fret. I'm sure it will all be sorted out."

"It's just not fair. We've done nothing but love these people. We've always respected them and been friends with many of them for over twenty years. Your father would do nothing to risk their lives, and he certainly wouldn't kill anyone or incite a war."

"I know, but apparently someone thinks they have proof against Papa. I'm sure it's wrong, but we'll have better luck if we are there to plead our case. Just remember, we have powerful allies in Washington. If need be, we can call on them to help as well. I'm certain Uncle Dean would rally many of his friends, even the president, if need be."

Her mother pulled several of her father's shirts from the wardrobe. Her eyes filled with tears. "This is just such a nightmare. I want only to awaken and find that it's nothing more than that."

Connie nodded. "I want that too, but we have to be strong, Mama. God won't leave us without guidance and counsel. We must put our trust in Him. Many times you've told me that, and I believe it."

"I do too, but I don't understand why He didn't keep this from happening. I can't see anything good in it."

"Perhaps the good will come later. Maybe through this, our faith will increase, and we will become even stronger in the Lord." Even as she spoke the words, however, Connie wasn't sure she believed them. Why *was* God allowing this?

After they finished packing, Connie went in search of Tom. She found him in the barn with her brother—speaking in hushed whispers.

"Am I interrupting?" she asked.

They both startled. Isaac shook his head. "No, come join us."

"I wanted to say good-bye. I know you're both staying, but I wish you were coming along. I'm afraid of what we might encounter. We have quite a distance to travel to reach proper civilization."

"I know, but I'm confident that the army will be able to keep you safe," her brother replied. "Still, if it makes you feel better, I could ride along until you reach Willamina."

"No, because then you'd have to ride back alone. I don't want either of you in danger. If you came with us to Portland, you'd be safer." She looked at each of them, hoping they would change their minds.

"We can't, and you know that. I need to help Isaac with the farm," Tom said, then looked at Isaac. "And Isaac is going to help me with our investigation. I told him about the house of guns. The soldiers have demanded that all of the Indians appear for a count in the morning. That will hopefully remove the guards from where the rifles are stored and allow Isaac and me to see what's what."

"Maybe you could take some soldiers with you," she suggested.

"We were just discussing that, and I think we will."

Connie nodded. "Good. I'm glad you'll have each other. I'm so afraid the uprising is going to start before we can figure it out. Having Papa arrested has been the worst that could happen."

"It's going to be all right, Connie," her brother said. "Pa's faith is strong. Mama's too. They'll get through this and be just fine. Now we need to do the same."

"I'm sure you're right. I'm trying to keep a positive spirit." She looked at Tom. "I couldn't bear it if something happened to you. Either of you."

"Nothing's going to happen to us," Tom said. "We're smart, and we'll be careful."

She felt tears trying to form. Her throat

ached as she fought back the urge to cry. "I hope so."

She turned and ran from the barn. She knew if she remained much longer, she would have begged them to leave with the rest of the family.

She slowed her pace when she reached the house. A dozen soldiers had formed two lines in front of her home. Connie knew it was time to go. There hadn't been time to go speak with Rosy and say good-bye.

Clint appeared from the back of the house. "I was just coming to find you. They're waiting on you."

"I know. I wanted to say good-bye to Isaac and Tom and ask them one more time to come with us."

"And will they?"

"No. They feel they must stay here. You'll be too busy to worry about taking care of our sheep or the other livestock. This way you won't have to concern yourself with it. I hope you will all be safe."

Clint laughed. "The army will keep the Indians in their place. My father is due here tomorrow, and they wouldn't dare do anything with a man as important as my father in residence. I found out that was the original reason for the army being here. Additional men will likely arrive with my father. The telegram delivering orders to arrest Adam and bring him to Portland was just happenstance."

"It's ludicrous, and you know it."

"Well, I want to believe that, but sometimes people just aren't who we think they are."

"I'm going with you, Uncle Lance. I have a picture of Mama and Papa, and we can show it to the man at the hotel before we go to the jail. If Papa can be arrested just because he supposedly signed a hotel ledger, then hopefully we can prove he isn't the same man who checked in."

Her uncle threw a pleading glance at his wife. Aunt Hope just shrugged. "You know how stubborn we can be." She looked toward the kitchen, where Mama and Faith were talking to Nancy. "You'd better head out, or you'll have the rest of the women with you as well."

He shook his head and gave an exasperated sigh. "Very well, Connie. Let's go."

The carriage was waiting for them at the curb. David, Nancy's full-time groundskeeper and stableboy, stood holding the horse.

"Thank you, David. I'll bring the carriage around back when I return." Uncle Lance helped Connie into the small carriage, then quickly climbed up and took the reins.

Connie said nothing until they neared the hotel. The front desk clerk had told police officers that he could identify Adam Browning as the man who had signed into his hotel. Connie was still uncertain how her father supposedly being at the hotel was linked to the killings of Berkshire and Lakewood.

Uncle Lance brought the horse to a stop in front of the Grand Hotel. The place betrayed its name by not being at all grand, even if it was in a decent part of town.

After setting the brake, Uncle Lance climbed down and then assisted Connie. He wore the same suit he'd used for travel. Aunt Hope had been up late, brushing the dust out of it and making certain it looked good. He had a particular set to his expression that was all business.

"Let me do the talking, Connie."

She nodded, knowing it would be hard to remain silent if anyone spoke out against her father.

They made their way inside to find the condition of the interior not much better than the exterior. Uncle Lance made his way to the front desk and rang the small bell on the counter. It was several minutes before an old man appeared.

"Yes, can I help you?"

"Are you Reginald Belfast?"

The old man shook his head. "He's my grandson. Do you have business with him?"

"I do." Uncle Lance smiled. "Is he here today?"

"He is. He ran some blankets up to 203 and should be right back down." He glanced toward the staircase. "In fact, that's him now."

"Thank you." Uncle Lance turned from the desk and made his way toward the approaching man. Connie followed. "I understand you're Reginald Belfast." Uncle Lance extended his hand in welcome. "I'm Lance Kenner. If you have a moment, I would like to speak to you."

"Sure, mister. What about?" Belfast looked at Connie and smiled.

She returned the smile, hoping it would keep him in good spirits. The whole time, however, she wanted to grab him and demand the truth.

"We can sit over here," Belfast said, pointing to the lobby, where a dozen or more well-worn chairs awaited. Connie and Lance followed him and took a seat. Belfast pulled up a chair. "Now, what can I do for you?"

"I am the brother-in-law of Adam Browning. I'm also his lawyer, and this is his daughter."

Belfast frowned. "I only told the truth."

"Why don't you tell me what you told the police?"

"Mr. Browning came to the hotel every so often. The night Berkshire and Lakewood got shot, he had been out most of the evening. He came back just long enough to get his messages, then told me he had a meeting with Mr. Berkshire and Mr. Lakewood. When he came back that evening, he had blood splattered on his coat and shirt. He said he'd been caught up in a street fight but hadn't been hurt. I offered to send his clothes to the laundry, and he told me to come up for them shortly."

"And did you?" Uncle Lance asked.

"I did. I took them to a Chinese laundryman I knew, and he agreed to work on them that night and have them ready by morning. In the morning he brought the clothes clean and pressed, and I personally delivered them to Mr. Browning."

Connie had to force herself not to blurt out that the man in question wasn't Mr. Browning.

"Why is it you've only recently shared this information with the police?"

"I didn't hear about the deaths of Mr. Berkshire and Mr. Lakewood right away. See, after Mr. Browning left the hotel, I left as well. We got word that my mother was ill and would probably die—she lives in California.

My grandfather arranged for a friend to run the hotel, and he and I left to be with my folks. I didn't think anything more about Mr. Browning until just a couple of weeks ago, when I saw an article about the police still trying to find who had killed Mr. Berkshire and Mr. Lakewood. The article mentioned that the police were certain that while the killer staged it to look like a murder-suicide, it was clearly murder. That's when I remembered Mr. Browning and the blood on his suit."

"Would you recognize this Mr. Browning if you saw him again?"

"Sure would. He stayed with us lots of times. I told the police I could point him out. I'm supposed to go do that this afternoon."

Uncle Lance looked to Connie and nodded. She pulled the photo of her mother and father from her purse and handed it to Uncle Lance. He glanced at it, then turned it around for Belfast to see. "Have a look at this."

Belfast took the photo and glanced down. He looked back up at Connie's uncle. "What about it?"

"Do you recognize the man?"

Belfast looked again, then shook his head. "Never seen him before."

"Are you sure?"

Belfast nodded and pushed the picture back. "I am. Who is he?"

"That, Mr. Belfast, is Adam Browning— the man you said was staying here at your hotel."

"No. That's not him. The Adam Browning I know had a completely different look."

"Come with us now, then," Uncle Lance said, getting to his feet. "The man they have in jail is this man. He's there wrongfully, and I want to see him released as soon as possible."

"I'll have to speak to my grandfather and make certain he can spare me, but sure. I don't want someone in jail on my word who isn't guilty." Belfast left them and went to the front desk.

Connie was so excited she could hardly keep from giving a yell. "I'm so happy. Mama will be too. This is such great news."

"Well, we haven't gotten him released yet. Hopefully soon." Uncle Lance handed back the picture.

A half hour later, the trio stood in front of a heavyset man who announced himself to be in charge. He listened to what Uncle Lance had to say and then requested to see the picture. Connie handed it over and waited while the officer reviewed it with a magnifying glass.

"That's him all right," the man in charge declared. He had already requested his officer bring Connie's father to his office. Now they waited. "That's the man we have in jail. You say this doesn't even look like him?" he asked Belfast.

"No, sir. Not a bit. The other man was bigger—broader in the shoulders. The hair is all wrong too."

Finally the officer returned, bringing Connie's father with him. She wanted to throw herself into her father's arms but saw that he was in shackles. Poor Papa. It was so uncalled for. He was a man of peace.

"Mr. Belfast, is this your Mr. Browning?"

The younger man got up from his chair and turned to face Connie's father. "No, sir. That's the man in the photograph, and like I said, that's not the Adam Browning who signed the ledger at our hotel."

"There you have it," Uncle Lance said, turning to the man in charge. "I demand you release my client."

Connie ignored the police officer and went to her father. She wrapped her arms around him only to have the officer pull her away.

"You can't touch the prisoner."

"But he won't be a prisoner much longer. You heard Mr. Belfast. My father isn't the right man."

"It doesn't matter," the heavyset man announced. "Your father isn't only here on charges of murder. He's also been arrested for supplying the Indians with whiskey and guns. We have two different men who produced signed receipts and said they personally delivered crates of rifles to your father."

"I assure you they weren't signed by me," Connie's father declared. "I've never seen a single crate at the reservation, much less witnessed their delivery and signed for them."

"It doesn't really matter what you claim, Mr. Browning." The heavyset man rose. "It matters what the evidence says."

Her father stepped forward, but the guard yanked him back. "Even if you don't believe me, I can prove my signature. Let there be a comparison."

"We'll get around to that soon enough. Take him back to his cell."

"No!" Connie hadn't meant to cry out, but now that she had, she wasn't going to take it back. "You can't lock him up. He's innocent."

"That's for a jury to decide," the heavyset man said, waving off the officer.

"Let's go, Browning." The policeman pulled on her father's arm.

"I love you, Papa. We'll get you set free."

He smiled. "Your uncle Lance can manage this. I need you to take care of your mother. I imagine she's frantic."

Connie didn't want to worry him. "She misses you, but she's stronger than any of us give her credit for."

He chuckled. "You both are."

"Are you sure this is the right direction?" one of the soldiers asked Tom.

"She said the house was located north of the big bend in the river. We've come directly north," Tom replied. "Maybe we should spread out more."

Isaac pushed his way through the trees and rejoined them. "I haven't seen anything that looks like foot traffic or crates being dragged."

"Over here!" another of the soldiers called. "I found a shack."

The men hurried through the thick vegetation as best they could. Tom prayed that the weapons had finally been located. It would be to everyone's advantage if they had.

They halted in the trees a few feet away from a clearing. "I never knew this was here," Isaac said in a hushed whisper.

The clearing was hardly more than twenty feet or so across. To one side, the little shack stood with plenty of prints in the dirt around it to show signs of activity. Tom and the other men advanced cautiously. Just because they didn't see anyone didn't mean there wasn't a guard present.

Clint had worked with the soldiers to see that a detailed count was taken of the Indians each day. This kept them occupied between eleven and noon, giving Tom and the others just an hour or so to seek out the weapons. They'd been looking ever since the army had taken Adam Browning away, and now it looked like they had finally managed to locate the stash. It was a huge relief.

Seeing no one in the area, Tom and one of the soldiers advanced and knocked on the door of the shack. There was no answer. Tom opened the door to find the shack was comprised of one large room, and in the room were stacked crates of what he could only presume were rifles. Hundreds of rifles, and no doubt as much ammunition as was needed for a war.

Tom spied a crate with its lid askew. He walked over and pushed back the lid to reveal the cargo inside. He picked up one of the rifles and held it up to catch the light coming in from the open doorway. How many people might have been killed with this weapon alone?

"They're here," the soldier called outside to the others.

Tom replaced the rifle and shook his head. "We've got our work cut out for us."

"At least the hotel clerk was able to state that Papa isn't the same man who signed the ledger using his name." They had just finished supper, and Connie was determined to give her mother hope. "He was quite certain about it."

"Well, of course he was. Your father was never there."

"Once I can get them to compare the signatures on the receipts to Adam's as well as the hotel ledger, hopefully they will release him for lack of evidence," Uncle Lance said.

"It's all too maddening." Connie's mother shook her head.

"Lance will see him vindicated," Hope assured her sister.

There was a knock at the door, and Seth excused himself to see who it was. Meanwhile, the ever-opinionated Bedelia Clifton spoke up.

"I believe you should tell your story to the newspapers." For a moment everyone fell silent and looked at the older woman. "It only makes sense," she continued. "There is a man out there posing as Adam Browning. It's possible that someone will remember him calling himself by that name, or that someone will have had dealings with him and would be willing to come forward and speak up on the matter."

"She's right," Uncle Lance said. "We could explain the situation and ask if there are any witnesses who might come forward to prove the man they dealt with also wasn't Adam Browning. I'll get on that in the morning. Hopefully we'll have Adam out of jail by the end of the day tomorrow."

Connie saw the hope in her mother's eyes. *Please, Father God, please let it be so.*

The door to Clint's office opened, and his father walked in as though he owned the place. He looked at Clint with a scowl. "What kind of mess do you have going on here? There are soldiers everywhere."

"I presume they're here because you are. After all, you're a very important man." Clint's sarcasm made his father smile.

"I am, aren't I?" He laughed. "I was afraid they were here to quell an uprising."

"Well, I'm sure that might have something to do with it."

"Your Indians . . . they won't be discouraged, will they?" His father raised his brow. "Back out on you?"

Clint got to his feet and laughed. "No, sir. Everything is still going as planned." He came around the desk and embraced his father. "Good to see you again."

The older man smiled. "I thought I should come pick out the land I intend to buy after your little Indian uprising sees them all dead."

CHAPTER 20

Connie sat up with a start and looked at the clock on the mantel. It was nearly six in the morning. She eased back against her pillow, trying to remember what had so shocked her. Then it started to come back to her.

At the police station, her father had said he knew nothing about the shipments of whiskey and rifles coming to the reservation. That he'd never even seen any crates, much less signed for them. But Clint had told her that night by the river that her father was well aware of it. That they had seen the deliveries together.

Clint had lied to her. He'd stressed to her she should say nothing about it. No wonder.

"He wasn't down at the river spying on the Indians. He was helping them." Why else would he have been there? It made perfect sense, especially with him not wanting her to speak to her father about it.

Connie jumped up and began to dress. She needed to let Uncle Lance know that Clint was in on all of this. She thought back through everything she had learned since reaching the reservation. They had felt certain that someone on the outside had befriended the Indians and arranged for the uprising. Instead, what if Clint was the one who had arranged it all? He could come and go at will, helping those on the reservation and purchasing goods on the outside. He regularly had meetings in Salem and Portland, supposedly with government officials. It was all so clear. Why hadn't she seen it before?

Connie hastily pinned up her hair, then hurried downstairs. Nancy's boarders were just sitting down to breakfast, and little Jack was in his father's arms at the head of the table.

"Good morning, Connie," Seth said. "I hope you're hungry. Your mother and aunt have been helping Nancy cook since dawn. I believe we're in for a real treat."

"Where's Uncle Lance?" She tried not to sound panicked. "I need to speak with him."

"He's in the front room, talking to Major Wells."

"Perfect." She didn't wait to see if he might protest her joining them. This was important, and it was all the better that the army major was there.

"Uncle Lance," she said, coming into the room. "I need to speak to you both."

The two men looked up from where they stood. Uncle Lance held a newspaper in his hand and quickly folded it as if to hide it from her. She looked at him and then at the major.

"What's wrong?" Uncle Lance asked.

"I could ask the same thing." She glanced at Major Wells, who quickly looked away. "Something isn't right. What is it? Please tell me, and then I'll tell you what I've figured out."

Uncle Lance hesitated, then unfolded the newspaper. The headline read, *Cherokee Encourages Uprising*.

Connie took the paper and read. "'Adam Browning, a half-breed who posed as a white man and once headed up ministerial and school studies at Grand Ronde, has been arrested on charges of inciting an uprising.'" She felt sick. Few people knew of her father's Cherokee heritage. She looked up at her uncle. "He's not a half-breed."

"I know, sweetheart, but it's not going to matter. It's going to be impossible to get much support for him. Especially when people are certain he's stirring up a war."

Connie glanced over her shoulder. "Does my mother know?"

"No, and we don't plan to tell her. This would be much too hard on her. You didn't read the rest of the article, but don't bother. The journalist found it necessary to point out that your father is married to a white woman—making their marriage illegal in Oregon. They also mention his illegitimate children."

Connie handed back the newspaper and sank into the nearest chair. "This isn't right. Papa is only a quarter Cherokee, and that's not illegal for marriage to a white woman. He would have to be half."

Uncle Lance squatted beside her. "I know. But it's also very hard to prove the percentage. I'll do what I can. Now, tell me what you came to say."

She tried to sort her thoughts into a comprehensible statement. "Something hit me in my sleep. Something that happened at the reservation. I overheard some of the Indian men planning to go down to the river to receive something after midnight. I couldn't hear all that they said, but I went down to the river that night by myself. I was sneaking along the banks and heard the men talking.

A boat had come, and they were unloading something. I moved to get a closer look, and someone grabbed me and pulled me away from the riverbank. It was Clint Singleton. He told me he was trying to figure out who was smuggling guns and whiskey onto the reservation. I asked him if Papa knew about it, and he assured me he did—that he and Papa had observed deliveries before. He also told me to say nothing to him." She paused only a moment. "Then yesterday at the jail, when they said they had receipts that Papa had signed—"

"Your father said he'd never seen any crates, much less signed for them," Uncle Lance declared.

"Exactly! Clint said they'd been watching together when other deliveries had come, but Papa said he knew nothing about it. Don't you see? Clint was lying. That means he must be involved. He comes to Portland and Salem whenever he wants on government business. He could easily have arranged all of this."

"She's right." Uncle Lance got to his feet. "No one outside our family knows Adam better than Clint Singleton. And he knows the reservation and the people there better than anyone save Adam. He also knows that Adam is part Cherokee. One of the few who know that outside of the family."

Connie shook her head. "And I'm sure our family would never have spoken of it to strangers or acquaintances."

Uncle Lance's expression darkened. "No, but something else comes to mind. When Lakewood was still alive, he forced the medical college to dismiss Faith because she was . . . supposedly part Indian. Lakewood had learned that her father, Isaac Browning, whom Connie's brother was named for, was a quarter Cherokee. Whoever told him didn't realize Faith was adopted by Isaac and Eletta Browning, so that rules out family. Clint must have been the one who told Lakewood."

"That ties Lakewood and Singleton to each other, if that's the case," Major Wells added.

Connie knew her uncle was being very careful to avoid revealing Faith's half-Cayuse heritage.

"At the time," Uncle Lance began, "we wondered who could possibly know and have told Lakewood, but at the same time not realize Isaac Browning wasn't her biological father. This makes so much sense."

"And if Singleton was coming here, posing as Adam Browning," the major said, "he could have easily pulled it off. He knew Adam rarely left the reservation, so it wasn't much of a risk that someone would question or recognize him."

"Exactly. And in the beginning, he would have known through the family about Nancy and her husband, Albert Pritchard. At least enough to connect with him." Lance shook his head.

Not only was Connie's father in jail because of Clint, but Tom was at the reservation. She knew Clint saw Tom as a rival. He'd made more than one comment about Tom being in love with her. What if Clint decided to have Tom killed just to be rid of him?

She jumped up. "You have to protect Tom. Clint hates him."

"There are already several companies of soldiers at Grand Ronde. No one is going to hurt anyone at this point," Wells replied. "Clint's father, Senator Singleton, has made a stop there on his way home to California. He's an avid supporter of the Indians and is even traveling with a newspaperman."

She shook her head. "His father being there won't stop Clint from hurting Tom, if he has a chance. He's jealous of him."

"Clint sees Tom as competition for Connie's affection," Uncle Lance explained.

"Tom's in love with me. And though it's taken me much too long to realize it, I'm in love with Tom." Connie hadn't meant to speak the words aloud, but now that she had, she knew they were the truth. She loved Tom. Loved him more than life itself, and the very thought of losing him was too much to handle.

"I've got a supply detail heading to the reservation first thing in the morning," Wells declared. "I could arrange for them to secretly pass information to Tom and for a group to escort him back to Portland. We could even say that he's under arrest."

"Clint would probably like that," Uncle Lance said, looking at Connie. "That should solve the problem."

She nodded, but already she was trying to figure out how she could be a part of the army detail. Now that she knew she was in love with Tom, she had to see him again. Had to tell him how she felt.

"Now if we can just figure out who the mysterious Mr. Smith is," Wells said, shaking his head. "We believe he's the top man—the one holding all the purse strings. The one who ordered Seth beaten and those others killed."

The name sounded familiar, and Connie tried to recall where she'd heard it before. Then it came to her. "Smith—that was the name I heard the night Clint caught me spying on the delivery. Someone asked where Mr. Smith was. I always presumed the Indians were asking about someone who should have been with the boat men."

"But what if they were asking for someone there on the reservation?" Uncle Lance suggested.

"What if Clint is Mr. Smith, as well as the hotel's Mr. Browning?" Connie murmured. "Maybe he used both names."

"What do you know about God listening to prayers?" Tom asked as he and Isaac slipped through the forested lands. They were making their way to a secret meeting of the Indian Legislature at James Menard's house. Few knew about the meeting, and that was the way Tom wanted to keep it. The last thing he needed was the army finding out and storming the place.

"What do you mean?"

Tom thought back to what he'd read in the Bible. "There's a passage in the ninth chapter of John. Jesus healed a blind man, and the Pharisees were all up in arms about it because He did it on a Sunday and that was against the law. I can't remember why, but at one point someone said that God doesn't hear the prayers of sinners, but that if a man is a worshiper of God and does His will, then God will hear him."

Isaac paused to catch his breath. "Well,

the Pharisees had all sorts of rules and regulations for how a man could be a good person. They followed the law, but Jesus was all about grace and forgiveness. He offered people a way for God to hear their prayers by coming through Him."

"Your father said something about that. What was the way?"

"To put their faith in Him. In Romans, it says that if you confess with your mouth that Jesus is Lord and believe in your heart that God raised Him from the dead—you will be saved. Pa always said it isn't nearly as hard as some men like to make it."

A noise disturbed the otherwise silent woods. Isaac put a finger to his lips, and he and Tom crouched down. A doe crossed the path directly ahead of them. She caught their scent and darted off through the trees.

"Come on," Isaac said. "We're going to be late. I sure wish you would have let us ride the horses."

"We couldn't risk being seen. You know that."

"I guess so. My feet think otherwise."

A half hour later, Tom and Isaac stood before the Indian Legislature. Tom had just explained that Adam Browning had been arrested. Apparently Clint had said nothing to the Indians about what had happened.

"Adam told me that we should come to you. He told me this before the army took him and his family away from the reservation. Adam told me you are all good men whom I could trust. I realize you don't know me, but Isaac Browning stands here as a witness to my character, and you know what kind of man he is."

"Go on," the eldest of the bunch said.

Tom drew a deep breath. "I need your help before disaster strikes."

"What is it you want from us?" another man asked.

"There are plans for an uprising. Your young men have been deceived by someone. This person has convinced them that if they rise up and kill the white men and soldiers, the government will have no choice but to set the Indians free. That simply isn't true. If you doubt me, think of what has happened to your brothers who have fought against the government in the past. None have won. They might have a momentary victory, but in the end they are captured and jailed—sometimes even put to death.

"We must stop the attack before it starts, but I need your help. You have power over your people. They respect you and look up to you. We must convince them to remain in their homes and not join the uprising."

"It won't be easy," an older man declared. "My son has been helping, and he is convinced this is the only way. He would rather die fighting for his freedom. I told him it was foolishness, but he said Agent Singleton had promised he would be victorious."

Tom's eyes widened, and a jolt shot through him. "Agent Singleton promised him this?"

The older man nodded. "He has guns for them and plans to poison the soldiers. Agent Singleton told him." He looked to the Legislature. "He promised that if we rose up together and killed the white settlers and soldiers, the government would set us free."

"Nothing could be further from the truth." Tom chose his words with care. The idea that Clint was behind this war was something he couldn't fully grasp. He'd had his suspicions about Clint, but it was still hard to believe. What was in it for Singleton? "Fighting against the law—the government of the United States—would not bode well for the Indians. They always end up losing everything."

"He speaks the truth," James Menard said. "This war is not to our benefit."

"But what can we do? Our young men's hearts are full of fire. They want revenge for their people," the old man countered. "They no longer care what the old chiefs say. They don't listen to us."

Tom knew what he said was true, but there had to be a way. "We have to try. Remind them what has happened to others who rebelled. Do whatever you can to encourage their peace. Explain that their house of rifles was discovered, so there will be no weapons. Explain to them that once I talk to the army colonel, Clint Singleton will be arrested. They will have no leader and no arms."

The men began to talk amongst themselves. Tom hoped it was enough to move them to action. While the Legislature discussed the matter, he prayed they would come to the right conclusion. Adam had told him this reservation lived peacefully because there were reasonable men in its leadership. He had to believe calmer heads would prevail.

"We will do what we can," the old man finally said after the discussion concluded. "We will go now and talk to our young men."

Tom breathed a sigh of relief and looked to Isaac, who offered him a smile. Hopefully the Indians would work together to dissipate interest in the uprising, explaining to the young men that war would not ensure their freedom but would guarantee their demise.

James Menard approached them. "We

will ride with you part of the way back to your house."

"We didn't bring our mounts," Isaac said. "We were afraid to be seen."

James nodded. "I will lend you horses."

"My feet will be very grateful," Isaac said, smiling.

The men from the Legislature rode a little more than half the distance back with Tom and Isaac. When they reached the first collection of closely built houses, they parted company. Tom and Isaac, now on foot, went different ways in order to keep suspicion to a minimum. Isaac needed to check on the family's livestock, but they agreed to meet at the army's camp.

Tom made his way toward the Browning house, where he planned to saddle up one of the horses in order to go in search of Colonel Bedford. He was an old-fashioned soldier who had refused Clint's offer of a room in his house and insisted on tenting with his men. With the soldiers camping at both the old fort and just beyond the church, Tom wasn't sure where he'd find Colonel Bedford. Nevertheless, it was imperative that he locate him and warn him of Singleton's plans to poison the soldiers.

Tom didn't know why it hadn't dawned on him sooner that Clint was the inside man on the reservation. Everyone thought he was of the same mind as his father and brother, but instead he'd been working against the Indians all along. Even Adam Browning had thought Clint in support of the Indians and a strong man of God. Funny how Clint had pulled the wool over Browning's eyes. It seemed he was good at deception. He'd toyed with Connie, and Tom doubted he even cared for her. He probably just wanted to use her for the short-term fun he could have.

Tom wondered if Connie was safe. The family would no doubt be staying with the Carpenters. Hopefully it would be a simple matter for them to clear things up for Mr. Browning. Once they did and this was all over with, Tom intended to ask for Connie's hand. He knew Connie cared for him—maybe even loved him a little. He intended to prove to her they belonged together. He'd never been surer of it.

Tom was deep in thought when he heard a rifle fire and felt an immediate searing against the outer part of his upper arm. He looked down at the blood already turning his coat crimson. Then another shot was fired, and Tom felt the bullet skim his head in the same spot where the soldier had hit him with his gun. There was an explosion of pain. He put his hand to his head and drew it back bloodied.

Dizziness and nausea flooded him at once, and he slumped forward and fell to the ground. He fought to stay conscious. It was funny, but of all the things that came to mind, he suddenly remembered a portion of a verse Adam Browning had shared at Tom's first morning devotional with the family. Part of a Psalm—one he'd reread several times since.

Hear, O Lord, when I cry with my voice: have mercy also upon me, and answer me. When thou saidst, Seek ye my face; my heart said unto thee, Thy face, Lord, will I seek.

Tom stared up at the sky and realized he very much wanted those words to be true.

Help me, God. I don't know you very well—but I do believe and . . . I confess with my mouth . . .

"Jesus is Lord." His voice was just a whisper.

The world was going black, closing in from the sides and leaving only a tunnel of light. Just enough to see the man who'd done this terrible deed rise up from the brush.

Clint Singleton.

Clint was about to check that Tom was dead when he heard a bugle being sounded. He'd never bothered to learn the various calls.

The army had already pulled out when he'd taken over as agent, and while he and the soldiers continued to have their encounters, the army was no longer a daily part of reservation life. Still, they were here and had to be dealt with.

The plan was easy enough. Clint had poisoned a large portion of beef and was even now having it made into stew for the army. The poison was fast-acting, as his trial run with the Indians' flour had proven. He smiled, remembering how no one had been able to prove what was wrong because he had cut the dose down so that it would only cause illness and not death.

Sam Sheridan called to him from the direction of where Clint had left his horse. He decided to see what Sam needed. He felt confident that he'd killed Tom. The last shot had been to the head, and few survived head wounds.

He made his way through the brush to where he'd tied his horse. Mounting, he saw Sam. "What's wrong?"

"There's trouble. The Indian Legislature met with Isaac Browning and that man who is making a record of the tribes."

"Thomas Lowell. I just took care of him, and he won't be any more trouble."

"Well, he was trouble enough. The leaders are spreading the word to abandon our plans. Apparently Lowell found our guns and took them."

Clint shook his head. "That's impossible. No one knew where they were except people I knew I could trust. Men who wanted this plan to work." He fumed and wished he could kill Lowell all over again. It wasn't like the guns would have been much use. Only a few had firing pins—the others were useless. But the Indians would have gone to war with them, believing they were of the best quality. "Did you check on the weapons?"

"No, but I sent others to do the job."

"Well, let's find out what the truth is and then modify our plans as needed. There's no sense canceling our plans until we know it's true."

Sam scowled, and his eyes turned dark. "We can still kill the soldiers with the bad meat."

Clint nodded. "Yes, we can do exactly that. Killing the soldiers might be enough. We can take their weapons and distribute them as the men gather for war."

The plan wasn't ideal. After all, he had never meant to give the Indians a fair fighting chance. Fully functioning weapons would mean more killing—more white deaths. Clint shrugged. The times called for tough measures, and if innocent people had to die . . . well, that was life.

Elias Carter sat down opposite a group of men he didn't know other than Major Wells. His conscience had bothered him terribly since the death of his friend Samuel Lakewood, and he found it impossible to continue with Mr. Smith's plans. Then, when he'd read in the paper that Adam Browning was being held for the crime of killing Lakewood and Berkshire, Elias knew he couldn't remain silent.

With a secretary writing down his every word, Carter explained his part in the planned Indian uprising. "I worked with Samuel Lakewood to raise money from among the wealthier men of Portland. We were determined to see the Indians moved far away from here. The reservation land would then return to white settlers, and Oregon would no longer have to have so many reservations."

He licked his dry lips. "We determined that if the Indians were warring against us, the government would have no choice but to move them. The threat against white settlers and towns would make it necessary. We paid off people at every reservation to help us get weapons into the hands of the Indians, as well as whiskey and anything else that won them over to our side. Samuel told me that Mr. Smith had seen great success doing things this way."

"Who is Mr. Smith?" Wells asked.

"It's an alias used by Senator Singleton's son, Clint Singleton. He went by the name Mr. Smith so that no one could tie them together. His father helped finance everything, and since Smith—Singleton—was an Indian agent at Grand Ronde, he was the perfect man to work with us. He helped us connect to the other reservations.

"The plan was that the Indians would rise up with faulty weapons. Most wouldn't have firing pins, but some would. We knew the Indians would kill some settlers, but it was necessary to force the government's hand. The Indians would be shot down by soldiers or by white men who had been let in on the scheme. The hope was that all of the Indians would be killed, and if not, then they would be rounded up from the various reservations and sent together to another location. We knew the public outcry would be enough to force the government to do as we demanded and get rid of the Indians once and for all. Then the reservation land would be available to us to purchase."

The poor secretary could hardly keep up.

"I never wanted to be a part of the scheme, but Samuel Lakewood threatened to destroy my business and see me bankrupt. I have a family to care for and could hardly ignore the threat."

"We understand that, Mr. Carter," Major Wells replied. "That's why we're offering you a deal. You tell us everything you know and agree to testify against Singleton, and we will protect you and your family."

Carter took out a handkerchief and mopped his perspiring brow. "I'm just so worried that we won't be in time. The attack is set for to-morrow."

CHAPTER 21

Realizing how long it would take to reach Grand Ronde with the supply detail, Connie changed her plans and chose instead to take the train to Sheridan. From there she could rent a horse and ride the twelve remaining miles to Grand Ronde. This would allow her to sneak back to her house without being seen.

It wasn't an ideal choice. There would be no moonlight to see by, but thankfully Connie knew the area quite well and figured that once her eyes adjusted, she'd get by fine. If only the government had carried through on one of their many proposals for spur-line connections, but it seemed that plan after plan either failed to materialize or went bankrupt trying. There was always river travel, but that required finding a boat headed the right direction and would let others know what she was up to.

On the train ride down, Connie thought about Tom. Why hadn't she allowed herself to see how ideal he was? There was, of course, his lack of belief in God. She knew it was wrong to be unequally yoked, but even so, she knew in her foolish heart she probably would have overlooked that had she realized the depth of her feelings for Tom. Maybe it was God's way of protecting her. She knew her parents would never have approved, and she would have had to defy them. Seven years ago, Connie could see herself going against everyone who said she couldn't marry the man she loved. The thought made her sad. Would she truly have ignored the Bible's warning and her own beliefs? Caught up in a moment of emotion, Connie feared she would have done just that.

"But now he believes in God—or at least he's starting to," she murmured to herself.

As the train neared Sheridan, Connie began questioning her plan. This was a very dangerous situation, and yet she'd thrown caution aside. She could have sent a telegram to Tom.

But a telegram would have been intercepted by Clint. He always had a favorite Indian runner bring him any and all telegrams before they were delivered. Even Father Croquet had his messages looked over. Clint said it was the right of the Indian agent. The way Connie saw it, it was just Clint's way of keeping track of what was going on.

In Sheridan, Connie managed to rent a horse only after the current livery operator brought his father over to the livery to confirm who she was. The old man remembered her after Connie reminded him of a few stories related to their livery experiences. Finally she was on her way, with a warning that the twelve-mile distance couldn't be managed easily on a moonless night.

"If that horse throws you, he'll make his way back here Johnny-quick. You won't have a chance to catch him," the old man declared.

"Then I'll make sure not to be thrown," Connie countered with a smile.

She knew the risks. She knew there were plenty of dangers, but if she didn't reach Tom, she feared there would be even worse things to come. The trip had given her plenty of time to consider all that had happened and all that might yet be done. Mostly, it had given her time to contemplate her feelings for Tom and how she could hardly bear their separation.

The horse snorted and sidestepped. Connie remembered the warning about being thrown and tried her best to soothe him. "It's all right, boy. We'll be there soon." She ran her hand along his neck and gave his sides a little nudge. He seemed to settle as they moved forward. This happened several more times during their dark journey, and always it unnerved Connie just as much as her mount. Were there men sneaking around in preparation for an attack? Was it just wild animals? The latter didn't frighten her nearly as much as the first.

She had no idea what time it was, but when the distant lights of Grand Ronde finally came into view, Connie breathed a sigh of relief. She could admit now that she'd been more than a little afraid on the deserted road.

Several mounted oil lamps lit the immediate area around the government house and church. The horse seemed as happy as Connie was to have civilization finally in view. He was less content when Connie took him in the darkened direction of her parents' house. A single lamp glowed from the kitchen window. Hopefully Tom and Isaac would be there to greet her.

She tied the gelding to a hitching post and made her way inside. "Tom! Isaac!" She moved through the dark rooms to the kitchen. There was no one there.

A shiver ran down her spine. Was it possible Clint had already arranged for them to be captured . . . or killed? She shook her head. She couldn't let herself think of such things. Tom and her brother were both smart. They knew how to take care of themselves.

Connie made her way out the back door and considered her choices. Maybe they were at the government house. Major Wells had promised he'd send a fast rider ahead of the supply detail. The rider would have a letter explaining the truth to Colonel Bedford, since they couldn't risk sending a telegram. Maybe the colonel had already taken Clint into custody, and her brother and Tom were giving evidence against him.

Taking the shortcut to the government house, Connie endured the blackness once again. At least here on the reservation she knew her way around even better than on the road. This had been her home for fifteen years. There was nothing to fear here. Well, not unless you counted a madman who wanted to start a war and Indians who had come to hate anyone who was white.

She shivered and cast a glance heavenward. The stars seemed so bright in the ebony sky. She smiled. Although their light wasn't all that bright, they brought her comfort all the same. The same God who had created the universe and put the stars in the sky had sent His Son to die for her. Surely He was with her now. He wouldn't leave her to face this alone.

Connie came out of the trees and crossed the open yard to the government house. There were at least two lights burning inside, as she could see light coming from the back of the house and from the front. She wasted little time reaching the back door, then snuck a peek into the kitchen area. Clint's living quarters were here, but he was nowhere in sight.

She had thought perhaps Tom and Isaac had gone to help take Clint into custody, but maybe it was worse. Maybe they'd been taken by Clint. She moved around to the front of the house and stopped under an open window. She listened. There didn't seem to be anyone inside.

The army was camped just beyond the church and school. Perhaps she should go there and explain why she'd returned. It was possible that Tom and Isaac were with the soldiers. That would make sense.

She started for the open yard, but someone grabbed her from behind and dragged her backward.

"I'm so glad you're home." Mercy wrapped her arms around her husband and sniffed back tears. She had prayed so long and hard that he would be set free, and now that he was here, it was all she could do to keep from sobbing.

"I'm all right, sweetheart. Don't cry. They took good care of me once they realized I probably wasn't guilty."

She pulled back and smiled. "Lance has worked hard to get you set free. He wouldn't rest, and neither would Connie."

Adam glanced around. "Speaking of Connie, where is she?"

Mercy glanced at the others, then turned back to Adam. "She's gone to Grand Ronde."

"What? With all that's happening? Mr. Carter said they mean to attack—that Clint is the one in charge. That even his father is a part of this."

Mercy nodded. "I know, and when Connie found out some of the details, she left to get to Tom. I've been very worried."

"When did she leave?"

"Earlier today. She left me a note—a very brief one, but she told me that she loved Tom and meant to ensure his safety."

Adam shook his head and looked at Lance. "What can we do?"

"It's already been done. We let Major

Wells know, and he's going to telegraph Colonel Bedford in the morning. Bedford is in charge down there. Of course, it's always possible that the telegram could be intercepted."

A heavy sigh escaped Adam, and Mercy put her arm around him. "What else can we do? It's not only Connie, but also Isaac and Tom. They're all at risk."

"There's nothing we can do. Major Wells has asked us to stay put," Seth said. He stood not far from Lance. "We need to honor his request. There are enough people running around Grand Ronde now as it is. Hopefully his men will find Connie before she even reaches the reservation, and they know that Tom and Isaac stayed behind. They should have already moved them to a safe place."

"I feel such a sense of defeat."

"Nonsense." Mercy understood her husband's feelings but was determined they focus on the positive at hand. "You're home now. That's a good thing."

Adam touched her cheek. "Connie being gone isn't our only trouble. Do you know what they said about us in the newspaper?"

Mercy looked at the others. She could see by their expressions that they were hiding something. Nancy wouldn't even meet her gaze, and Faith's eyes welled up with tears.

Faith's husband, Captain Gratton, put his arm around her as Hope came to stand beside Mercy.

It was clear that whatever the news was—it wasn't good. "Someone better speak up and tell me what's going on."

Adam shook his head. "It was reported that I'm half Cherokee and that our marriage is illegal."

Mercy had never expected even the remotest possibility of this. Her knees gave way, and Adam caught her and helped her to a chair.

"It isn't true," she murmured, shaking her head. "It isn't true."

"We know the truth, darling, but the facts are what they are. I'm part Indian, and you are white. Oregon state laws make our marriage null and void."

"But the law only applies to someone who is half Indian." Mercy still couldn't believe this was happening.

"You know it would be next to impossible to prove that I'm not, and besides that, what about the movements to push for the amount of Indian blood to be lowered to one-quarter, as it is with other races?"

"This isn't right."

"No, it's not," Faith agreed.

Mercy still shook her head. "Just when

I thought this nightmare might actually be over."

Tom woke up with a fierce headache and the memory of Clint Singleton standing nearby. It was pitch black, and Tom felt around and found only thick brush. His thoughts were rather jumbled by the pain, but he knew he had to reach Colonel Bedford. The minute the solders started eating whatever meal Clint had poisoned, it would be too late to save them.

He stood, holding fast to a small sapling. The darkness was good cover, but just as it aided him, it would also aid Singleton and the Indians. Tom hesitated.

Then something he hadn't expected happened. A bugler was blowing formation. Was it possible the army had received word about Singleton? He maneuvered on shaky legs toward the sound. If he could just reach the camp, the doctor there could treat his wounds, and he could make certain they knew what was going on.

He pressed on until he saw the lights of the central reservation. He knew the smaller group of soldiers was just beyond the church. He could make it there and then get someone to send for the colonel. Tom's hope surged.

It seemed to take forever, but Tom finally reached the camp. There was a large tent with lighted lanterns in the center. He stumbled inside and blinked, giving his eyes time to adjust to the light.

"I need to see the colonel," he said.

A man looked up at him from where he sat at a table with a map rolled out before him. His eyes widened at the sight of Tom. "Good grief, man, sit down before you fall." He turned and called to a young man at the far end of the table. "Private, get the doctor."

The boy jumped to his feet. His eyes widened at the sight of Tom. "Yes, sir, Captain." He rushed from the tent, pulling on his cap as he went.

Tom sank onto a camp stool. "Captain, I have information you need to know. Singleton is the man you're looking for, the white man who has been bringing guns and whiskey to the camp."

"The senator is responsible?"

"No. I mean, I don't know if he's involved." Tom strained to think. Was the senator involved? He couldn't remember. "Clint Singleton plans to poison your food supply. I was in a meeting with the Indian Legislature. They told me it was part of the plan. Clint set the entire thing in motion to set off the war. We found the guns, however, and they won't be a problem. Most of them appeared to be non-functioning anyway. We moved them—hid them from where Clint had stored them." He paused. "But you probably know that. Your soldiers helped."

Tom pressed his hand to his head to stave off the dizziness and tried to collect his thoughts. The doctor entered with his bag in hand. Tom closed his eyes but continued to speak. "The Legislature agreed to stop the Indians. At least the ones who would listen to them."

"Just be still, son. Let me examine these wounds. Private, bring me hot water and towels," the doctor commanded. The young soldier did so quickly, then stood ready for his next order.

Tom paid them little attention. He wanted to make sure the soldiers would be safe. "Captain, don't let your men eat whatever Singleton has arranged. He plans to poison you all."

"Private, get over to the mess and tell them the men are to eat nothing until I say otherwise. Tell them the food is poisoned, lest the men be tempted to ignore orders. Then ask Colonel Bedford to join us," the captain said, then looked at Tom. "We received a telegram telling us to take Singleton into custody earlier, and word must have reached him. He hasn't been seen anywhere."

Tom relaxed and gave a sigh. "Good. Thank God." The words came so easily from his lips that Tom couldn't help but smile. It was the first time he'd ever thanked God for anything.

"Tom!" A very worried Isaac rushed to his side.

A wave of relief flowed through Tom. Isaac was safe. He closed his eyes again and winced as the doctor began swabbing his head wound.

Isaac looked at Tom with grave concern. "They said you'd been shot."

"Afraid so. It seems Clint Singleton wanted me out of the way."

"Where is he now?" Isaac turned to the captain.

"We haven't been able to locate him. However, we will. Rest assured."

"I'm happy to help," Isaac declared. "I came to warn you that your food has been poisoned." He looked down at Tom. "Or did you already tell them?"

"He did, and we should be able to dodge that attack. Thank you both. But I think now you need to stay out of the way and let the army do its job," the captain replied. "Singleton is obviously dangerous and will require men with training to bring him down."

Isaac didn't argue but exchanged a glance with Tom. They were hardly the kind to sit back and let someone else take care of their problems.

CHAPTER 22

Clint dragged Connie into his house, then let go of her with a push. She stumbled but righted herself quickly. "What are you doing here?" he demanded.

Connie appeared to be wrestling with her fears. Clint hated her all the more. He had no time for such nonsense. She was no longer useful to him.

"I asked you a question," he pushed.

"I was afraid for Tom . . . and Isaac . . . and you."

"Afraid for us? Why?"

She seemed to be thinking over her answer. Her pretense at innocence annoyed him.

"Never mind. I don't need any more of your lies," he said.

"When have I lied to you?"

Now she sounded angry. Clint almost

laughed. "Your whole appearance has been a lie. Don't think I didn't know you were trying to prove your mother and father innocent of inciting the Indians to war."

"But they are innocent, as you well know."

"And just what is that supposed to mean?"

She planted her hands on her hips. "It means that my parents are innocent. And I didn't lie. I came here to chronicle the Indian tribes. It just so happened that I wanted to help my folks as well. I didn't lie about my investigation. I just didn't bother to tell you about it."

"And why not? Don't you trust me? I thought you were madly in love with me."

She shook her head and backed up a pace. "I didn't trust you then, and I don't trust you now."

This time Clint did laugh. "So you're a private investigator now, eh? Little Connie Browning playing Pinkerton agent."

"Why are you treating me like this? I thought the tables were turned and you were in love with me now. What about that?" She raised a brow.

"Ha, that'll be the day, when I fall in love with an Indian. You're an eighth Cherokee, after all." He could see her surprise. "Didn't think I knew that, eh? I've known it since you were a child throwing herself at me."

"So that's why you didn't return my love or even show an interest in me." She nodded. "It all makes sense now."

"That and the fact that your crazy father would have had my hide if I so much as looked at you with serious intent. He knew you were smitten, but he talked to me long and hard about it."

"He did? I never knew. I guess he could sense your bad character." She crossed her arms. "It's funny how a God-fearing man has insight no one else has. My father apparently knew you were nothing but trouble, even back then."

"Just as I knew he was nothing but another Indian. I kept his secret as long as it served me to do so. Of course, it no longer does."

"I saw your false report in the Portland newspaper. It couldn't have come from anyone else, so don't bother to deny it."

"I wasn't going to." Clint leaned back against the counter and smiled. "I take full responsibility."

"Well, you could have at least gotten the facts right. Father is only one-quarter Cherokee."

"I know, but *half-breed* sounded so much better." Clint shook his head. It really was a pity. If not for that Indian blood, he might have done other things with Connie instead of thinking how he might kill her. Her boldness was appealing.

She raised her chin. "All I care about is that your plans are foiled. Someone in your group of cronies came forward to the army and police and told them everything. They know all about your plans—that you killed those two men and probably more."

Clint narrowed his eyes at the thought of Elias Carter's betrayal. It had to be him. No one else knew enough to cause any real fuss. Still, it was like a stab in the heart. He'd thought he could trust Carter. Thought he had him so frightened he would never say anything about any of it.

Connie continued. "And what does your father think about the harm you've caused so many people? The harm you planned against the Indians he's fought so valiantly for all these years?"

"You really don't know anything, do you? My father was in on all of this. He doesn't hate the Indians as much as I do, but neither does he hold them in any admiration. He simply took advantage of them. My father saw my brother's compassion for the Indians and how a great many easterners who'd never had to deal with them also felt that way. He simply decided to use it to his benefit. Once the Oregon Indians started a war, my father was going to lead the charge to remove all Indians in this state and those in reservations in California and Washington Territory as well. Seeing how well that would be received, especially after word came of all the white people who had been killed, my father intended to present a bill that would remove all Indians from the entire country. He was the one promoting the relocation to the far north. I thought it quite brilliant, myself."

"It's cruel and you know it. The Indians would never survive another forced march. That's thousands and thousands of miles through nothing but vast Canadian wilderness. They would have died before they ever reached Alaska."

"And that would have solved the problem nicely. No Indians to resettle, just bodies to bury."

"And skeletons to sell. I suppose you were a part of that as well."

"You are truly naïve. I've been at the center of it all. Selling artifacts and skeletons—whatever made me money. I've amassed a small fortune because of the bizarre interests of others."

"You really don't care about these people at all, do you?"

"Why should I? They've been nothing

but trouble. Pitiful little children, with their superstitions and ridiculous beliefs. The sooner they're dead and gone, the better for all of us."

"And does that include me, since I'm one-eighth Indian? Will you kill anyone with the slightest bit of Indian blood?"

The kitchen door opened, and Sam Sheridan filled the doorway. Clint had never cared for him, but knowing he hated Browning had made him an ally. At least a temporary one. Clint had particular plans for Sam's death after he had served his purpose.

"What do you want, Sam? Are the troops dead?" Clint asked.

"No, and neither is Mr. Lowell."

Clint could see the relief on Connie's face. He burned with anger. "So your precious Tom is still alive. I knew I should have shot him one more time to make sure he was dead."

"You shot him?" Her voice was shocked.

"I did, and I meant to kill him. My mistake for not seeing the job through. I won't make that mistake again."

"Tom has done you no harm," she protested.

"He's ruined my plans."

Sam nodded. "He warned the soldiers. They won't be eating that stew you provided.

I heard one of the soldiers announce this at their eating place."

Clint let out a growl. "It was all planned. It was perfectly laid out. I told my father it was going to be done tonight."

"Your father has also been taken by the soldiers."

Clint whirled and punched the cabinet behind him. "Where are your men? We have a few rifles left and plenty of rounds. I want them to sneak out and kill all of the nearby settlers. Tell them to kill any soldier they can—but only if they can do it and get away unseen. I don't want to lose what loyal men I have."

"You don't have any loyal men. They are my men," Sam declared.

Clint looked at him. The hatred on Sam's face was obvious.

"If that's the way you feel, then I must end our association." Clint pulled his gun and pointed it at Sam.

Without warning, Connie threw herself in front of Sam. "I won't let you kill him. You'll have to kill me first."

"Stupid girl. And why do you think I won't?" He could see out the window that it was already starting to get light.

Connie had the audacity to smile in the face of death. "Because, Clint, you need me.

I'm your only hope for getting out of here alive. You need me as a hostage."

Mercy and Adam sat in the boarding-house's front room, waiting for news on Connie, Isaac, and Tom. Mercy hadn't been able to eat a bite of breakfast, nor had she been able to sleep the night before. The thought of her only daughter and son being subjected to whatever horrors that were planned made her ill. She had seen the Indians at war. They were a skilled people—a proud people. They had endured oppression and inferior treatment for decades. They would not be easily persuaded to stand down.

Glancing at Adam, she could see he had the same thoughts on his mind. They met each other's gaze, but Mercy felt no reassurance. The only emotion in Adam's eyes was dire worry. She squeezed his hand.

The hours passed with them doing nothing but sitting and waiting. Mercy tried to pray, but the words wouldn't come. She knew God understood her heart, but she had so little strength left. She'd spent her entire life loving this man that the government of Oregon now wanted her to put aside. She had given him children that the world also condemned. How could people be so cruel, so unfeeling? How could they imagine that tearing her family apart would serve any good purpose?

Nancy came to announce lunch, but even now Mercy wasn't hungry. She shook her head at Nancy's continued encouragement.

"Aunt Mercy, you have to eat. You'll make yourself sick, and what good will that do?"

"She's right," Faith declared, coming into the room. "Neither of you will be of any use to Connie, Isaac, or Tom if you are malnourished and dehydrated. As a physician, I'm ordering you both to the dinner table." She smiled. "Please."

Adam nodded. "We're coming." He stood and reached for Mercy's hand. "Come on, we have to try. We won't be any help if we're both sick in bed."

Mercy let Adam lead her into the dining room. He pulled out a chair for her, and she sat. She knew her nieces were right but wasn't sure how she could eat when all she really wanted to do was cry.

Bedelia Clifton sat at Mercy's left, and to Mercy's surprise, the spinster reached over and took her hand. "Sister and I have been in prayer for you all morning. I know you must be afraid."

Mercy nodded. "I am."

"God laid a message on my heart for you, so I will share the verse I felt He wanted me to share." She pulled a piece of paper from her pocket. "It's Isaiah forty-one, verse ten."

The words were penned in the most beautiful script. Mercy read them to herself and then noticed everyone was watching, as if waiting for her to share.

She cleared the emotion from her throat. "'Fear thou not; for I am with thee: be not dismayed; for I am thy God: I will strengthen thee; yea, I will help thee; yea, I will uphold thee with the right hand of my righteousness.'"

"Amen," Adam said. "Those are the exact words we needed to hear, Miss Clifton." He looked around the table. "We're so grateful for all of you and your prayers."

"I believe we should offer up a special one," Seth declared. "When we pray together, it seems to add strength, and I, for one, have benefited from those prayers. Adam, if you would permit me, I'd like us to offer up our prayers for you and your family—here and now."

"Of course," Adam replied, looking to Mercy.

She nodded and glanced around the table at the family and new friends who so willingly offered to support them in this way. "Thank you."

CHAPTER 23

Y ou can't kill him, Clint." Connie stared down Clint and the gun as if she were defending her own brother. "Sam is a good man, and he just lost his wife and son."

Clint snorted. "Good. Then he can join them, and we'll be rid of yet another Indian."

"You must have some compassion left in you, Clint. You can't go on like this. The army already knows what you've done, and the government is taking charge. You need to cooperate so they'll have mercy on you."

"They're not going to have mercy on me, Connie. I've killed men and arranged for the murder of others. I killed your cousin's first husband when he threatened to stop helping me and ordered her second husband beaten. Did you know that? I planned for Seth Carpenter to be killed at the hospital once he started to recover, but your two cousins moved him home so they could take care of him, putting a stop to my plans. So you see, there is no reason for me to cooperate, only to be hanged."

"But perhaps if you put a stop to all of this, I can tell the court you showed compassion, and maybe they won't hang you."

"I've committed treason. They aren't going to care that I held back from killing one Indian. You should have never come back here, Connie."

"I had to." She looked at Clint. His eyes were wild with hate. "I had to help Tom. I love him. That's what people do when they love someone."

He laughed. "You love anyone you think might show you the slightest bit of attention. Even when you first arrived here, I could see that you were questioning your feelings for me. That's why I played on them. It was just a game, but an amusing one. I actually did think about the benefits I might get, but then I remembered that Indian blood of yours. I couldn't see myself married to a squaw." He paused and looked as though he'd just gotten the most brilliant idea. "Say, maybe Sam could marry you! Because after Tom finds out that you're part Indian, he's not going to want you any more than I do. No decent white man will ever want you."

Sam suddenly shoved Connie aside. The next thing she knew, the two men were battling. Sam was doing his best to push the gun away.

Connie didn't know what to do. The way the men were wrestling to get control of the pistol, she knew it could go off at any moment. Just as that thought came to mind, the gun fired. She ducked down behind a chair, wondering if either of them was hurt. She carefully raised her head. Neither man appeared injured, as they continued to fight. She started to crawl out of the room but then saw the gun lying on the floor. Clint must have dropped it. She had to get it out of their reach.

As Sam laid a punch into Clint's stomach, Connie scrambled around the table and chairs to reach the revolver. Clint slammed Sam to the floor, but Sam was too quick for him, and the minute Clint dove on top of him, Sam flipped him over and reversed their positions.

Connie reached the gun just as two soldiers entered the room and demanded a halt to the fight.

"On your feet," one of the soldiers commanded, taking hold of Sam. The other grabbed Clint, who tried to fight him off. Another soldier came inside to help restrain Clint.

Several additional soldiers entered, and behind them came Tom. He had a bandage on his head in the same spot where the soldier had wounded him that day at the Menards' house.

"Tom!" Connie leapt to her feet, forgetting all about the pistol. Pushing her way through the soldiers, she wrapped her arms around the man she loved. She'd never been so happy to see anyone in her life. "Are you all right?" She reached toward his bandage, then stopped. "Are you in pain?"

"A little bit, but not so much that I failed to hear your declaration. Is it true?" He looked so serious.

Connie wasn't sure what he was asking. "What . . . do you mean?" She met his blue-eyed gaze. "Do you mean am I really part Cherokee?"

He shook his head. "I already knew about that. It was the other thing. I heard you say that you love me."

She smiled and breathed a sigh of relief. "I do."

"It took you long enough to come to that conclusion."

Her brow raised. "I hardly had any incentive to consider it."

The soldiers were removing Clint and Sam from the house.

Connie held up her hand. "Wait!"

One of the soldiers looked back at her. "What is it?"

"Sam Sheridan is a good man. He did his best to save me from Agent Singleton. I hope you'll show him mercy."

The soldier looked at Sam. "He saved your life?"

"Yes. He pushed me out of the way when Singleton had a gun aimed at me." She didn't bother to say that Clint's intent was to kill Sam.

Sam fixed her with a stern gaze. "You are a good woman. My wife called you friend . . . now I will call you friend. You are welcome at my home."

Connie smiled. "Thank you, Sam. Maybe one day our fathers will be friends again too."

The soldier in charge motioned for the others to take him. "I'll write what you said in my report."

She nodded. "Thank you. I'll come by and speak with the colonel on Sam's behalf." When they were gone, she turned back to Tom. He was so pale. "You need to sit down." She left his side and drew up a chair. "Please."

"Not until I get a few things straight." He swayed but held his ground. "I've loved you practically from the moment we met. You

were all sass and fire, but there was a sweet-
ness about you too. I couldn't help myself."

She blinked. "But you never said a word."

"I knew it wouldn't do any good. Your
uncle told me you'd never marry a man who
didn't believe in God."

"And yet that didn't change your mind?"

"It agitated it a bit." He grinned. "But
your uncle Dean said I couldn't pretend or
play at a faith in a God I didn't believe in. He
said you'd know the difference, and so I loved
you in silence. Then, when you stopped talking to me about God, I feared it was because
you no longer cared."

"I always cared. I will always care. You
were always my dearest friend, and I loved
you. I just didn't realize I was falling *in* love
with you."

"When Clint shot me, I didn't think about
you," Tom said, not taking his gaze from her
face.

Connie felt a burst of disappointment.
"You didn't?"

"No. God was all I could think about.
Your father told me how to be saved, and I
had been considering it long and hard. As I lay
there, I recalled a verse from Psalm twenty-
seven. It was one your father read on that first
day at breakfast. It said, 'Hear, O Lord, when
I cry with my voice: have mercy also upon

me, and answer me. When thou saidst, Seek ye my face; my heart said unto thee, Thy face, Lord, will I seek.' Then I remembered another verse your father had shared with me when I asked him how I could be saved. The one you shared with me."

"You did?" Connie felt her heart skip a beat. Now that she had feelings for him, the only thing that had stood between them was his unwillingness to believe in God and accept Jesus as his own.

"I don't know where it's found, but it said that if I would confess Jesus as Lord and believe that God raised Him from the dead, I'd be saved."

"Yes. Romans ten, verse nine." Connie couldn't keep the joy from her voice. "And did you?"

He grinned. "I did."

Connie wrapped her arms around him once again. This time Tom moaned. She pulled back. "Did I hurt you?"

"My arm was grazed by a bullet. The doctor said it was fine, but it hurts when you grab me."

"I'm so sorry, Tom. I'm just so happy."

"It's all right. I like it when you hug me."

"I'll be more careful." She put her arms around his waist this time and laid her head on his chest. "I love you." Then she did what she would never have thought to do before. She lifted her head and raised up on tiptoes. "I love you more than life." She kissed him on the lips with great tenderness.

When she pulled away, she smiled, but Tom's eyes were closed, and he was sinking down even as she held him. Thankfully, the chair was right there. Connie helped him sink down into it.

"I kiss you, and you faint." She shook her head and smiled. "But at least I kissed you."

"Thank you, Rosy, for helping me with Tom." Connie tucked the blanket around him and smiled. "He's a good patient with proper incentive."

Rosy chuckled. "It will be good for me to take care of someone. I am a great nurse."

Tom looked at Connie and shook his head. "I don't need a nurse."

"You passed out, and if I hadn't been able to commandeer a couple of soldiers to carry you over here, you'd still be sitting in Clint's kitchen."

"I just got dizzy. And besides, you kissed me. It shocked my system."

Connie laughed and brought him some hot tea to drink. "This is my mother's favorite tea for headaches. I'm hoping it will ease your misery. The army doctor told me you wouldn't take laudanum."

"It makes me want to sleep. I had it once when I was suffering from pneumonia. I was pretty sick. The doctor dosed me up, and I think I slept the better part of three weeks. They kept waking me up to roll me into different positions and make me cough. Then they'd give me more medicine, and back to sleep I went."

"That's terrible, but it was probably because you were a difficult patient." Connie looked at Rosy. "I'll be back as soon as I telegraph my parents and let them know we're all okay. I sent Isaac for more blankets. He should be back soon."

As if summoned, Isaac waltzed in with a stack of blankets. "Here they are, just as you ordered, sister."

"That will be perfect." Connie grabbed one and unfolded it. "We don't want Tom catching a chill. I was just about to head out and telegraph Mama and Papa."

"No need. I already sent one. Colonel Bedford sends his compliments. We had a long talk about everything you told me. He's releasing Sam. In fact, he's turned the Indians over to the Indian Legislature to be dealt with. Since there was no real uprising, they aren't concerned with imposing martial law or anything like that. However, they're going to leave a company of soldiers here to help enforce whatever the Legislature decides. They've also let Washington know that they'll need to send someone to replace Singleton as Indian agent."

Connie placed the blanket over Tom. "Too bad you've already got a job."

Tom frowned. "After all this is dealt with, I don't know that I will. I can't imagine they'll want us to stick around. We might only remind the Indians here about the failed uprising."

"I don't want us to lose our jobs." Connie looked to Rosy and then her brother. "We were just starting to make friends."

Isaac crossed his arms. "Well, there's also the issue of Mother and Father. We need to ensure their names are cleared and see what the government plans for them. Besides, they've got the legal issues of their marriage to sort out."

"It's ridiculous." Connie shook her head. "I don't want to think about it. Tom, as soon as the doctor says you can travel, we're heading back to Portland to see to this matter."

"Yes, ma'am." He feigned a salute.

She gave him a look. "Are you suggesting that I'm in charge?"

Tom chuckled and pulled the blanket up

under his chin. "I think we both know the answer to that."

Connie walked outside with her brother. It was already midday, and she couldn't remember the last time she'd eaten anything. "I don't know about you, but I'm famished. I'll bet Rosy and Tom are hungry too."

"You're going to cook?"

"Of course. Why not?"

Isaac shrugged. "I didn't know you could. Ma said you spent the last seven years with your nose in books."

"I also learned more about cooking and sewing. Aunt Phinny is an amazing woman. She enjoys a beautiful home and servants, but her modest upbringing taught her many skills. Where Mama's training left off, hers picked up. I can make some of the most amazing dishes you've ever tasted. There's one chicken dish in a mustard sauce that—"

"Stop," he begged. "Don't talk anymore, just cook." He pushed her toward the shortcut through the trees.

She laughed. "Go kill me a chicken."

CHAPTER 24

Connie sat between her mother and Tom as they waited for Mrs. Helen Hunt Jackson to be introduced. Connie was delighted to be able to hear her speak about the Indian plight. It held special meaning in light of everything that had happened.

When Faith came onto the stage, the audience began to applaud. She was dressed in a blue evening gown with a tightly corseted waist. The three-quarter sleeves were trimmed in ivory lace, as was the square-cut bodice. Nancy and Connie had both helped her arrange her hair in a much fussier fashion than Faith normally wore, and she looked gorgeous.

"Ladies and gentlemen," she began. "I am honored to introduce Mrs. Jackson this evening. Having heard her speak in Colorado,

I can tell you that you are in for an evening of great information and a rousing presentation." She continued to tell the audience some of Mrs. Jackson's background.

"Isn't she beautiful?" Connie whispered to her mother. Mama gave a nod, but it was Tom who leaned in to answer.

"Not nearly as beautiful as you are."

Connie's cheeks grew hot, and she threw a quick sidelong glance his way. "Hush."

He gave a low chuckle, then ran his fingers over the back of her gloved hand. Connie couldn't even focus on what Faith was saying. This romance stuff was enough to completely dislodge one's thoughts.

"And now I give you Mrs. Jackson."

There was thunderous applause as a stylish older woman walked across the stage. Connie was anxious to hear what she had to say after hearing Faith speak so highly of her. Yet for all her desire, she was more than a little aware of the handsome man at her side.

"Thank you, ladies and gentlemen. I am delighted to be able to speak to you this evening. Many of you who are familiar with my work know that my heart is to better the fate of the American Indian. Tonight, I would like to speak about what I have learned as I've traveled this fair land.

"At this time, there are between two hundred and fifty thousand and three hundred thousand Indians in America, not including Alaska. Many tribes are now extinct due to war and disease, but of those remaining, there are around three hundred separate tribes."

She stepped to the side of the podium. "Many were annihilated at the hands of white men determined to rid the world of those they called savage. Looking at their deeds, I wonder who truly was the savage."

Mrs. Jackson continued speaking. Her comments made Connie think of Clint. He was sitting in jail and certain to be found guilty and hanged. The thought of someone she'd grown up knowing, someone she had once loved, being hanged sickened her. She knew he had done wrong—had even threatened to kill her—but Connie couldn't find it in herself to want him to die.

Still, she knew Clint was responsible for at least three men's deaths, possibly more. He deserved to hang. Her father had gone earlier in the day to act as a spiritual advisor to Clint, but Clint wanted no part of it. He said God was immaterial to him. That saddened Connie even more. Whom could he turn to for comfort as he faced death, if not God? How did people without God even manage to face daily life, much less death?

"Stories are told," Mrs. Jackson continued, "of the cunning Indian waiting for the cover of darkness to kill those foolish enough to wander into their traps. Others paint pictures of the lazy Indian who is unwilling to learn a trade, much less go to that job each day and produce for himself a good living with which he can support his family. Lies abound when speaking of the American Indian because they have no one to defend them. I am here to do just that.

"It might surprise you to know that the Indians of most reservations are self-sustaining. They raise crops and hunt. They utilize various parts of animals killed for making clothing, furnishings, food, and medicines. They even manage in many locations to raise or catch animals and fish that they sell to white men for additional income. They are, of course, cheated at every turn by those who feel they are undeserving of a fair price.

"If I might dare read from Isaiah fifty-three—a verse that referenced our Lord Jesus, but a verse that well applies to our poor Indian brethren." She moved behind the podium again and opened a Bible. "'He is despised and rejected of men; a man of sorrows, and acquainted with grief: and we hid as it were our faces from him; he was despised, and we esteemed him not.'"

Mrs. Jackson looked out over the audience. "I put it to you that the American Indian is despised and rejected of men. They are well acquainted with grief. Only a few short years ago, a terrible massacre occurred in the Arizona Territory, brutally taking the lives of Apaches who had long been peaceful and under the direction of the authorities at Camp Grant. Women and children were murdered without leaving a single babe alive. This terrible act was accomplished by white people from nearby settlements and towns. When the camp doctor was sent to lend aid, he came back to report that there was no one alive to whom he could minister.

"The Indian has been despised, and 'we hid as it were our faces from him.'" She paused and closed the Bible. "Please do not think me blasphemous or think that I am comparing the Indian to our Savior and Lord. It is just that these Scriptures depict the heart of the matter when we reject those whose skin is not the same color as ours. Now, you might say, 'But, Mrs. Jackson, the Indians also attacked and made war on the white people.' This is true, but I challenge you with this question. At what provocation?

"There are many stories passed down regarding Indian attacks during the wild frontier days, massacres and wrongs done to innocent white families. I do not suggest that either side is perfect, but I do suggest that we are more than willing to look away—completely forget the wrongs our own people have done. Well-respected military officials have testified on record that in nearly every case of attack by the Indians, we were the ones who made the first act of aggression."

Mrs. Jackson spoke for nearly an hour, and when she concluded, there was thunderous applause, and everyone stood to honor her. Connie thought her marvelous. She had defended her beliefs not only with great passion, but with statements of proof from documents provided by honorable men, including more than one president. Connie hoped and prayed her teachings would educate the people and cause them to give up their desire to drive the Indians to the far north. Perhaps in time, if the two peoples could just find common ground, they might learn to work together.

"Wasn't she marvelous?" Mama said.

Connie gave a brief nod. "I was just thinking that. I hope we have a chance to meet her."

"Faith said she would try to introduce us, but I believe the entire audience is hoping for that chance. We may simply have to be content with having heard her speak."

"I am glad I didn't miss it," Connie admitted. She looked over at Tom. "Did you enjoy her talk?"

"Not as much as I enjoyed sitting next to you." He grinned.

Connie smiled as he raised her hand to his lips and kissed her gloved fingers. A shiver ran through her body. She still found it hard to believe the change in her feelings for Tom. She could hardly wait to see where God took them.

On October first, Connie sat with her family and Tom while Clint's sentence was read. She listened to the judge as he listed the charges for which Clint was found guilty before continuing with the sentencing. Connie waited, hoping for leniency.

"And so it is the decision of this court that on October fifteenth, two weeks hence, you will be taken to the gallows and hanged by the neck until you are dead."

Connie didn't hear anything else. She knew it was a just decision, but it still tormented her to think of Clint dying. She wondered what he thought. Was he afraid? Angry? His father had received little more than a reprimand, with all of the blame being put on Clint. Senator Singleton denied any knowledge of an uprising, telling the court weeks earlier that he had only come to visit his son as he made his way back to California. The lawyer he had was much too quick with words and a long list of people who were happy to speak out on the senator's behalf, including his other son, who worked for the Bureau of Indian Affairs in Washington, DC.

It wasn't as if Connie knew the truth about the situation one way or another. Clint could have made up his father's participation, thinking to take the pressure off of himself. The prosecution had plenty to use against Clint, however, and no amount of double-talk by his defense lawyer had been able to save him.

The judge dismissed them, and everyone rose as he left the room. Connie glanced toward Clint and was surprised when he looked her way. He smiled as if amused by the entire situation. She couldn't help being shocked and didn't even try to hide her surprise. This only made him laugh. Perhaps he had gone mad.

She left the courtroom on Tom's arm. He was commenting on the beauty of the day, but Connie couldn't put aside Clint's reaction.

"What's wrong?" Tom asked when they reached the carriage.

"He was smiling." Her voice was barely a whisper.

"Who?"

She met Tom's gaze. "Clint. He was smiling as he left the courtroom. How can a person smile when he knows he'll die in two weeks?"

"It's the shock," her father said before Tom could reply. "It's his only way of dealing with it and still appear as if he's lost nothing."

Connie touched her father's arm. "You will go to him and talk to him about God again, won't you?"

Her father's expression turned sympathetic. "Of course I will. I think once he's actually facing the noose, Clint will be far more willing to turn to Jesus."

Connie nodded. "I know he's guilty, and I hate that he tried to kill Tom and see you jailed, and that he'll be killed for murders he committed, but I don't want to see him lose his soul."

"Ever my compassionate daughter." Papa kissed the top of her head. He stepped back and smiled. "Speaking of Tom, when do you intend to marry him?"

Connie's eyes widened. "Marry him? I, uh, don't know. He's never asked me." She looked at Tom. "I think his head injury caused him to forget his feelings for me."

"Hardly." Tom dropped to one knee right there and then. Chuckles could be heard from the family members gathered around.

"Constance Browning, will you become my wife?"

Connie put on a thoughtful look and paused for a long moment, as if having to truly consider the question. Finally, she smiled. "I will happily become your wife, Thomas Lowell."

Tom looked at her father. "May I kiss her as a pledge of my intention?"

"Yes, I suppose that would be acceptable," Connie's father said with a stern expression. Moments later, he burst into a laugh.

Tom rose and pulled Connie into his arms. He leaned forward, and Connie closed her eyes, awaiting his kiss.

Before he pressed his lips to hers, Tom whispered against her ear, "Let's see who faints this time."

That evening Connie and Tom talked about the future as they relaxed before a fire in the front room of Nancy's boardinghouse. Most of the extended family had returned to Oregon City, and the boarders had gone to bed, but just as she thought she might have Tom to herself for the rest of the night, Connie's mother and father entered the room. After all these years, they still looked at each other with an expression one might find on the faces of newlyweds. They were still very much in love.

"I thought you two had gone to bed," Connie said. "Come join us."

Tom was already on his feet out of respect for Connie's mother. "Please. We were just discussing the future."

"That's very appropriate. Your mother and I have been doing the same." Papa led her mother to the sofa and, once she was seated, sat down beside her.

Faith and Captain Gratton appeared in the doorway. "Might we join you?" Faith asked.

"Of course." Papa motioned her into the room. "I want you to hear this, as well as Nancy and Seth."

"Did I hear our names mentioned?" Seth asked, drawing Nancy into the room alongside him. "We were just coming to say good night."

"Please stay a moment. Mercy and I have an announcement to make."

Nancy sat on a wooden chair while Seth stood behind her. He was so much improved from the injuries he'd received earlier in the year that there was talk of him soon returning to work at John Lincoln's law office.

"What is it you want to say?" Connie asked.

"We know that after you and Tom marry, you are being relocated to a reservation in the Washington Territory."

Connie nodded. "Yes, just after the first of the year."

"Well, your mother and I thought . . . if you don't mind, we'd like to follow you there and start a new church in the small town nearby. I've corresponded with the town mayor, and he assures me that a new church would be quite welcome."

"That's wonderful. I'd love for you to be close by." Connie looked to Tom. "Wouldn't you?"

He smiled. "I want whatever makes you happiest. Your mother and father have become more like parents to me than my own ever were. After we're married, I'm looking forward to calling them mine."

"We already consider you our son," Mama replied. "But speaking of weddings, have you set a date yet?"

Connie and Tom had talked of nothing else all evening. "We thought just after Christmas, while everything is still decorated and beautiful. We'd like to marry here at Nancy's. Right here in front of the fireplace. She told me she intends to set up a large tree in that corner over there." Connie pointed. "I think it would be quite charming."

"Would that be all right with you two?" Tom asked, looking at Nancy and Seth.

"I would be honored to have your wedding here. I only hope there's enough room." Nancy looked to Seth. "Will that be all right with you?"

"Of course." He put his hands on Nancy's shoulders. "I'm sure we can squeeze anyone and everyone in here."

"It'll only be family . . . and the ladies of the boardinghouse," Connie said. "We don't want a big affair."

"Then maybe you shouldn't invite the entire family," her father murmured.

"It's true," Faith replied. "We have become quite large."

"But why wait so long?" Mama asked.

"Well, I know it will take time for Aunt Phinny and Uncle Dean to clear their schedules so they can come. They would want to be here."

"Of course," her father said, nodding. "They would be devastated if you left them out."

"Perhaps we could have a double wedding," Connie suggested. "With all the nonsense about you not really being married, we could prove once and for all that you are."

"We already know we are," Papa said, taking her mother's hand. "I don't feel the need to prove it to anyone. Washington Territory has no such foolish laws, which is another reason we want to move there. We want to be done with any accusations. We just want to live in peace and help people find their way to God."

"I have a feeling," Seth interjected, "that Oregonians are quickly going to tire of this nonsense as well. I think as they listen to more speakers like Mrs. Jackson, they will start to see the truth."

"On the other hand," Nancy added, "a lot of the men and women who live here remember the Rogue River Indian Wars just twenty-five years ago. The Whitman Mission massacre was only thirty-three years ago. There are too many people living with too many memories. Generations may have to die out before people will rethink their feelings toward the Indians."

"Nancy's right," Faith replied. "I think it will be a long time before the people of Oregon forgive and forget. But until then, I will do what I can to help further the cause. Of course, I might have to delay serving any causes for a time." She smiled at her husband. "We're going to have a baby."

Connie jumped up and went to hug Faith, as did Nancy and Mama. "This is such wonderful news, Faith. When do you think the baby will be born?"

"Sometime in March." She was positively glowing with joy.

"Congratulations," Mama said, kissing her cheek. "Nothing can cheer a day like weddings and babies."

Everyone agreed.

While the others continued to congratulate Faith and Andrew, Connie and Tom slipped closer to the fire. Tom took hold of Connie's hands. "In case I haven't told you lately, I love you."

She smiled. "You tell me every hour of every day in the way you look at me and the way you treat me, but still I love to hear it. I love you too, and I'm sorry it took me so long to see it."

Tom shook his head. "I think it had to be this way because I was so blind to the truth of who God was. I know you stopped talking to me about my beliefs and yours, but you never stopped being my friend, and for that I'm so grateful."

"I'm sorry that I stopped defending my faith. I was so confused about what that faith really meant to me. Now I'm confident and will happily discuss and argue points with you anytime—anywhere."

"I don't think there will be any need for arguments. I find myself in complete agreement with what you believe."

"And why not? The same man led us both to the Lord." She glanced past Tom and looked at her father. The expression on her face was full of love. "I'm glad they'll be close by. I hope you truly don't mind."

"Not at all. I still have so much to learn. I know your father won't lead me astray when I ask him questions. We will be so blessed to attend your father's church."

"Oh goodness, don't call it that," Connie replied. "Papa has always been quick to correct anyone who suggests such a thing. The church belongs to God alone. *Soli Deo Gloria.* To God alone, the glory."

He thought about that for a moment. "You know, Gloria might make a pretty name for a baby girl."

Connie blushed and looked at the floor. It endeared her to him all the more.

CHAPTER 25

On the twenty-seventh of December, Connie stood in the same pale-yellow gown she'd worn to her last ball in Washington, DC. Aunt Phinny had brought it with her so Connie could use it for her wedding dress.

Mama totally approved. "It's just the loveliest gown. So beautiful against your complexion and eyes. Are you sure you don't want us to create some kind of veil? Nancy said she has some extra tulle and lace. I'm sure between me and your aunts, we could come up with the perfect notion to go with it."

"No, I don't need anything else. I've already let the lot of you give me fussy hair." She grinned. "But I like it, and I'm thinking Tom will too."

"Well, then, I believe it's time for us to

join the guests and get this thing done," her father declared from the door. "It's nearly nine o'clock. If you wait much later, we'll be serving lunch instead of a wedding breakfast. And frankly, I'm starved."

They all laughed at this, and then Mama kissed Connie's cheek. "Be happy, my love. Never go to bed with anger between you, and always put the Lord first."

Connie swallowed the lump in her throat. "Oh, Mama, Papa, I'm so blessed that you're both here. So many have lost their family or parents. I get to have you both here as well as my aunts and uncles and cousins. It's such a joyous celebration, and I'm particularly excited to see how Cousin Meg gets along with Aunt Phinny. I just know Meg would love living with them in Washington, DC."

"Well, don't push. Let it develop or fall apart on its own," her mother warned. "Now, come on. Your father is right. It's time."

Connie took her father's arm while her mother made her way ahead of them. Connie looked up and saw that her father's eyes were damp. "Are you crying?"

He smiled. "I suppose I am. I never thought about giving my daughter—my only daughter—away to someone else."

"Oh, Papa, you know better. You aren't giving me away at all. You're taking on Tom as your son. You're just getting to know him, but I've known him for seven years. I can tell you from experience that he can be quite opinionated and bossy, but I'm sure you can handle him."

Her father chuckled. "I just hope he can handle you. I wonder if Tom has really considered what he's getting himself into."

She leaned close. "Shh. We don't want to scare him off."

He laughed softly. "It'll be our secret."

Everyone in the cramped front room stood as Connie and her father entered just behind Mama. Connie smiled at everyone, confident and not a bit afraid. This was the most important day of her life, and she didn't want to shy away from a minute of it. She wanted to memorize what everyone looked like.

Near the fireplace, Tom stood waiting. He was so handsome in his dark blue suit and tie. He watched her as if mesmerized. Connie wondered if he was nervous. He looked completely captivated with her, but she knew Tom was very good at concealing his fear.

Papa handed her off to Tom and then took his place before them. He was the only one in the world Connie had ever wanted to perform her wedding ceremony. She had thought about it since she was a little girl.

"Please, everyone, be seated," her father declared. "At least those of you who have chairs." Everyone chuckled.

There was a rustling sound as people took their seats, but Connie found it impossible to take her gaze from Tom's face. She was marrying her best friend, the man who had always been there for her when no one else was. The one she could tell her troubles to and feel neither condemned nor belittled. He was the only one in the entire world with whom she could imagine spending her life.

"Thomas and Constance—Tom and Connie —we have come here today to witness your joining in holy matrimony." She glanced at her father, and he winked. "But first, let us pray."

Connie thought it the most perfect ceremony. She made her vows and pledged her heart and life, then listened as Tom did likewise. She didn't feel at all afraid to face the future. Her life with Tom so far had been full of adventure. She had no doubt it would continue to be so as they faced the next year and the ones after that.

They laughed and talked throughout the wedding breakfast with family and the boardinghouse ladies. Everyone seemed to be having a wonderful time. Bedelia Clifton had worn a fancy lace collar, and her sister, Cornelia, had placed a lovely pink bow and cameo at her neck. Even Alma stood faithfully beside Mrs. Weaver.

"Was the fussy hair your idea?" Tom asked Connie when they finally had a moment to themselves.

She smiled. "You know very well it wasn't. The gown, however, was. Aunt Phinny brought it and several others that I had worn in Washington. This was always my favorite."

"It's the one you wore to the fund-raiser ball just before we left for Oregon."

"Yes. How do you remember that?"

He looked at her with what she had come to recognize as love mingled with admiration. "I remember everything about you that night. I thought briefly of telling you how I felt, but something about it just wasn't the right time."

She reached up to touch his cheek. "I'm glad you waited."

He covered her hand with his. "It wasn't easy, let me tell you." He took her hand and drew it to his lips. He kissed her fingers with great tenderness. "I love you more dearly every day I draw breath."

"I still can't believe you've loved me all these years. I loved you too, as a friend, but I never suspected the way you felt."

"I worked hard to keep it hidden. I knew there was too much standing between us, and I couldn't bear to think of declaring my love only to have you refuse me." Connie relished the warmth as Tom drew her in his arms. "I know it would have been my undoing."

"Well, you needn't worry about that, Mr. Lowell. I will be now and always happily your wife and love, excited by the possibility of all that we will see as we walk life's paths."

"You're starting to sound like a poet, Mrs. Lowell." He lowered his mouth to hers and kissed her.

Connie felt all the butterflies and fireworks that had failed to come when Clint Singleton had forced his kiss on her. Tom's kiss was more like a promise of things to come—a life of love that would forever bind them to one another.

"There you two are," Nancy declared. "Come see your wedding cake. All of us had a hand in it, including Jack, who just put his hand in it."

Connie and Tom pulled apart, laughing.

"You'll just have to ignore the handprint," Nancy said. "Now, hurry. We're all in the dining room." She left them with a quick backward glance and smile.

"I suppose we'd better follow, or they'll all come see where we've gotten off to," Tom said with a sigh.

Connie laughed and led him off to see the cake.

Two weeks later, they boarded the *Morning Star* with the Brownings and Faith. Captain Gratton welcomed them aboard, heartily kissed his wife, then ordered the men to make ready to depart. It was very cold, and the dampness chilled Connie to the bone, but Tom was more than happy to wrap his arms around her as they waved good-bye to the family standing on the dock.

"You know, Tom, Mercy and I were married at sea," Connie's father announced.

"I'd nearly forgotten that," Connie replied before Tom could speak a word.

"I hadn't," Faith said. "I was there. I thought it very romantic, and for a long time I wanted to get married on a ship. Instead, I get to live on a riverboat—at least for a while. Andrew wants to buy a house for us in Portland."

They waved to the family who remained. Captain Gratton signaled with the horn, and Connie blew kisses.

"Don't forget, you promised to come see us," Connie called.

"We will when time permits," Uncle Dean promised. He put his arm around Connie's cousin Meg. "We shall be quite busy while we get this one settled at the seminary."

"Come see me when you get a chance," Isaac added.

"When everything settles down, I'm sure we'll find time to come," Adam Browning called to his son. "Meanwhile, I'll pray things go well with the farm."

As the riverboat began to move away from the dock, Connie snuggled up closer to Tom. He pulled her tighter. "We should go inside. You're freezing."

"In a minute. I won't see them for a very long time, and I want this moment to last."

The riverboat found the current and began to move more quickly. Tom watched with Connie until the city was nearly out of sight. Everyone else had gone into the salon to warm up, leaving them alone on the deck. Tom turned his wife in his arms and saw that she was smiling.

"Are you ready to start this grand adventure, Mrs. Lowell?"

She nodded and stretched up on tiptoe to offer him a kiss. "I am. What of you, my darling husband?"

"Wherever you go, I'll be forever by your side."

Author's Note

The Bureau of Ethnology was established by Congress in 1879. The purpose was to transfer archives and other materials related to Native Americans from the Interior Department to the Smithsonian Institution for safekeeping and further study. Within this bureau, it was decided to catalog and study the various tribes of the United States so that their history wouldn't be lost. The Bureau of Ethnology changed its name to the Bureau of American Ethnology in 1897, and in 1965, the department merged with the Smithsonian's Department of Anthropology.

As for the laws against interracial marriage, Oregon set some very strict guidelines. In 1866 a law was passed that read:

Be it enacted by the Legislative Assembly of the State of Oregon:

Section 1. That hereafter it shall not be lawful within this state for any white person, male or female, to intermarry with any negro, Chinese, or any person having one-fourth or more negro, Chinese or Kanaka [Pacific Islander Native] blood or any person having more than one-half Indian blood; and all such marriages or attempted marriages shall be absolutely null and void.[1]

These Oregon laws against interracial marriage weren't repealed until 1951, sixteen years ahead of the United States Supreme Court's repeal of all anti-interracial marriage laws in the United States.

And sadly, although the Fifteenth Amendment passed in 1870 and granted all US citizens the right to vote regardless of race, many states still refused that right to Native Americans. The Snyder Act (passed in 1924) admitted Native Americans born in the United tates to full US citizenship. However, the Constitution left it up to individual states as

1. This is taken from "The Act to Prohibit the Intermarriage of Races," *The Oregonian*, November 2, 1866. For more information, visit https://oregon historyproject.org/articles/historical-records/act-to -prohibit-the-intermarriage-of-races-1866/#.Xnz 1C4hKiUk

to who had the right to vote. It took over forty years for all fifty states to allow Native Americans the right to vote. Utah was the last state to legalize voting for Native Americans in 1962.

Tracie Peterson is the award-winning author of more than one hundred novels, both historical and contemporary. She is often referred to as the "Queen of Historical Christian Fiction," and her avid research resonates in her stories, as seen in her bestselling HEIRS OF MONTANA and ALASKAN QUEST series. Tracie considers her writing a ministry for God to share the Gospel and biblical application. She and her family make their home in Montana. Visit her website at www.traciepeterson.com or find her on Facebook at www.facebook .com/AuthorTraciePeterson.

Sign Up for Tracie's Newsletter

Keep up to date with Tracie's news on book releases and events by signing up for her email list at traciepeterson.com.

More from Tracie Peterson

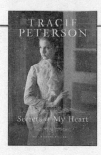

Reunited with childhood friend and lawyer Seth Carpenter, recently widowed Nancy Pritchard must search through the pieces of her loveless marriage for the truth behind her husband's death after his schemes come to light. But as they pursue answers, their attraction to each other creates complications, and dark secrets reveal themselves.

Secrets of My Heart, WILLAMETTE BRIDES #1

You May Also Like . . .

In this sweeping companion to the Hallmark TV series *When Hope Calls*, Lillian Walsh rushes to a reunion after discovering the sister she believed dead is likely alive. But Grace has big dreams beyond anything Lillian is prepared for. Can Lillian set aside her own plans and join her sister in an adventure that will surely change them both?

Unyielding Hope by Janette Oke and Laurel Oke Logan, WHEN HOPE CALLS #1

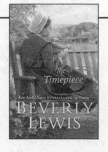

In this continuation of *The Tinderbox*, when young Amish woman Sylvia Miller's world is upended by the arrival of Englisher Adeline Pelham—whose existence is a reminder of a painful family secret—Sylvia must learn to come to terms with the past while grappling with issues of her own. Is it possible that God can make something good out of the mistakes of the past?

The Timepiece by Beverly Lewis
beverlylewis.com